MW01593098

Reclaimed Life

Tyler Valley Mountain Series, Volume 1

D.W. Alder

Published by D.W. Alder, 2023.

RECLAIMED LIFE

First edition. February 1, 2023.

Copyright © 2023 D.W. Alder.

ISBN: 979-8215915301

Written by D.W. Alder.

To Bob, who never failed to encourage me and believe in me. You are my happily ever after.

No book is made without a team of professionals, and I would like to thank:

Misha Carlstedt of Verity Ink Editorial for developmental editing, The Atwater Group for copyediting, and April Bennett of The Editing Soprano for proofreading.

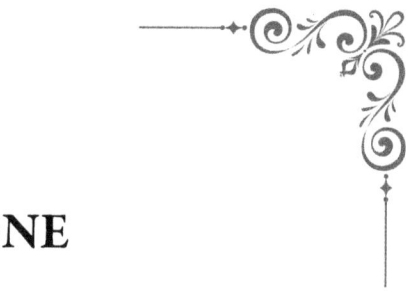

ONE

~Dixon~

BLACK.

Black hair. Black dress. Black shoes.

She looked like any other woman in the place. But then she turned toward her friend, her face in full view. A smile. Round, rosy cheeks.

It was the smoldering look in her eyes that made my heart stop. And my feet.

"Hey, what the—"

Ryan bumped into me, and my beer sloshed over his arm. I guess that's what happens when you come to a dead stop in the middle of a crowded country bar on a Friday night. He caught where my gaze was stuck and laughed.

"Yeah, keep dreaming. She's outta your league, Dixon. Come on, the game's on. Let's grab a seat and watch your team lose. You're gonna owe me some big bucks, buddy."

I was too busy trying to remember how to breathe to give him any shit back about the game. And then I was too busy thinking about how to approach her without looking like your typical barhopping jerk looking for a one-night stand. Although, I wouldn't object to it. I'd just have to try not to be a jerk. Emphasis on try.

I didn't have a reputation as a steady guy...unless it was a steady flow of ladies, one right after the other. I just wasn't into relationships. A good time? You bet. An hour or two of stress relief? Sign me up. But getting to know someone...letting someone in? Nope.

I wanted to know her. My mouth on her mouth, my hands on her body, her cry of satisfaction—my dick was totally in for that. Something about those eyes caught my attention. It tugged at my heart...something that hadn't stirred in years.

This was the last thing I expected...or wanted.

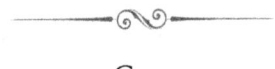

~Cora~

BLACK.

That's what caught my eye when I turned toward Wendy.

Black leather jacket. Black jeans. Black hair.

But those piercing eyes...they watched me, captured me.

It took Wendy's snapping fingers in my face to break the spell.

"Hey, you there? What do you want this fine gentleman to buy for you? A margarita? Or are you ready to kick it up a notch and do some shots?"

"What? What gentleman? Oh." The guy behind Wendy was clearly checking out her ass as she leaned against the bar. He swung his gaze to me...and then he proceeded to check out my front. *Jerk.*

"No, nothing for me. I think I'm ready to head out."

"Come on, Cora. Stay for a drink...a real drink this time, not a club soda." Wendy glanced back at her admirer before returning her gaze to me. "Please, don't leave me. He's probably harmless, but..."

Guilt. She gets me with it every time. "Okay. But, seriously, just a club soda for me. I've gotta get up early tomorrow."

Wendy wiggled her fingers at the bartender, Jake. When he got within shouting distance, she ordered her margarita and my soda, with a pointed look to Mr. Jerk.

"Here, let me get that for you beautiful ladies. Another Coors for me, too." He slapped a twenty on the bar. Mr. Jerk smiled, apparently gearing up to show us his best stuff. Although, I had to admit, when he smiled and looked you in the eyes, he was almost bearable. Almost.

That was ruined when he opened his mouth again. "So, what are you two doing later tonight? Maybe we can all find a room and—"

Wendy pushed away from the bar, her voice rising with each sentence. "What? Are you thinking that just because you bought us a drink—one of them a damn club soda, for Christ's sake—that we're gonna fall all over you and do you in some sleazy fleabag hotel? You think a soda and a margarita and a smile is gonna get you two women who have standards? Think again, pal!"

Typical Wendy answer. I admired her ability to have a comeback for just about every situation. A skill I lacked.

Jake showed up at the bar with the drinks. "Problem here?"

~Dixon~

THE ENCHANTRESS AND her friend were waiting for their drinks, probably courtesy of the scumbag checking them out at the bar. Jake, my stepbrother, took the order and walked away to make the drinks.

Jake owned the bar, which was convenient because it gave me a place to crash after a night of drinking, which was every night these days. He had a few rooms upstairs and let me couch-surf there while I was figuring out what the hell to do with my life. Right now, I was working construction with Ryan Chatfield, my old high school buddy, back in Tyler Mountain Valley in Connecticut, where we'd grown up. Better than the hourly temp jobs and warehouse jobs I'd been doing for the past six years after high school but definitely not what I wanted to do forever. It got me enough dough to pay the bills and buy some beers. Hey, I've got priorities.

And right now, my priority was still figuring out how to introduce myself to the beauty at the bar without being a schmuck. Actually, my priority was making sure that asshole at the bar wasn't going to beat me to the punch. It sure looked as if he were trying. Her friend pushed away from the bar and her voice rose, although the jukebox distorted her exact words. Was that *Do you in a sleazy fleabag hotel*? What the hell?

My feet hit the ground and before that jerk knew it—hell, before *I* knew it—I got up in his face. "Hey. You need to learn some manners, dude. That's no way—"

A hand on my arm stopped me. My brain short-circuited at the electric touch.

Jake was behind the bar, watching me. Clearly, he'd already been ready to take care of the situation. I suppose, being a bar owner, he'd seen his share of sleazy come-ons and knew how to get a lady out of a jam with a drunk asshole.

But my gaze was stuck on that hand. Delicate. Fair skin. Manicured. I followed it up until I looked straight into gorgeous green eyes.

"Thanks. I think we are leaving." Green Eyes glared at her friend.

"Yeah, I think I've had enough of this...this gentleman's attention." The friend gave the death stare to the dumbass who now stood—well, wobbled—and attempted to reach for the ladies.

"Andrew, sit your ass down. You're gonna have a real problem if you try anything but picking up this coffee. The ladies are off-limits." Jake's commanding tone had the drunk flopping back into the barstool.

"And you, Dixon. Why don't you take Wendy and Cora here out to their cars? I'll make sure lover boy here keeps his ass right here."

And with that, my dreams started to come true. I had a chance to talk to my enchantress. And I almost had her name, too. I just had to figure out which name belonged to who.

~Cora~

"YOU'RE SHAKING. I'M so sorry, Cora. I didn't think he'd get so ballsy."

"I know. Look, I'm ready to go." Getting walked to my car by this man in black had me shaking, not the idiot in the bar. Jake knew him—he wouldn't have suggested a perfect stranger should walk me to my car, right? But something about this man's penetrating gaze had my heart stuttering and my head spinning. He took wide steps, with a steady gait to keep any would-be harasser at arm's length.

And he was right behind us, listening to every word. I couldn't tell Wendy the real reason I was shaking. The heat of his stare burned through my dress; I wanted to feel the heat of his hand at the small of my back. And somewhere else, too.

"Hey, I parked right out front. Where are you?" Wendy had her keys out and beeped her doors. The headlights flicked on and the interior lights lit up.

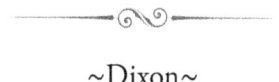

~Dixon~

CORA. HER NAME WAS Cora.

Cora and Wendy walked out of the bar and to the parking lot, me two steps behind. I had to hand it to Jake for getting me in the door and giving me the excuse to watch Cora from the back. That knee-length black dress hugged her every curve and had me itching to put my hand on her back, to lead her somewhere besides her car.

I listened to the friends talk—I couldn't help it, being so close—and let the soft tones of Cora's voice wash over me. I could listen to her voice forever...soft, lilting, tender—until her words garbled and became moans, calling my name as she came. *Shit.* I had to stop drifting off into the fantasy of her and pay attention to the real her, the right-here-and-now her.

Cora said her car was parked at the back of the lot. Right where there weren't any lights. Jake needed to take care of that little detail.

"I'll make sure you get there safely." The words were out of my mouth before my brain could stop them. Hopefully my brain could do a better job keeping my mouth shut in the future. But it sure as shit seemed to be out to lunch right now.

And after Wendy instructed Cora not to do anything she wouldn't do, my mouth beat my brain again: "And what does that limit us to, Cora?" I smiled at her, hoping my dirty thoughts weren't leaking out of my gaze. A drunk at a bar had basically propositioned her, or her friend...or maybe both; I didn't think she'd appreciate another pass from a stranger. I wanted to sleep with her, sure, but I didn't want to be a stranger.

"Well, Wendy's always been more of an adventure junkie than me, so I'm afraid that bar is pretty low." Her smile lit up her face, and some of the stress of the past half-hour seemed to fade from her features.

We still stood under the parking lot lights. I was about a head taller than her; a tendril or two of her straight, midnight-black hair lifted in the spring breeze. Her face flushed—whether from thoughts of Wendy's exploits or from something else, I couldn't tell—and she looked down, tucking some hair behind her ear.

"Hey, I just realized we never got introduced. My name's Dixon. Dixon Reed." I offered my hand to her. When her hand came up, so did her gaze. Her smooth, smaller hand was enveloped in my callused palm. That electric tingle shot up my arm again, zapping the few brain cells I'd managed to hold on to.

"Cora. Cora Stetson. Yes, like the hat." She blushed.

"Well, Cora Stetson, like the hat, it's nice to meet you."

"My car's over there." She looked over at the edge of the parking lot and then back to me. Her eyes, as deep green as a sparkling gem, brightened under the lights.

"Well, let's get you there." How could I drag out the sixty-second walk across this parking lot? I needed more time...and to step up my game. Any second now, she'd be in her car and out of my life. The click-clack of her heels echoed in my head as I followed her.

Then: "Ouch! Damn!"

If I hadn't been mesmerized by the sway of her hips, I would have seen why she twisted her ankle and dropped to the ground.

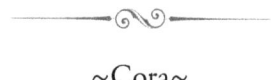

~Cora~

I WALKED AWAY FROM his stare and that rumbly voice that bounced around my head. All I needed to do was get to my car, and then I wouldn't feel overheated and the fluttering in my stomach would settle down. Dixon was sending my system into overdrive or something. I tried to concentrate on closing the distance to my car as quick as possible. But the heat of his stare was still there, and I still wanted to feel his hands there.

That was why I wasn't looking at my feet or the chewed-up pavement in the parking lot. "Ouch! Damn!" My body was flailing, right until it smacked into the hard dirt—no pavement anymore—and my left ankle twisted. On a three-inch heel, a twisted ankle was a bitch. This hurt...and would hurt for more than a few minutes. There were some minor scrapes on my hands from trying to break the fall, but my damn heel was broken.

The only light now was from the almost-full moon; we were too far out of the streetlight lamp's reach. My ankle was at a bit of an angle, and it was swelling. This night was too much, and another curse slipped out. "Motherfucker, that hurts!"

Dixon knelt and tenderly lifted my leg.

I jumped at the contact, but not because it hurt. Well, there was my hurt pride and my hurt ankle, but the reaction was pure attraction. He caressed my calf to my ankle, as his fingers ghosted their way down, fluttering softly and at a leisurely pace. His warm hand was callused, but not too rough. A tingle skittered over my body.

"Looks like a sprain. Can you wiggle those little piggies?"

My eyes were fixed on his fingers, watching them dance on my skin. I drew in a sharp breath and wiggled my toes—all ten of my Summer Reign-painted toes—inside my heels.

"Yup. A sprain. You need to elevate and ice that before it really gets bad. You live nearby?"

No. No way was he going to find out where I lived. Much less take me there. "Not really." I gulped back my nerves. "Do you live close by?"

A smile took over his face. "Why, Ms. Stetson, are you trying to get invited to my place? You know, you didn't have to fall to have a reason to visit." His grin grew larger, and a laugh escaped. "I'd be happy to take you back to my place, Cora." His eyes sparked at his words as he watched for my reaction.

There was that heat again, and I was certain it was in my eyes, too.

~Dixon~

BY SOME TWIST OF FATE—OR rather, by twist of the ankle—I now had Cora in my arms as I walked back toward the bar.

"Umm...Dixon, I know I might need ice, and maybe the bourbon to go with it, but you do realize you are taking me back to the bar, right?"

Cora's teasing words had me tightening my arms under her to hold her closer. "I live over the bar. Well, live might be a stretch. I've got a room there...a temporary thing while I figure some stuff out. The stairs are on the other side of the front doors—you'd hardly see them if you weren't looking for them."

"Oh." She thought about that for a second. "What do you do? I mean, if you're just living here temporarily?"

"Right now, I rescue ladies in distress." I tried to keep her steady as I approached the front doors to the bar. A spring scent, like fresh-cut grass, swirled around. She was as light as a flower petal falling to the ground. The entire experience was like the day after the first rain of spring, full of promise of what was to come.

The bouncer, Dave, sat on his stool, keeping an eye on the inside from the propped-open door. The closer I got, the more sure I was that Jake would hear about this by the time I got to the upstairs door. Me carrying a lady across the parking lot was bound to catch Dave's eye; about two seconds after that, Jake would get the news from him. I nodded to Dave as we passed by. "Tell Jake it's just a sprain—no big deal."

"No big deal? Hey, this is going to make things difficult for me. I've got—"

"I don't want Dave here thinking you were trying to worm your way into my apartment. Or worse, Jake thinking it." What I meant was I was covering my interest in getting her into my bed—apartment, I mean.

"Oh. I see your point, I guess." Her nose scrunched. "Maybe I should go to a walk-in clinic or something. You really don't need to take care of me."

But, to my surprise, I'd be damned if that wasn't exactly what I wanted to do.

TWO

~Cora~

THIS WAS GETTING WORSE by the minute, and not just the pain and embarrassment. I shouldn't go to his place. Really, I shouldn't. But I wanted to. He held me gently, but firmly. I was safe there: safe from drunks hitting on me, safe from broken heels and twisted ankles. Safe from people trying to run my life. But possibly not safe from the heat I now felt—not imagined—from his hands on my skin.

But his steps continued, around the corner of the bar and up the stairs to the second floor of the building. He didn't break a sweat, or have to catch his breath. As though he'd been carrying women up flights of stairs his entire life.

"Now, don't judge me on how it looks. It's a temporary thing, remember. But I'm sure I've got some aspirin and ice for your ankle. We can prop it up on some pillows and rest it a bit before you try putting any weight on it."

He fumbled for the keys in his pocket—quite the feat while he kept me in his arms. Once he found the right one and got the door open, he clicked on the light.

I wouldn't judge him, but it was…well, plain would be generous. Beige walls, beige counters, beige appliances, beige couch, beige carpet. As if someone was afraid to put color into their life…or didn't care about the place.

He set me down on that beige couch. It might look boring as hell, but it was a comfy couch.

"Here, put your foot up on this coffee table. Use one of those pillows on the couch to lift it up some." He plucked a beige (of course) pillow off the edge of the couch, set it on the coffee table, and moved my leg to get it settled.

That little zip zinged again. *Wow.*

"Let me get that ice." He turned to the kitchenette a few steps away to rummage in the freezer for ice. "Ice, ice, baby...where are you, ice?" His mutterings filled the quiet as I took a moment to examine him from behind.

And what a behind it was. The jeans hugged his butt—none of that baggy jean crap where you'd see the guy's underwear. My gaze wandered up to his broad shoulders and that onyx hair—a slight wave to it, cut short but not a buzz cut—that my fingers itched to run through. He was about six foot, a good five or six inches taller than me. The perfect height to snuggle my head under his chin and breathe in his sandalwood cologne.

Stop. No running fingers, no broad chest to feel, no scent to inhale, no ass to hold as he...*NO. Just stop.*

He spun around. "Found it! I'll get a plastic baggie and then a towel to wrap around it. And two aspirin, coming up."

The smile on his face only grew as my face heated. He'd caught me looking at him.

~Dixon~

I DIDN'T MEAN TO EMBARRASS her, but damn. That look she was giving me—her gaze traveled up and down my body, and she parted her lips. I wanted to sink into her and never let go. But

I sensed a one-night stand wasn't her style, so I tried casual teasing instead. "Why, Ms. Stetson, were you checking me out? Tsk, tsk. Trying to take advantage of your knight in shining armor?"

"Umm..."

I laughed. "Well, let's see if I can dig up that aspirin before I call myself a true knight in shining armor." I headed to the bathroom and rummaged through the medicine cabinet. I figured an hour or so of elevation, ice, and the aspirin would get her on her feet. So I had sixty minutes to find out everything about her, not be a jerk, not throw myself at her, and definitely get her phone number. If my brain would engage before my mouth—or my dick—I'd be all set.

I was doomed.

"Here you go. Dr. Dixon says to take two and call him in the morning." Yeah, so much for the brain engaging before the mouth did.

"Doctor, huh? You strike me more as a Boy Scout—you know, always prepared." She took the aspirin from my hand and swallowed them with a gulp of water.

The flash of heat from that simple touch had me flustered. It traveled straight to my dick, getting it to stand to attention. And more of my brain cells fried, I swear. I tried to get back into the conversation at hand.

"Well, I never made it to the Boy Scouts. Got kicked out of Cub Scouts." I shrugged.

She looked at me, her lips pressing together. "What could you possibly do to get kicked out of Cub Scouts?"

"Well, it used to be you had to pay dues. Each week, my mom'd give me the money and off I'd go to the meeting. I'd spend the money on the way there—you know, gum, candy, video game. Whatever sounded good. I'd tell the den leader that my mom and I were poor and couldn't afford the dues. After a while, he contacted my mom and told her not to worry about the dues. I was totally busted. She told the guy she'd given me the dues money, and that was the end of that. They kicked me out."

She tried to swallow her laughter. "Did she ground you or anything?"

I smiled. I hadn't thought about that story in a long time. It was one of the few good memories I had of my mom. Before everything went to shit. Before she was gone. My smile disappeared, and my shoulders sagged as that familiar hollow feeling of despair settled in.

This...this was why I never let anyone in. There was shit I did not want to think about, much less talk about.

"Nope. She was cool about it." I left out how my stepfather reacted, though. It was the first time he'd lost his temper with me, the first time he'd hit me. Getting grounded was a new thing, too.

Time for a change of subject. "So, tell me, Ms. Stetson like the hat, what do you do? Besides go drinking with your friend and try to finagle your way into a stranger's apartment?"

Her sultry lips—God, her mouth was just begging to be kissed—turned into a full smile.

"That's not all I do. In fact, I don't do that at all." The smile became a pout.

Still begging to be kissed.

"I...work downtown."

~Cora~

HOW PATHETIC WAS THAT answer? Very. But I didn't know what to say. Certainly not the truth. That would lead to questions, questions I didn't want to answer. What I wanted was his mouth on my mouth, my hands on his body, his... *Shit, this had to stop.* I'd never been this disoriented around a guy before. I usually had more control. Well, that's not true...I never required control until I met

Dixon. And that meant more trouble for me, for sure. Something I seriously did not need. Dealing with Mark and my father was more than enough testosterone in my life already.

"Downtown, huh? Like at an accounting firm or a lawyer's office? Come on, Cora, what do you do?" He stretched his arm out over the back of the couch, his fingers inches away from my shoulder. He turned toward me, a curious look on his face.

"Something like that. Actually, you never answered my question from before. What is it that you do? Why are you living above Jake's bar?" I hoped redirecting the attention would work, and he'd leave the subject of my career alone.

"What, you don't believe I rescue ladies in distress?" A grin tugged at his kissable lips. "Like I said, I'm just here temporarily. Jake's my brother—well, stepbrother—so when I needed a place, he offered this up. I'm working construction with an old high school buddy right now, but that's probably temporary too. Not sure exactly what I want, but I know it's more than that or this crash pad over a bar." He scratched his cheek. "I'll figure something out soon, I guess. I like being here with Jake, so maybe it's time to stop wandering around and settle down. Maybe get a real place of my own. Find a direction for my life."

Well, that explained how he easily carried me across the parking lot and up the stairs. And the broad shoulders. And the muscled arms.

He tapped his fingers on the back of the couch, and all I wanted was them on my arm, smoothing away the day's cares. Somehow, my body shifted just enough that his fingertips did brush my shoulder. I gulped at the spark the touch elicited and drew a deep breath. "How long have you been here? I mean, living over Jake's?"

"A few months. Came into Allentown in February to catch up with Jake and see his place. He offered me a job tending bar, but it's not my thing. I'd be happier drinking than handing out the drinks.

Or I'd spend too much time watching the game and not paying attention to the customers. Didn't think I should abuse Jake's good nature that way. The apartment is more than enough to ask."

He leaned over to check my ankle. I still had my shoes on; I wasn't sure whether it was better to take them off or keep them on. And right now, my head wasn't interested in figuring out that medical mystery. I had more pressing issues, like how his touch singed my leg as he caressed the ankle. I couldn't help but jump a bit at the feeling.

"What do you think? Want to watch some of the game while we let this rest some more? I'm not sure that aspirin kicked in yet if it hurts when I just touch it."

What could I do? Tell him it was his touch that had me so jumpy? That I wanted to grab him and never let him go? That I wanted to experience that tingle all over as his hands wandered my body?

"I should go. You must have had plans before I crashed them." Getting out of there before I gave in to any temptation would be the smart thing to do.

~Dixon~

I COULDN'T LET HER go. Plans to watch a game with my buddy or the chance to get to know Cora? No contest—Cora'd win every time. And I couldn't stop touching her, either. That twisted ankle was a blessing in disguise for me. I'd gotten to feel her calf, touch that silky skin; I'd gotten to carry her in my arms for a good two minutes; I'd gotten to brush her arm on the couch. Mostly little touches, but the rush was incredible. No way I'd want to give that up. Each caress created more compulsion to explore her body, to find those secret places that would have her shuddering in surrender.

"No. Stay. You've hardly let that ankle rest. We'll give it some more time and see how you're feeling in a bit. Want something to drink or eat? I can offer...let's see..." My words rushed out as I got up and checked out the cabinet next to the sink. "A bag of Cheez-its that feels like it's all crushed...some chocolate chip cookies, which may or may not be stale...a chocolate bar..."

"Oh, chocolate cures anything. As long as it's real chocolate and not that fake stuff."

I turned back to her and grinned. "Fake chocolate? You think I'd offer a beauty like you fake chocolate? Nothing but the best, m'lady." I handed over the Cadbury bar. "I'm partial to the Cadbury Eggs, too, but I missed them this year."

"Ew. The crème eggs? Those are so disgustingly sweet. I'm a Cadbury Mini Eggs fan, myself. Now, that's some good chocolate. I can't tell if I'm happy or sad they are only available for Easter."

I took the few steps back to the couch.

"Oh, that's much better. I never ate before I met up with Wendy tonight. I was busy—" The smile disappeared from her face, along with whatever she was going to say next, and she bit the inside of her cheek. She fidgeted with the chocolate wrapper.

"Busy? With what?"

"Nothing. Never mind. Thanks for the chocolate. But I really should go." She lifted her foot off the coffee table and set it on the ground, readying herself to get up.

And leave.

As she put her weight on it, she let out a little gasp, so I reached out to catch her before she fell. She listed over to the side, and I tightened my hold on her waist.

"Whoa there. I think you need a bit more rest before you go running out of here. Or even walking out of here." I stood there and stared into those green eyes. More of my brain cells fried as her eyes widened in surprise. And then sparked with desire.

I let my hand drift up her side, then along her neck. I traced her jawline with my fingers. Tingles shot through my arm. Everything seemed to come to attention, especially my dick. Just a breath away...just a little farther and our lips would touch. Her breath came in quick spurts, and my heart beat a mile a minute. She clutched my shoulders.

Then she leaned back and sat down. "I guess I should stay a bit longer. It doesn't feel like I could put too much pressure on it right now."

Damn. So close. But I wasn't about to give up.

~Cora~

DAMN. THAT WAS CLOSE. Too close, in too many ways. I'd almost kissed Dixon...given in to the temptation he was clearly becoming. I'd almost spilled about my day... about myself...and I'd almost spilled over the couch. *If he hadn't been there to catch me...* Enough of that line of thought.

I still had that chocolate bar in my hand. I snapped off a piece and let it melt in my mouth. It'd help me keep my mouth shut...stop me from talking about myself and stop me from kissing him. Even if that's all I wanted to do. Those blue eyes watched me, shimmering with intensity, as if he were trying to see my soul. And damn if I didn't want to bare it to him.

If I couldn't leave his couch right this second, I could at least lead the conversation. Or try to.

"I can practically hear you thinking over there. You okay?" He was back in the kitchenette, opening a beer bottle. "Want a beer? It'll take your mind off the pain."

I wasn't sure it was the pain I should forget or the way he looked at me. I probably needed my wits about me to get through this night. "Sure. A beer'd be great. But just one. After all, a chocolate bar dinner isn't exactly going to balance out more than one beer." One beer wouldn't be the end of the world, right?

Our fingers brushed again when he handed me the longneck. And damn if that tingle didn't run up my arm and down to my girly parts. This was getting unreal. Forget getting...it just was unreal. But I didn't want it to end. Even though it'd be for the best. I didn't have time for a relationship—even a fling. I needed to focus on my goals: My bed-and-breakfast. Getting out from under my father's sphere of influence. Make my own destiny, not follow his.

I took a swallow of the beer and tried to rein in the fluttering in my chest.

THREE

~Dixon~

"GO FISH."

"I can't believe it. I'm losing at Go Fish." I took a swig of my beer and grabbed the top card. "How can I be losing at a kid's game?"

"Maybe you're just a kid...who sucks at Go Fish." Cora giggled. "Do you have an eight?"

That giggle kicked me in the gut. I looked over the cards in my hand and met her stare. How could she be so serious about the game but still be tipsy and giggly? And how did someone get tipsy on one beer?

"You know I do. Damn it. I really suck at this game." I handed over the card, trying my best to avoid touching her hand. There'd be more sparks, and I wasn't sure I could trust myself to not turn a casual touch to a stroke, and then to a full caress, and then the possibilities seemed endless. Or, actually, they seemed like they'd end in bed. Which, I knew, would be a beautiful mistake. But still, a mistake. She was the kind of woman who deserved more than a one-night stand, and that's all I'd ever done...all I was willing to do.

"Do you have a..." Cora seemed to be lost in thought. "A queen?"

I licked my lips. "Ah...no. Alas, I have no queen in my life, or in my hand."

A pink blush covered her face as she reached for the deck. "That's not what I was axing...I mean, asking." Another giggle escaped before she took a sip from the longneck.

All I could do was watch as she tipped her head back, put her luscious pale-pink lips on the bottle, and swallowed the liquid. Her skin practically shimmered as she sighed.

"Yummy. I forgot how much I like beer." She whispered the words, as though it were some kind of personal confession. Then she broke out into a wide smile. "Can I have another?"

"Sure, I guess. You sure you can handle it?" From the looks of things—the way she held her cards loosely, the way she seemed to drift off, the way she was mixing up her words, the way she giggled at the slightest thing—she was definitely a lightweight.

She peered up at me. "I can handle it." A delicate belch punctuated her assertion.

I stood to get another beer for each of us. "How's that ankle? It's been about an hour since you had that aspirin."

"What ankle?" Cora giggled. "You mean this ankle?" She lifted her leg off the coffee table and rotated her left ankle. "Shit! Ouch! Damn!"

"I'll take that as it only hurts when you move it. Here, put it back down and rest it some more. I'm sure kicking my butt at Go Fish will improve your disposition." I put the beer bottle next to her cards and moved to get her leg back on the pillow on the coffee table. I was jonesing for my next fix of touching Cora, and I wasn't about to miss out on my chance to feel that silky soft skin under my fingers.

"So, Dixon…if you could go anywhere in the world, where would you go?" Cora watched me holding her leg, making sure it settled softly on the pillow.

Her calf muscle was firm, probably from those high heels. God, I'd love to see her in them…and nothing else. Thoughts of her body, wet and ready for me, filled my head. Shit, she was waiting for an answer…what was the question?

"Where would I go? I dunno. I like it here, right here with you. Something like this would be fine with me."

"Seriously? Right here? In a bachelor pad, over your brother's bar, in a room so beige it could put you to sleep, where you can practically be in every room in two steps...that's your dream travel destination?" She cocked her head, her mouth pursed.

"What can I say? I've got lofty goals." I picked at the label on the beer bottle. I could sense her stare, demanding to know the truth. "Well, I suppose, if you made me choose, the place I'd like to go isn't really what you'd call a travel destination. It'd just be a place, a place of my own, out in the country a bit. Nothing big or extravagant. Simple. Easy. Out of the hustle and bustle. Somewhere I could see the moon and stars, hear the crickets, catch fireflies."

I looked up and was blown over by the smile on her face. All dreamy, like she was right there in my little travel fantasy.

"Fireflies? I loved catching fireflies when I was a kid. At my grandmother's cottage..." She swallowed and grew quiet for a few seconds. She reached for the bottle at her side and took a long drink. "Got any sexes in your hand? Sixes. Sixes, that's what I mean." Cora looked at the cards in her hands, a soft pink blush covering her cheeks at her slip.

I grinned. Damn straight I had some sex. And later, I'd be having the kind of sex a guy like me, hung up on a dream woman, had...the self-serving kind, jerking off in the shower and imagining it was Cora with me, not my hand.

"No sixes in my hand." I thought about offering some of that sex she drunkenly said she was after, and my mind wandered right back into the gutter. But again, some inner voice reminded me she deserved more than a one-night stand. God, this was going to be a long night. "Go fish."

Her hand trembled as she reached for the deck to pick up her card.

"So what about you, Cora? What would be your dream travel spot? The Greek isles? Australia? Iceland?" I took a quick swig of my beer and tried to focus on the game or the conversation, not the way she held the cards in her small hand or the way she bit her lip in concentration. "Do you have a five?"

"Hmmm... I've been to so many places already that sometimes it seems like there's nowhere new to go. One of the perks—" She jerked her head back.

Why, I had no idea.

She grabbed the longneck and took a sip, as if to cover for her sudden stop in conversation. "Nope, no five."

"Darn. I was sure you had some secret stash of fives in that hand of yours." I tried to joke to lighten her mood. Whatever she didn't want to talk about was fine with me as long as she was still right here in front of me. "But that's okay. Everyone's entitled to their secrets."

"I think I should head out soon. I've taken enough of your night." Cora moved as if she were going to get up again.

Even though it shouldn't bother me, her continued efforts to leave had my heart sinking. I put my hand on her leg. Those damn tingles started up again, but I couldn't let myself get distracted. Between her ankle and the two beers—and her apparent lightweight status—I wasn't sure driving home was a good idea, and I told her so. "I dunno. You might want to rethink that. I'm not trying to be bossy here, but you're probably in no condition to drive home. If you were down in Jake's, he'd call you a cab or something. But you're up here, all comfy on the couch. Your leg is up and icing. Maybe you should stay here tonight."

She stared at me. Or rather, at my mouth. I held my breath as I waited for her to respond. God knew I wanted her to stay. I mean, really wanted her to stay. I promised myself I'd be a gentleman—against my instincts that demanded I show her the benefits of *not* being a gentleman—but I figured she needed to hear that I wasn't trying to get her into my bed. Even if that was my usual game.

"Honest. No hanky-panky. Just a safe place for you to crash. No need to drive impaired or try to deal with your ankle. I'll take the couch and you can have the bed. Scout's honor."

"Scout's honor?" Her laugh exploded. "You mean, the kicked-out-of-the-Cub-Scouts-honor?" She hiccupped and tried to catch her breath. She lifted her leg off the coffee table and placed it on the floor. After putting a little pressure on it, she eased back into the couch. "Maybe you're right. It's not giving me a ton of problems, but it's still sore. Some more ice and keeping it up sounds good to me. And yeah, I'd be happy to not deal with driving or taking a cab." She grinned and held her bottle up. "And I can indulge in one more of these."

"You sure? You look like you might have hit your limit there."

"If I'm not driving, and I'm not going to walk down any stairs tonight, I can handle one more beer. Honest." She dangled the empty in front of me again. "Come on. One more." She smiled, and my heart stuttered. "I promise I won't get too wild on you."

I wasn't worried about *her* getting wild; I was worried about *me* getting wild. Definitely time for me to switch to water. I could hold my liquor, but I wanted to make sure she'd be all right for the rest of the night, which might be more difficult if I kept drinking.

"All right...one more beer coming up. Then it's off to bed with you, little miss." I couldn't miss the widening of her eyes and the breath she gulped at the mention of bed. "By yourself, I promise." I couldn't help the words that barely qualified as a whisper: "This time, at least."

After grabbing one more beer for her and my bottle of water, I headed back to the couch and sat next to her. "So, how often do you hang out at Jake's? It seemed like you knew my brother a bit there, at least enough that he wanted to make sure you got to your car okay."

"Jake? Yeah, we've—that's me and Wendy—have been coming to Jake's for a while now. She found it first, and then decided we should make it our regular spot. Jake's been a great guy—always keeping his eye out for any morons, like the guy tonight. It doesn't happen often, but he's been known to throw some people out before they even get a foot in the door. He worked hard to change the atmosphere at the bar. It used to be a real bloodbath kind of place until he took over."

"And you know this how? Hanging out at all the biker bars now, huh?" I'd known Jake had turned the former pit of a bar into something decent, where anyone could cool off with a drink and good food, but to hear it from someone else was nice.

"Hey, bikers are people, too, you know." Her bluster was accompanied by a big smile, so I was pretty sure she was teasing me. "But no, I'm not exactly a fixture at biker bars. Hell, I'm not sure I've ever been to a biker bar. But Jake's is a nice place. Despite what some people think." Her smile turned into a frown.

"What's that mean? Who doesn't like Jake's?"

She seemed lost in her thoughts. "Hhmm? Well, let's see...my father, for one." Her voice lowered. "'Young lady, that is not an appropriate place for you to be spending time. You are more than welcome to have a drink at the club with me and Mark.'" She cleared her throat. "My father's a bit...opinionated. And stubborn. And looking to run my life." Cora grabbed the bottle and took a long pull. "As if I'm five still, and only he knows what's best for me," she muttered.

It was difficult to not hear the bitter hurt in her voice. But there was the other thing that caught my ear, too—Mark. *Who the fuck was Mark?* Did she have a brother? Please, dear God, let it be a brother or something and not a boyfriend. I took a quick look at her hands, just to double-check. *Please, not a husband or a fiancé.* Mark had to be a family member. It'd be the only way I'd stay sane. To meet Cora and fall under her spell...and then have to keep away because she was already taken? Fate, for all its cruel ways, surely wouldn't do that to me on top of everything else.

"And Mark. He's just as bad. 'Cora, join us for a nightcap.' He just wants me to sit there, like a porcelain doll—looking pretty and without a thought or ambition of my own. Don't speak unless spoken to—and nobody speaks to me. They want a bobblehead, someone to agree with every witty, smart, genius thing that comes out of their mouths." Her mumbling took on a life of its own, growing from a faint murmur to a pissed-off, ready to rumble, damnation oration.

And I sensed there was more where that came from. I was about to ask more about Mark, but she took another gulp from the bottle—God, that really was going to be a favorite image in my head from now on—and then she kept on going.

"Those ass-clowns wouldn't know an intelligent idea if it grabbed them by the balls and squeezed them until they were blue in the face. If they'd only listen to me, they'd see I have more to offer than just a pretty face or a family name to carry on. But nooo...." Her volume drifted off and mumblings took over.

I couldn't make out what she was talking about, but it was something that got her going. I wouldn't want to be on the receiving end of that frustration—whether she was drunk or sober. Time to take the bottle away. I reached out to grab it out of her hand. Not too surprisingly, it was empty.

"All right. Let's get you settled for bed. Need to use the restroom first? I might have an extra toothbrush somewhere in there, too." I reached for her hand, ready to pull her up and get her back in my arms. It'd been too long since I'd been able to sneak a feel of her, and I was itching to touch that flawless skin again, even if it was for the four steps to the bathroom.

Cora stood, keeping her weight off her left leg. She looked around awkwardly. "I can hop my way over there." As she lifted her foot completely off the floor, she wobbled.

I quickly got my arms around her waist. "Yeah, I don't think so. You're getting the royal treatment, my lady...an escort until your ankle is better and you can stand on your own two feet without falling over." I was close enough to breathe in the scent of her. It reminded me of spring...fresh-cut grass, flowers ready to bloom, and sunshine warming the laundry on the line. Full of promise.

After offering my arm to act as her crutch as she balanced, we made a hop-skip-jump shuffle to the bathroom. It was a tiny space, with a toilet, a small pedestal sink, and a narrow shower. I rifled through the medicine cabinet again, this time looking for a spare toothbrush and the toothpaste, and grabbed the clean washcloth and hand towel off the wall rack. "Here. Brush your teeth and wash your face before you hit the hay."

"Ummm...I need some privacy." She had a funny look on her face.

"To brush your teeth? Seriously, I've seen teeth before. You can trust I'll be quite the gentlem—" I stopped when her gaze darted around. "Oh, right. Not to brush...those three beers are catching up with you. Well, be careful on that ankle." Trying not to laugh or embarrass her further, I stepped out of the bathroom, closed the door, and made my way to the kitchenette sink to rinse out the bottles...and give her a curtain of noise to cover up any of her activities.

After a minute, the toilet flushed and then the faucet turned on. It didn't take long for her to wash up and open the door.

"Dixon, I'm not feeling good. I think I'm ready for that bed now." She stood—well, slumped would be a better description—in the doorframe of the bathroom, looking a bit out of sorts.

"Well, let's get you taken care of." God knew I wanted to take care of all her needs, but it looked like all that was on tap for her tonight was a bottle of water and more aspirin—for both her ankle and the headache she was sure to have in the morning—and a cold shower for me.

I put my arm around her back to guide her and took the few steps to the bedroom. "The light switch is right there." I nodded in the right direction and she reached out to flick the light on. It wasn't much, but the full-size bed had clean sheets and a comforter. A lamp on the nightstand acted as more of a nightlight than an actual light source.

I set her gently on the bed, fluffed up the pillow, and pulled down the covers for her. Kneeling, I reached down to take off her shoes, first the right and then the left. On the left, I brushed over the ankle to check the swelling. Okay, and to feel that soft skin one more time. I lifted her legs up and tucked them under the covers. "Well, it seems to be improving. You hardly flinched this time when I touched it. I bet a night of rest will have you right as rain." I'm not sure how I did it, but I controlled my urge to run my hands up her legs, up into the promised land under that dress.

"Make sure you take another sip or two of the water before you fall asleep. And if you wake up in the middle of the night, take the extra aspirins. It'll help. Trust me."

"Sir, yes sir," she mumbled, settling into the covers. A slow smile spread over her face. "So what Cub Scout badge do you earn for putting damsels in distress to bed?"

"Well, Cub Scouts don't earn badges like Boy Scouts, but their motto is—" A light snore stopped me. I whispered the rest: "Do Your Best!"

I couldn't seem to stop looking at her, sleeping in my bed. That pull from earlier, when I first saw her in the bar, kept getting stronger. I couldn't get enough of Cora, and whatever she was willing to give me. I started to wonder what my best would look like—what life with Cora in it would be like.

FOUR

~Cora~

THE SUN POKED ITS WAY under my eyelids. It was not a comfortable feeling. Actually, not much was feeling comfortable. I stretched in the bed...but it wasn't my bed. An avalanche of memories—fuzzy memories—dumped over my brain and landed in a lump in my throat.

I was in Dixon's bed.

I'd hurt my ankle.

I'd had too much to drink. *God, I hope I hadn't said too much.* A quick mental review reassured me that no major details had leaked out. But I flushed at the thoughts that I'd had about my rescuer. The very naughty thoughts.

I swiped at the gunk in the corner of my eyes and looked at the bedside table clock: 6:47. If I got up now, I'd have time to get to my car and get to my place, dignity mostly intact. If I timed it right, I could sneak in during the changing of the guard.

But first I had to make sure my ankle was up for the walk to the car. And that I could find my purse and phone. And what was I going to do about Dixon? Sneak out? Wake him up? Write a note or disappear forever? At that thought, my heart clenched. The memory of those blue eyes staring into my soul made the decision for me. I couldn't just ghost him. Maybe there was room in my life for some fun; it didn't have to be anything serious.

I pushed up and sat, swinging my legs down to the floor. A gentle pressure was followed by getting ready to fully stand up. Success! I could stand on my bare feet with no issues. Now the real test—those damn three-inch heels. They sat on the side of the bed, waiting to be strapped on and torture my footsies. Although, with the left one broken, walking would be a lopsided affair.

As I grabbed the current bane of my existence, it was clear the water and aspirin late last night had worked their magic. No headache, no stomach ache, no dizziness. I'd gotten lucky and the hangover gods had wreaked their worst on someone else last night. I shouldn't have had that second, much less the third, beer. Maybe someday I'd build up a tolerance, but clearly I was still a lightweight. Oh well. There were worse things to be.

Like sneaking out of a man's—a practical stranger's—apartment, ready to do my walk of shame. Except, there was no shame. I hadn't done anything wrong, despite any dirty thoughts that wandered through my drunken mind. And Dixon had kept to his word—no funny business from him. Although, maybe it would have been a little gratifying if he'd tried a little funny business.

I stood and put my full weight on my feet. Nothing more than a little discomfort, so I made my way to the closed door. I turned the handle slowly, aiming to be as quiet as possible.

Creak.

So much for that effort. The squeaky hinges gave me away. Or they would have, if the snoring man on the couch could have heard it over the sawing action going on. But I stopped in my tracks. Not from the squeaky hinge or the buzzing of Dixon's snores. It was the man himself.

His long legs draped over the end of the couch—one over the arm and one that landed on the floor at a weird angle. An arm rested on his forehead, the other on his stomach. His bare stomach. His bare, muscled, six-pack stomach. His fingers were curled in the blanket twisted around his hips. A hint of a boxer band peeked through the folds of the blanket. The steady up and down of his breathing was accentuated when a snoring jag set in.

With his eyes closed, I could take my time looking at his face without being mesmerized by his gaze. There was a bit of stubble there, but also full lips. Kissable lips. Lips that could work magic. A mouth that could whisper sweet, dirty words full of teasing and then deliver on those promises.

"See anything you like?" Those lips lifted into a playful smile as he dropped his arm off his forehead. "Good morning, Cora. I've gotta say, it's good to see you on your feet this morning. Any problems with the ankle? How's your head?"

"G-Good morning." Crap, he'd caught me. I guess either he wasn't really sleeping or that damn hinge did give me away. "It all seems fine. You were right—a night of rest was all I needed. But I sure could use a coffee to wake myself up some more." I looked away from his naked chest and toward the kitchenette. "Any chance there's an espresso machine in there, ready to give me a caffeine boost?"

"Not exactly. I've got an electric kettle and instant coffee. Not sure there's any creamer. Should be okay on sugar, though." He sat up, the blanket still wrapped around his middle. His arms went up in the air, stretching overhead while he yawned. "Water might be better—get you hydrated, not dehydrated." He moved to get up, and the blanket shifted on his lap.

Not ready for that sight—well, I wouldn't really complain—I motioned for him to stay where he was and took the three steps into the kitchenette. "Maybe you're right. Water sounds fine." And would provide a quicker exit; no need to wait for water to heat up and make awkward small talk. Or avoid questions. Or make an idiot of myself and latch onto his shoulders and rub up against him. You know, typical morning activities. Or what sounded like fun morning activities. But I had a job to get to.

I grabbed a water bottle from the fridge and turned around, ready to make my escape. But I was caught in Dixon's arms.

"Hey. You in a rush? How about some breakfast?"

"I-I've got to get going. Thanks, anyway. Actually, thanks for everything...last night...the ankle thing...the place to crash..." I blushed furiously, now even more aware of his bare chest and arms as he held me in a loose embrace. Thank God he had shorts on over those boxer briefs. Although now I could see his muscled legs.

I moved to get out of his arms, feeling the loss of his heat immediately. Before I could think too much of it, I stopped and looked him in the eyes. Blue pools of hazy heat caught fire and I couldn't think for a second. Or two. Hell, it could have been sixty seconds, for all I knew. Like some kind of magic, words poured out of my mouth, surprising me. "I've got to go, but I'd like to see you again. No twisted ankles, no rescuing required. Call me, okay?" I rattled off my cell number and hustled to the door, breathless. A lightness grew in my chest. It felt right to tell Dixon I wanted to see him again, consequences be damned.

Just as I had my hand on the doorknob, he answered, his voice thick with emotion.

"I'd rescue you anytime, Cora. You can count on me, any day of the week."

IT WAS GOING TO BE difficult, but I was hoping against hope that I wouldn't run into Wendy at the front desk. If I was lucky, I'd hit it just right and Jasper would still be on shift, waiting for her to show up.

I parked the car in my assigned spot and took a deep breath. A quick check in the rearview mirror for any wayward hair out of the hasty ponytail I put it in and I looked at my lips. The ones I wanted Dixon to kiss...to nibble... *Ugh.* I needed to get a grip. There was no room in my life right now for Dixon or any of the complications a new relationship would bring. So why did I give him my phone number? I remembered the way my heart pounded when he looked at me and how my body tingled at his slightest touch. I'd never felt that with anyone before, and I wanted more of it.

His parting words circled in my brain, like a kitty roller toy—round and round, unending. I wouldn't mind some rescuing from certain parts of my life. But there was plenty of my life I liked, and plenty I was looking forward to. Once I made my plans more public—meaning, filling in my father and Mark on what I was going to do, regardless of what they thought I was going to do—I'd be doing my own rescuing of myself. In less than a year, I'd be turning twenty-six and it'd be Independence Day. No man needed. Just me, a bed-and-breakfast, and no one making decisions for me.

The front glass doors slid open as I approached.

"I guess you did do what I would have done," Wendy chirped from the front desk.

Damn.

"For your information..." I paused and looked around for any other Stetson Suites employees. With the coast clear, I informed my best friend in what I hoped was a calm, normal voice, "No, this is not a walk of shame. I only spent the night there because I hurt my ankle. Damn heels got caught up in the dirt and down I went."

Wendy snorted. "Sure. Shoe problems. Happens to me *alllll* the time." She motioned me closer. "No, really. Tell me everything. Spare no detail."

I pulled my shoes off my feet—barefoot in the lobby might not be the best idea, but it was time to stop walking on two different heel heights. "Seriously. Shoe problems." I dangled the broken shoe in front of Wendy for effect. "No walk of shame. Now, I'm heading up to my place. I'll tell you what there is to tell—which isn't much—later. I've gotta hustle to grab a shower and then head next door before Dad gets in." With that, I headed for the elevator.

One of the "perks" of being who I was—the only daughter of the owner of Stetson Suites—was a penthouse suite in the original namesake hotel. Yeah, it's soooo hard to have room service and maid service. But there's also the security cameras—so my father can find out my every move in and out of my apartment...and who is coming or going—not to mention the staff watching everything I do. God only knew who reported to him on all the gossip about me, but someone did. There was no way he could know the things he did without somebody telling him, and it sure wasn't me. It wasn't a big deal most of the time; the most salacious thing that ever happened was a late night out with Wendy.

It wasn't Wendy, though. We'd met in college eight years ago during our freshman year and had some hospitality courses together. She'd been a whiz at the restaurant management class I struggled with, and I helped her with the marketing classes. We were as thick as thieves, and we each kept the other's secrets. Nope, it was someone else on staff, looking to brown-nose, who'd leak details to my dad.

But no time to worry about that now. I plucked my key out of my purse and let myself in. The car keys landed in the bowl in the entryway and I took a moment to gaze out the floor-to-ceiling windows at the view of downtown. The spring morning was well on its way, and I needed to get a move on to beat Dad to the office.

After a shower—a pure bliss of hot water, soapy suds, and a massaging shower head—I pulled my hair up into my "professional" look of twisted up on my head in a bun. Original, I know, but simple and classic. Add in the boring, traditional charcoal-colored pencil skirt, white blouse, and low heels, and I was now your average office drone. Even if I was the boss's daughter.

I didn't have much to compare it to, but my commute—which consisted of out the door, to the elevator, down to the lobby, out the doors, crossing the street, entering a lobby, heading up an elevator, and getting out on the seventh floor—was brief. No time to listen to more than one song; no podcasts or radio talk shows. But also no traffic jams or speeding tickets, no accidents.

After the break-in at our family home, my father insisted I move into Stetson Suites. My mother had been home alone—I was a freshman in college and Dad was traveling—when the intruders broke down the door. The aftermath—her coma for six months and subsequent death, the trial of the suspects, the appeals of the convictions—had my father stressed out and worried.

He wasn't the only one. I almost flunked out my freshman year. The only reason I didn't was because Wendy made sure I had notes for classes I missed, and did her best to keep me on track. She even took me to her home for school breaks, and was there for every breakdown—in the middle of the day or the dead of night. Wendy did everything my mother would have done for me if she were alive.

My father threw himself even more into running the business. He stopped visiting the campus and our sporadic contact became almost nonexistent. The only thing he did insist on was that I had to let his office know whenever I left campus, and then he arranged for me to live at Stetson Suites after graduation. I could count the number of times we spoke in person in the four years of college on one hand, with the occasional text wishing me a happy birthday or a Merry Christmas.

By moving from my college dorm right into Stetson Suites (both the job and a place in the hotel), I hoped to keep my father happy. It was a simple solution. Besides, I had no desire to go back to the home that no longer felt safe, where my mother had effectively been taken from our lives. I wasn't even sure Dad spent nights there anymore, either.

After a quick wave to Wendy at the front desk, I made my way across the street to Stetson Suites corporate headquarters. I started to think about the projects on my plate...but Dixon kept popping into my head. Dixon seemed like a great guy, but I needed to focus on work. Not his piercing gaze. Or gentle hands on my leg. Or the way he tucked me in last night...

The elevator doors opened on the seventh floor. The serene, quiet atmosphere settled my mind and turned on my concentration. I was working on a huge presentation for the upcoming social media ad campaign, something my father didn't see the value in. He'd built up the hotel chain on traditional ad campaigns—print, radio, television—but he had yet to explore what he could achieve with a more contemporary outlook.

I'd loved my marketing classes at Cornell, so working in the marketing department was a natural fit for me. But I wasn't one to coast in on my last name, despite Mark's opinion of my contributions to the company. For someone who wasn't directly involved in the hotel business—he was one of the outside legal team my father used, as well as the son of my father's best friend—he had an opinion about everything and never worried himself about whether he had any right to express those opinions. And the fact that my father was pushing some kind of "alliance" between our two families also meant Mark had no problem expressing his opinion about my life and how it should conform to his expectations.

Fortunately, Maeve, the department VP, treated me like every other staff member in the department, even if hiring me hadn't exactly been her choice. And she was committed to moving the company in the right direction—the future, that is—and hoped that having the boss's daughter give the presentation to the senior executives would at least mean they'd be willing to listen.

I popped my head in Maeve's office. "Hey, I'm going to have a draft ready for you later today or tomorrow. I need a few graphics and to run the text through another set of eyes to proof it."

Maeve stared at me over her glasses low on her nose. "Fine. We can do a run-through tomorrow at..." She glanced at her computer. "How's two sound?" She had her hands ready to enter the time on her schedule.

"Perfect." I made a mental note to add that to my calendar and headed to my office.

My low heels hardly made a noise as I walked down the hall, but Dad still heard me.

"Cora. Good morning."

His office door was fully open, so there was no way to avoid stopping or pretending I didn't hear him. I could only hope his spies were behind the times and hadn't updated him on my late—early?—arrival back home. I was an adult, and it was annoying that my father still kept tabs on me as if I were a teenager who'd taken the family car for a joyride and couldn't be trusted.

"Hi, Dad." I stepped into the plush office.

He sat behind his mahogany desk, a single computer screen and keyboard on the surface. Although he smiled at me, I couldn't see anything but a man crushed by time and circumstance. He looked every one of his fifty-seven years...and maybe a few more, too. The light I had seen there as a kid was gone—long gone—and now all he had in his eyes were expectations. Ones I wasn't willing to fulfill.

"I hear that social media thing you've been wasting your time on is up for discussion soon. I don't see why Maeve pushed you to do this. Everything is fine the way it is...it's always worked for us before."

"Dad, we can't get stuck in the past. There're ways to incorporate these new strategies without a huge impact on the stuff you've always done. It's not a total replacement, just a way to reach out to a younger generation, become their hotel of choice...build their loyalty when they are young so we'll have a future client base. You want the company to be around for another fifty years, right?" He'd resist change, but he would also fight tooth and nail to ensure the company was viable for future generations...which was a sticking point on my end of things. But one battle at a time, right?

He grunted. "Well, I guess we'll see what you've come up with and go from there."

Hardly a ringing endorsement, but I'd take what I could get on this fight.

"So, will you be at the club tonight? I hear the Franklins are hosting a dinner. Maybe tonight will be the night Mark finally gets you to agree to marry him."

Ugh. And here was another battle. One I wasn't able to side-step, much less win, this morning. Or ever. He'd been banging this drum ever since I had agreed to that first date with Mark. "I have other plans tonight. Mark knew that a few weeks ago, so he didn't invite me to his parents' dinner tonight." I purposely didn't address the marriage part of his question. "What charitable cause are they championing tonight? Debutantes Without Prospects? A shelter for pampered princesses who break their nails?"

I couldn't help the snark. Mark was insufferable, but he came by it honestly. His parents were the most hoity-toity people I'd ever met, only concerned with their status and bank account. And their tax write-offs. A by-product of being lawyers, I guess. His father, Martin, was the corporate lawyer for Stetson Suites—and my father's college roommate, best man, and best friend. His mother, Lila, handled international law for their law firm, Franklin, Franklin, and Langdon.

A stern look was his only response. Figuring I'd pushed past my limits, I turned and waved goodbye to him before I was out his door.

FIVE

~Dixon~

"SERIOUSLY? THERE'S nothing wrong with this kitchen."

Ryan swung the sledgehammer and the cabinet buckled under the pressure. "Yup. But we're getting paid to demo it and install the new stuff." He grinned and hefted the sledgehammer again, ready to rain down some more destructive force. "So, did you strike out with that babe from last night? I didn't see you come back to the bar, but man, I just can't figure you got anywhere with her. You must've wanted to back out of our friendly little bet, huh? No dice, man...cough it up. Your team lost, nine to zip."

"Well..." I wasn't sure how to answer him. Actually, I wasn't sure I wanted to answer him about Cora. True, I hadn't gotten anywhere close to what I usually wanted from a woman, but with Cora, over the course of one night, I wanted more than just a one-night stand. Thoughts of anything more than that were foreign, so it kind of threw me off my game. Not that I would say as much to Ryan.

"Yeah, here's your ten bucks. Enjoy a beer on me, dude." I picked up my crowbar and concentrated on the countertop. It had to be granite, glued with some super adhesive. Between the weight of the material and the strength of the glue, I'd be lucky to get any leverage to pop it off the cabinet bases. But damn if I wasn't going to try. I'd already cut away the caulking around the edges and had my shims ready to place between the granite and cabinet base. Now it was time to apply some pressure.

I was familiar with pressure today. My morning wood was compounded with the lovely Ms. Cora featuring in my shower daydreams. Like I'd suspected last night, the closest I got to my goal of getting some was in my hands, my head full of snippets of midnight-black hair and green eyes. And those lips on my cock. Shit, this was not the time to slip into those thoughts. I had shit to rip out, not a chubbie to rub out.

I appreciated Ryan getting me this job, but it wasn't something I enjoyed. I'd been destroying houses with him for the better part of a month and it was getting kind of depressing. Yeah, this time around we had the install part of the job, too, but mostly we worked as a demo team for the construction company Ryan's parents owned. There was enough destruction in the world—especially my world—that I was starting to think I needed to build something up, not pull something down.

That kind of heavy, philosophical thinking got me into a funk—that's what was going on right there. But the other kind of thinking—the kind where my mind filled with dirty thoughts and fantasies about a certain black-haired beauty—wasn't going to pay the bills either, so I refocused on the granite countertop and pried that perfectly fine granite off its foundation.

The black granite had speckles of different colors in it, but my eye was caught in the green flecks. Thoughts of black hair and green eyes filled my head again. *Cora.* Damn, I couldn't get more than five minutes without my wandering mind going back to her. I could picture that dark hair splayed on my pillowcase, those green eyes staring back at me, her words haunting me. *So what Cub Scout badge do you earn for putting damsels in distress to bed?*

"You gonna stare that granite off that cabinet base, or you gonna put your back into it? It's almost lunchtime, and I'd like to have that done before we break." Ryan's amused tone cut through my distraction.

"Yeah, yeah." I wiggled the crowbar farther between the slab and the base. With a hefty heave, I worked my way around the counter. "Okay, let's lift this section out."

Ryan stepped close and grabbed the other end of the sink cutout. "As good a place as any to stop. Gonna grab the lunches from the truck. Be right back."

As Ryan left the room, I stared at the black granite, a grain of an idea forming in my head. Inspired by Cora, I thought about her surrounded by the material, the green flecks in the granite picking up the green of her eyes. If I turned the piece sideways, the cutout could serve as a deep recess for a chair, the rest of the slab as a desk area...or a makeup vanity. Legs made of some ornate scrolled wrought-iron...

"You still off in la-la land? Man, you got it bad." Ryan slapped me on the back and handed me the lunch bag.

"Hey, you think it'd be okay to take some of this demo'd stuff? They're not using any of it for anything else, are they?" All I needed was a place to store it until I could find the pieces for the legs. And a chair. And a mirror. Okay, this might be a bigger project than I first thought.

"Sure, I don't see why not. Otherwise, it's headed to the dumpster and then the landfill. I can check with George to make sure it's not a big deal, but I'm pretty sure it's free and clear, dude."

As Ryan headed off to talk to George, the jobsite manager, thoughts of the project swirled in my head. I had no idea where I'd find any of the stuff I might need, but maybe Jake could help me out with that.

"WHAT HAPPENED WITH Cora last night?" Jake wiped the bar with a rag and gave me a quick look. "I heard from Dave you took her up to your place. And he didn't see her before the place closed down."

Jake wasn't one to nose in my affairs—not that much, anyway—so I was surprised. "Nothing. Didn't he tell you she twisted her ankle?" I gulped some of my beer. "I just gave her a place to crash for the night. Nothing happened." I wasn't sure why I wanted him to know that...but I did. Cora didn't want anyone gossiping about her.

"Nothing, huh? I saw the way you looked at her." He stopped his cleaning and gave me a pointed look. "And I ain't ever seen you hold back when you were interested in a girl—back in high school or from what I've seen recently."

Girl? Cora was all woman. And yes, I could admit that my reputation of going after what I wanted was warranted. But something held me back when it came to Cora. Stalling for time, I pretended to be mesmerized by the label on the beer bottle and picked at it a bit. "Well, maybe she's different. Maybe I can show a little self-restraint and get to know her a bit. Maybe it wouldn't be the end of the world if I knew more than her name and what she drinks."

"Maybe." Jake grinned. Then he turned serious. "But don't fuck it up. She's a nice lady. And if you hurt her, I'll have to hurt you."

"Geez, glad you have my back. And how exactly do you know she's so nice?" I refrained from asking how he'd hurt me because I didn't even want to imagine that. He'd never laid a hand on me growing up, but he could get all badass when provoked.

"I see things. I hear things. I know things. She's a good person. She and her friend have come in over the past few months. Let's just say that anything she might have told me—or that I overheard—is covered by bartender-customer confidentiality."

"Bartender-customer confidentiality? What bullshit is that?" I smirked. "Next you're gonna tell me you're taking confessionals before happy hour." After another pull from the bottle, I fiddled with my phone. I had her number, but I hadn't called Cora yet. I didn't want to seem desperate...even if I was. I sat at the end of the bar where I could see the door, and with every glimpse of light when the door opened, I held my breath, waiting for her to appear there. Something that didn't go unnoticed by Jake.

"You know, you could just sit at the table by the front door. It'd be easier than trying to pretend you're not looking for her."

"Bite me." I checked my contacts on my phone. There it was: Cora Stetson. All I had to do was push a button and call. Or send a text. I wasn't sure why I had nerves about it. I'd called plenty of women. I'd texted—okay, sexted, too—some of them. My mushed-up brain processed something Jake had said.

"What do you mean—what did she tell you that would need to be kept secret? She married or something?" Worry and doubts crowded into my head. Surely, if she was unavailable, she would have said something, right? Would have made it clear she was in a relationship? *Mark.* Fuck, I'd forgotten to ask who the hell Mark was. Now worry and doubt twisted into something darker, something that clenched my gut. The feeling was unwelcome; I'd never had issues like this when anyone I was interested in was just for fun, just for a night or two.

"Look, like I said, she's a good person. Anything else, you're going to have to ask her yourself. Now, you gonna sit here all night and mope, or call her?"

Self-doubt—and something more—settled into my bones. "Jack and Coke. Keep 'em coming." I picked again at the label on the empty beer bottle, my fingernails not quite catching the paper. The memory of Cora's smile invaded my brain, and some of that negative thinking lost its grip on me. "On second thought, just another beer. And you got a pencil I can use?"

I'd only met Cora last night. I didn't need to get obsessed over things I didn't know about her. But I needed to draw out some sketches that had been knocking around my head since today's idea about the granite vanity table. I could use the napkin and spend a few minutes on that to give my brain a rest from constantly thinking about Cora. Except, of course, the reason I was thinking of this project at all was Cora.

"I can see your mind working a mile a minute there. What kind of trouble is this going to get you in?" Jake rummaged under the bar counter for a pencil and even pulled out an old order pad. "Here, take this."

"No trouble. I think, anyway. Just an idea for a table that popped into my head today. I can't believe what some people will throw away." Even though I'd done okay in my high school wood shop classes, I hadn't done any drawings or drafts of projects in forever.

Shayla interrupted our little discussion. "Jake, we're running low on the IPA bottles. Can you grab another case out of the back?" the petite strawberry-blonde asked.

"If you are running low on something, get Sam to get it for you." Jake didn't bother to look at her as he said the words; he just kept cleaning the bar in front of him.

"Sam was on his break. That's why I let you know instead of going in there and making a mess of your stockroom. I know how you are about everything going in its place, and everything's got its place...and my place is out in front, taking orders, not in the back, tearing apart your precious stockroom." She huffed, and her bangs blew up.

Jake clenched the towel.

Interesting.

"I'll take care of it. You'd better head over to table fifteen. They're looking antsy."

"Oh, and Dixon...if you are looking for some cool things people are getting rid of, you should check out the Trunk. It's a huge flea market about an hour away. Open Sundays at five a.m. until two in the afternoon. It's amazing what you can find there." With that, Shayla turned on her heel and headed over to table fifteen.

"The Trunk? You ever hear of that, Jake?" I kept sketching out the dimensions of the granite, and I tried to figure out what kind of legs would be needed for support.

"Yeah. Shayla's right...you can find just about anything there, from antiques to dollar-store crap and everything in-between. Vendors change all the time, so it's different each week. What are you planning out, anyway?"

I tilted the paper toward Jake and filled him in on my idea to re-purpose the demo'd granite slab.

"Cool. But where are you going to work on this little project of yours? And keep all the supplies and tools you're gonna need? And what, exactly, are you going to do with it once it's done, huh?" His teasing grin was back.

"Shut up." I pulled the paper back. "I think Ryan's got some space at his place where I can put all the stuff until it's ready to come together. I've got to find the right legs, and then a chair. And I wouldn't pass up the right mirror, either." I took another drag of my beer. "But I'll have to figure out what tools I'll really need and where to get those. Maybe I can find some of that at the Trunk, too."

I dropped the pencil and looked back to my phone. Picking it up before I could stop myself, I dialed Cora's number.

"Hello?" The sweetest sound met my ears after three rings.

"Hi. It's Dixon. Dixon Reed. Your Cub Scout savior from last night."

"Oh. Hi." Her breathy response gave away her surprise at my call.

"I wanted to make sure you didn't have any problems this morning. With your ankle, I mean, after you left."

"Thanks for checking on me. Nope, it's all fine. No problems."

"So, you'd be up for some walking? Say, walking into Jake's and having a beer with me tonight?"

Her laugh echoed through the phone. "Well, I guess that's direct. Thanks for the invite, but I can't tonight. Work."

My heart plummeted. "Work? It's after six. What kind of horrible bosses do you work for, anyway? You never said."

"I've got a big project up for review tomorrow. Once I give the presentation to my boss, we're giving it to the owner of the company early next week. I might have to work Friday night and over the weekend to polish it up before Monday."

"Working over the weekend? Sounds harsh. I've got a better idea." I had no idea what I was doing, but I didn't want any more time than necessary to go by before I saw her again. "Come with me on Sunday morning. Surely you won't be working Sunday morning, right?" I tried not to sound desperate, but by her laugh, I wasn't too sure I succeeded.

"How early Sunday morning are we talking? I mean, a woman's gotta sleep in sometimes."

"How early is too early?" I countered.

"And where exactly do you want me to go with you? Got some Cub Scouts you're guiding into ruin by way of video games and junk food?"

"Nothing so nefarious. I save that for second dates. I heard about a flea market about an hour away that I want to go check out. I'm in the market for some unique items." I wasn't going to tell her those unique items were for her.

"Glad to hear you're not in the market for fleas...I was almost worried about you. Are you talking about the Trunk? I've been there a few times, and it's pretty cool. Never know what you can find there. Sounds like fun. But seriously, what time? 'Cause I'm not looking to be one of the diehard junkers, getting there at the crack of dawn."

"How about I pick you up at eight, we grab some breakfast, and then head out? We'd be there a little after nine, so all the diehards will be out of there and we can take our time looking around."

The phone went silent, and I held my breath. Was she going to say no? Was it too early? Was—God forbid—she going to say she'd check with Mark? Or worse, have him come, too? I rubbed the back of my neck. I was about to offer a later time when a breath whooshed over the line.

"Yeah. I could make that work. But I'll meet you at Jake's. It's more on the way, so you won't have to come to get me and then double-back in the right direction." There were muffled voices in the background, and her attention seemed to leave our conversation.

"Cora? You there?"

"Yeah. Sorry. Look, I've got to run, but I'll see you Sunday at eight at Jake's, okay?"

"Sure...whatever you want...if that's easier." I was about to say goodbye, but she had one more thing to say.

Her voice softened. "Thanks for asking, Dixon. I'm really looking forward to it."

My heart pounded. *Not as much as I was.*

SIX

~Cora~

"WHAT DO YOU MEAN, YOU'VE got a date tomorrow morning?" Wendy demanded. "We were supposed to hang out all day. Nobody goes on a date on a Sunday morning." She stopped to drink her latte. "And who exactly is this date with? I can't imagine it's Mark, so that just leaves Hot Guy from the bar. I thought nothing happened?"

"Nothing happened. I swear, other than twisting my ankle and getting tipsy, it wasn't any big deal." I was such a liar. Well, maybe it was nothing big, but I felt things...things I shouldn't be feeling. I grinned as the picture of Dixon's smile, the sparkle in his eyes when he looked at me, popped into my head. The way he made me laugh, feel light inside. And that incredible pull to kiss him...to straddle him... Ugh, I was officially in trouble.

"And yes, I'm going out with Hot Guy—I mean, Dixon. He wants to check out the Trunk, and I said I'd go with him." I pulled out a light-blue long-sleeve scoop neck blouse and held it next to my jeans. "Hmmm...does this go together? Or should I try this one?" I grabbed the multicolor raw hem sweater. "Wendy, help me out here...which one looks better?"

"Well, they both look fine with jeans, but the shirt shows off your...ah, assets...more. So definitely the shirt." She winked at me. "Maybe he'll check out your trunk, too."

I threw the shirt at her, laughing. "And what, exactly, is my 'trunk'?"

She wiggled her butt. "You know, that big ol' thing you swing when you walk." She straightened up. "Have you told him about Mark yet?" Gone was the laughter in her voice. Apparently it was time for Serious Wendy to show up.

I loved Serious Wendy, but she could be a real party pooper. Bringing me back to the reality of my life. Bummer.

"There's nothing to tell. Mark exists. As much as I wish he didn't. I keep putting him off. He continues to act as if everything is fine, like we're still together. But we're not."

"Well, maybe if you told your father it was over, he'd stop pushing you two together and actually support you in your decision." Wendy frowned. "I know—he's more invested in your relationship with Mark than you ever were. But he's got to hear from you that Mark's just not the one for you. That you're not going to marry someone just to make him happy. Or fulfill some dream he has of setting you up for life with a rich husband with a good name."

I dropped the sweater back into the dresser and closed the drawer. "I know. I know. I need to tell both of them, somehow, in some way, that they each hear me. I swear, every time I try to bring it up with either of them, they shut me down or walk away. It only gets worse when they're together. Last week at the club was unbearable." I plopped on the bed, bouncing lightly, and flung myself back.

Mark and I had grown up together but last year, my father had pushed me to date Mark. I'd given in to the pressure and said yes to a date. It felt like going out with my brother, only ickier and grosser than that. He was a few years older than me, and we'd always been in each other's lives. Mark was polite, cultured, dressed well. But he was also a snob, only interested in status. And the law. He was a stickler for the law. He saw the world in black-and-white—no shades of gray. Or, actually, any color at all. He couldn't understand why I'd wanted to paint the walls in the penthouse. My royal-purple bedroom walls seemed to repulse him but they comforted me. That and the mountains of pillows propped at the head of my bed.

But now my father was doing more: he was actively trying to get me to marry Mark. And he'd enlisted Mark in this scheme. To be fair, it probably didn't take much arm-twisting. In all likelihood, he'd been planning to ask my father for my hand—that's the kind of thing he'd think was the proper and correct thing to do—and then inquire on the dowry. Get a prenuptial agreement drawn up. Find a huge, gaudy ring that I'd be afraid to wear for fear of either losing it or blinding people with it. Then, possibly, maybe, he'd remember to ask me. Or, more likely, tell me we were getting married. Mr. Romance, he wasn't.

And he didn't fit into my plans to run my own business. The thought of Mark being approachable and welcoming to a bed-and-breakfast guest was laughable. There was no way he'd encourage me to spread my wings and make my dreams come true.

I just needed to find a way to get Mark—and my father—to realize that neither of them controlled me or the trajectory of my career, my life. What that was, I had no idea.

BRIGHT AND EARLY SUNDAY morning, I guided my car to Jake's parking lot. It was mostly empty, so I had my pick of spots. This time, I parked close to the doors, on the side where the door to Dixon's apartment was. No ankle twisting this time. Of course, I wore much more sensible shoes for this outing—my trusty Keds, not the heels from hell. The whole day promised to be casual, so the shoes matched.

As I gathered my purse and backpack—it was easier to carry my finds in that rather than dozens of bags—a knock on my window made me jump. A quick twist in my seat, and those pools of blue heaven stared back at me.

"Hey, sorry. Didn't mean to scare you there." Dixon's sheepish smile brought the corners of his eyes up as his whole face joined in the smile. "You ready? I thought we'd take my truck. You never know what kind of treasures you can find at a flea market, right? At least this way, we can be pretty sure we'll be able to get it all home."

"Sure. Sounds like a plan. Do you know the way, or do you need a copilot?" I stepped out of the car and beeped the locks. As I stood close to him, the scent of sandalwood drifted over. And something intoxicating...something that was all Dixon.

He stared into my eyes, quiet for a moment. I started to drown in those pools, silently letting them wash over me. How did he do this to me? How could one person draw me in, make the rest of the world fade to black while I was captured in his sapphire eyes?

He cleared his throat. "Umm...yeah, sure, I could use a copilot. Every good expedition has a crew, right? Unless you'd rather be the Ginger on this three-hour tour." His eyes sparkled with his teasing.

"Yeah, right. More like Mary Ann. And what does that make you—the Skipper or Gilligan?" I laughed, trying to picture Dixon in either a black skipper hat or the bucket hat Gilligan never seemed to be without. But neither of those characters had the physique that Dixon had, and my laughter died as I considered what Dixon would look like on a tropical island, shirtless...

Get a grip! You hardly know the man! But my dirty mind steamrolled over any weak objections some small, sane part of my brain tried to put up. Those abs would be lickable, for sure, and his arm muscles could hold me—protect me—for hours. Or hold me down as he pounded into me, over and over.

A sense of heat crawled up my face, now flaming red, I was sure.

"Hmmm...never thought of myself as either of those two. Although, that professor had it pretty good. Good-looking, smart..." He grinned.

"Not smart enough to fix the boat or build a raft that worked. But I would agree he was the best-looking of the bunch." I stepped away, determined to keep my hands to myself, and headed for what I assumed was his truck parked close to the apartment stairs.

"I know this great little diner on the way to the Trunk. You ever been to Tony's?" Dixon was clicking his seat belt in and stopped to watch me pull mine over my shoulder. "They have some of the best waffles I've ever had."

"I've never been, but waffles sound good. Let's go there and we can plan out how we're going to attack the flea market."

Dixon started the ignition. "Attack? You make it sound like we're headed off to war."

"Well, you have to know how you're going to approach it. Is it just an easy, laid-back stroll through rows and rows? Are we looking at every vendor, or just at ones that catch our eye? Are we starting at the back row and making our way forward, or starting at the front and working our way to the back? All very important questions, I think."

"Wow. I never would have thought you'd need to plan so much just to check out a flea market. I guess this is a conversation to have over waffles." He glanced over at me and those blue eyes twinkled at me. "Here we are, my liege. Let's go plan our attack."

The diner was tucked between an antiques store and a bakery, a hole-in-the-wall kind of place. Definitely promising—I'd never had a bad meal at a small mom-and-pop place like this.

Dixon held the door of the diner open—a little bell tinkled to acknowledge our entry—and the smell of bacon hit me.

"Oh my God. Bacon. We're definitely having bacon with those waffles." I glanced back at Dixon, who now held the door open for an elderly couple coming in after us.

"Thank you, young man." The woman's crinkly face crinkled some more when she smiled.

"Now Barbara, don't go smiling at him. Your smile can melt a man's heart, and how's a young'un like him gonna be able to take that first thing in the morning? Me, I'm man enough for you, any time of the day." The old man grabbed her hand and pulled it to his lips, giving it a kiss.

"You're welcome, Miss Barbara. You can smile at me anytime." Dixon winked at the old woman and looked up at me. "But you might have competition in the heart-melting department."

My heart *did* melt at the look he gave me. Just a little. I cleared my throat and prayed I wasn't blushing too much. "Okay, enough flirting with the ladies. Time to plan for battle and fortify ourselves." I turned back and found a booth in the corner.

After some of the best waffles I've ever had, some crispy bacon—the only way one should have it—and a debate on Mrs. Butterworth syrup versus authentic maple syrup (Vermont maple syrup all the way!), we talked about the Trunk and what we were looking for. Turned out he had very specific ideas on what he wanted. So we were going to be looking at a lot of furniture, which kind of dovetailed into my plans for the B&B. I wasn't opposed to getting ideas for how to furnish my bed-and-breakfast, and I hoped the flea market would give me inspiration.

We left the diner, and the next forty minutes of drive time passed in a wink. I learned what kind of music he liked (eighties hair bands and boy bands of any decade as opposed to my love of country music), how he got his job (his high school buddy Ryan's parents owned a construction company), and his middle name was Ray. Before I knew it, we were pulling into the parking lot at the Trunk.

"You ready to score?" The words slipped out of my mouth before I could catch them. Never mind that my body hummed from being so close to him for so long. Never mind that I imagined his hands not on the wheel but on my body. That was not what I meant. "S-score some deals, I mean."

He gave me a heated gaze. "Yeah, I'm ready to score...some deals."

His stare fired up my body up even more, and his hand was now touching mine, causing a tingle to shock me into a silence. Okay, maybe my body meant what it sounded like. But my head was in charge here, right?

A grin—one I was quickly looking forward to—grew on his face. "Let's get it done."

We'd decided to start in the back and work our way forward, so we headed off to the back corner without stopping at any booths. It took a good ten minutes of walking to find our starting point.

"Geez, after that quick march, it's really like we are in a military campaign!" But the sun felt wonderful, and it was warming up to be a beautiful spring morning in Connecticut.

"Hey, this was all your idea. I wanted to start in the middle and go out in concentric circles—well, squares...whatever—but you nixed that idea. So no complaining about the hike." Dixon wagged his finger at me, pretending to lecture me while his dimples fought to stay hidden.

"Yeah, but this way, we won't miss anything. We have to go past it all to get back to the truck, right? Let's go, Mr. Cub Scout."

The first few booths were little more than someone's tag sale leftovers: plastic housewares, kids' toys, and strangely enough, a toilet. A note on the porcelain throne said: Please do not use toilet.

"I wonder who it was that made that sign necessary." I poked Dixon in the ribs to draw his attention to the sign. Oh my God, not an ounce of fat—pure muscle. That construction work definitely had some side benefits.

"Probably some kids goofing around. I can picture myself around ten or eleven, being just enough of an idiot to dare one of my friends to use it."

"Oh, look! This is a cool chair." I almost ran over to the next vendor. A classic Craftsman chair, with dark leather and walnut wood, caught my eye.

"It reclines." The vendor stepped forward. "A true Craftsman classic. Here—sit down and lie back. You can have all the great quality and design and still lay back like a Lazy-Boy."

I sank into the soft leather. "Oh my God. This is so comfortable. And," I reached to move the handle, "such a smooth motion to lay back. This is awesome."

"Just two hundred bucks. We can help you get it to your car, no charge."

The man could see the sale coming, but I had to shut it down. "Sorry. I really don't have room for it at my place. I love it, though. It's got great lines, and it's in great condition. But I can't take it."

Dixon jumped in. "It is an awesome chair. But we're just starting out on our flea market excursion. Do you have a card? Maybe I can sweet talk her into splurging and call you later on."

"Sure. Here you go. But don't wait too long...a chair this good won't last long."

I reluctantly got out of the chair. As much as I loved it, I couldn't take it home. Frankly, there wasn't any room, and I didn't want to hear from my father about my habit of collecting chairs. There were a dozen or so at our family home I'd had to leave behind when I moved into the hotel after college. A few made it into that new space, but not all of them. I'd held myself back this time, but something about the varied ways a thing as simple as a chair could be made amazed me every time. I wanted them all. Silly, I know, but some chairs just called to me, to be part of a home, part of someone's life. A place at a kitchen table. A place to cuddle in. A place to relax. A place to hold a crying baby. To make a home. All things I wanted someday.

We wandered over to the next booth, which looked like a Home Depot tool department surplus store. I recognized hammers and screwdrivers, but had no names for the power equipment and other tools. But Dixon scrutinized the tables, obviously looking for something.

"See something you like?" I ran my fingers over the tools, trying to figure out what the sharp objects might do.

Dixon grabbed my hands. "You have no idea where those tools have been. They could be full of rust and dirt, and if you cut yourself on any of this, it's off to get your tetanus shot update. No more flea market for you, young lady." He pulled them close to his chest, pulling me along with them.

I could only look into his eyes and once again fall into those heavenly pools of blue. Just the smallest taste of being his full focus, and I could barely think, much less speak. "Oh. Yeah. Right." I thought I was breathing, but the little gasps that came out weren't enough to get oxygen to my brain, apparently. I sensed I should tug my hands away from him, but the urge to hold tight overwhelmed me. Maybe I could stay like this, hands on his chest and staring into his eyes, for a minute or two longer. *Or much longer than that.* I shook myself at that thought.

Taking a deep breath, I found the willpower to pull my hands back to my sides. "Yeah. I'm not a big fan of needles, so I'll take your advice." Somehow I was colder now, without the warmth he telegraphed into my body.

SEVEN

~Dixon~

ONCE HER HANDS LEFT my chest, there was an immediate loss of heat. I'd been concerned about her getting cut on some of those tools, but now I was thinking about how she could hurt me. I just had to make sure I didn't let anything real develop. That way, there wouldn't be any damage, right?

"Come on. Let's hit the next one. There's nothing here I'm looking for." I smiled at Cora, trying to reassure her it wasn't a big deal. "Look—there's another chair you can say no to." I pointed to the gaudiest, ugliest chair I'd ever seen. The mustard-colored fabric stretched over the padded seat and high back, with wooden armrests. But what truly set it off was what was on those armrests...and legs, too. It looked as if someone had gone to town with a BeDazzler. There wasn't an inch that wasn't covered in colored gemstones. Many colors. In the sunlight, it was practically blinding.

But Cora was still drawn to it, like a moth to the flame. "Oh...my...God. It's incredible!"

Incredible? More like unbelievable. "Seriously? That is the ugliest chair I've ever seen." Her interest in the chair only seemed to grow when she sat in it and sighed, closing her eyes. "Yeah, I'd have to say, closing your eyes is about the only way you could sit in that thing."

Her eyes flew open, her mouth ready to open and fight back, I could tell. "But it looks sturdy. And comfy. Is it comfortable?" I tried to find something, anything, that could redeem that monstrosity.

"It is pretty sturdy and comfy. Want to see for yourself?" She popped off the chair and motioned for me to take a seat.

Cornered, I had no choice but to sit. Quicker than I could react, Cora had whipped out her cell and snapped a picture of me on the chair.

"OMG! I can't believe you sat in that one!" Cora doubled over in laughter. She proudly held the phone. "Jake is gonna love this!"

I jumped out of the chair. "Hey, no fair. You pretended to like that chair to get me to sit in the ugliest chair of all time. Delete that photo!" I tried to get the phone out of her grasp, which only landed me closer to her again. "All right, all right...at least let me see it before you show the world."

She let go of the phone, and I could see the photo on the screen. Not bad...if you could somehow make out my features in between the glow of the colored gems in the sunlight. But thankfully, that was a goal most couldn't achieve. "Hey, I've got an idea."

Phone still in hand, I dragged her back to the chair, sat in it, and pulled her onto my lap. "Let's get a selfie. Something for posterity to ponder as they marvel at the campaign at the Trunk where mere mortals were able to withstand the power of the Jeweled Gem Throne of Horror to blind its victims into submission."

She snuggled into my lap, giggling. "The Jeweled Gem Throne of Horror, huh? Are you the conquering hero, ready to save more damsels from twisted ankles and hangovers?"

I held her phone up and snapped a picture. "Yup. That's me, claiming the spoils of war." Without thinking, I kissed her cheek and hit the photo button for another shot. A jolt of electricity seemed to shock both of us. She immediately stopped giggling and squirming, and I could only stare into her eyes. Breathing seemed like an impossible task, unless she came to my rescue and performed mouth-to-mouth resuscitation. I was sure I needed her to make my heart pump, my lungs take in air.

The moment was broken when a rough voice said, "You interested in that chair or just scaring off serious buyers?"

We both broke our stare and turned to look at a heavyset man with an unlit cigar in his mouth.

"Um...how much?" I had no intention of buying this chair, but I'd at least pretend to make sure this guy didn't lose it on us. Although, it had given me the opportunity to get Cora in my arms again.

"It's a steal at four hundred bucks." The man grabbed the cigar out of his mouth and coughed, then stuck it back in, like some kind of stopper.

He had to be kidding. Four hundred bucks? For a BeDazzled chair with the ugliest color of fabric imaginable? "Too rich for my budget. But it's a real piece of work." That was about the best I could do to be polite and get out of his crosshairs. I turned to Cora. "Let's keep looking. I'm sure we'll find something, sugar bear."

As I pulled her away from the vendor and the Jeweled Gem Throne of Horror, Cora burst into laughter.

"I can't believe he wanted four hundred for that. I mean, I know you're supposed to haggle, but starting out at four hundred seems like a stretch." Cora kept her hand in mine as we walked to the next set of tables, quickly bypassing the offerings of used textbooks and a table with cosmetics.

I'd had some luck on my list of items. I'd found an old mirror that looked perfect. The vendor told me it was a margin mirror, in the Arts and Crafts style. I could picture Cora in front of it every morning, looking back at me in the reflection with a smile on her face. It might be a dream, but it was one that was getting stronger, starting to come into focus. Spending time with her strengthened that pull I had to be near her. Every smile she gave me, every silly pose with some French beret or fur stole, every time I took her picture in every chair she sat in warmed a part of me that had been so frozen, it'd been as though I came in from a blizzard but hadn't even known how cold I was.

But still on my list was those damn legs. I'd seen some older furniture that gave me ideas on how to "rescue" it, too, but nothing had quite what I was looking for in legs to use for my project. Plenty of wooden legs, but the granite needed something with strength.

"Oh, look at this!" Cora pointed at—well, it looked like old farm equipment or something.

"What? That wheelbarrow skeleton? Or the chicken wire?"

She bent over to move some boxes and showed me a pair of perfect legs. I mean, her perfect legs caught my attention until her fluttering hand had me looking at black metal legs lying on the grass. The pair of them had a sturdy top base for a table top to rest on, legs that curved in toward each other, and feet that were long enough to be stable but short enough that they didn't stick out past the top base. I had my legs, and now my project was ready to become a reality. I just had to haggle with the guy selling them and then get them to the truck.

"How much for the legs over here?" I tossed the question over my shoulder to the young guy with the baseball cap on backward. I tried to keep the interest out of my voice so he wouldn't gouge me on the deal.

The guy rubbed his whiskered chin. "I dunno. Gramps wanted to clean out the barn...not too picky about pricing, I don't think. How's twenty-five bucks for the pair?"

I had to swallow my surprise. I nodded in agreement before any words could form, and my hand reached for my wallet. "Done."

Cora, however, wasn't as subtle, and jumped in excitement. "Awesome! You've been looking at just about every booth to find something, but I never thought you'd find it, the way you kept looking and looking. What are they for? Oh, look—here's some more!" She smiled brightly at me as she unearthed another set of legs, this time ones that looked like the letter V with a narrow base at the bottom, a larger base at the top, and a support shelf in the middle.

"I can let those go for twenty-five bucks, too," the guy offered.

I grabbed three twenties out of my wallet. "I'll take them both. If you can haul them up to my truck, I'll give you another ten for the trouble." I wasn't prepared to haul both sets back to the truck, and there was no way I was going to ask Cora to carry a set.

"You bet. You ready now or want to come back to grab them before you leave?"

I turned to Cora. "You ready to go? Or you still want to walk around?"

"I'm ready whenever you are. We can catch lunch on our way back and you can tell me your plans for these finds."

I had a grin on my face at the ideas rolling around in my head and how Cora figured into them.

DICKIE'S TAVERN BOASTED the "best BBQ in the state" on its outdoor sign, and it didn't disappoint.

I reached across the table and wiped some BBQ sauce off Cora's chin. "You've got a little something there..." My grin disappeared as that ever present tingle ran down my arm at the feel of her skin.

Her lips parted, those kissable lips I wanted to devour, before she grabbed her water and looked away. After a quick sip, she wiped her lips with a napkin. "Well, barbeque isn't a good look for a first date. I guess this is technically our second date, so you can see me at my worst now." She grimaced. "Although, I guess you've already seen some of my worst."

"I dunno...I wouldn't call that your worst. I mean, it was just a twisted ankle."

"You're not mentioning my lightweight status—gee, thanks. I know I may have gotten a little silly." She cleared her throat, fidgeting in her seat.

I grinned. "A little. But it was cute." Hell, it was more than cute. All that sass—and that ass—had me all tangled up inside. But there was still so much to learn about her. "So, come on, you never told me what you do. What is it? You've got a tattoo shop downtown? Work as a shoeshine gal on the corner? Oh my God, you run a bar downtown, and you go to Jake's to check out the competition—Wendy's a hired gun to pretend to be your friend. Am I right?" I fake-whispered the last, trying to hold back my laugh.

She cleared her throat. "No, you big goof. I'd never stoop to checking out my competition under false pretenses." Her tone turned serious. "Actually, I work for my dad in the family business. Ever hear of Stetson Suites?"

"Stetson Suites? Isn't that the huge hotel chain around here?" I whistled, low and long. "Geez, a real real-estate heiress, huh?"

"Not exactly, but yeah, we have about fifty-five or so locations, mostly on the East Coast and Mid-Atlantic region. The flagship hotel and corporate headquarters are downtown." She ran her fingers through her hair and she bit her lip, as if she didn't want to share this much information, but she kept going. "I work in marketing, trying to get my father into this century. It's been a fight, but at least I have a manager who listens to me and doesn't pull any punches because I'm the boss's daughter."

That's why she emphasized the Stetson hat connection when we'd met—so I'd not think of the hotel famous around here. Sometimes the baggage your last name brought with you was more than you wanted to deal with—I could definitely understand that. Jake and I had had our own brush with that type of thing, and it still got me defensive and protective.

"Well, my buddy Ryan works for his parents, so I've seen how that can be tricky sometimes. It's like he can't always just be himself, but an extension of his dad. The crew gives him a hard time every once in a while but he tries to brush it off as no big deal. But I can tell it bothers him." I took another bite of my baby back ribs.

"Yeah, there's always someone who gives you a hard time. Or dismisses you out of hand because you're family—like you couldn't possibly have earned the job instead of landing it because of your name. It doesn't help when your own family puts your ideas down as silly or unrealistic." The bitter tone from the other night crept back into her voice.

"At least you have some family around. I mean, your dad must like to be a part of your life if you are in business with him, right? Do you guys hang out much?"

Cora dropped her fork on the plate. "'In business together' would be a stretch. Like I said, I'm in marketing and he's not my direct boss. Any 'hanging out' we do—well, we don't do it the way we used to when my mom was alive." Her voice cracked on the last few words.

Shit. I had no idea that her mom was gone. Add that to the list of things we had in common. Not that I'd wish that on anyone. "God, I'm so sorry. I didn't think—"

"No, it's okay. It's been a few years now. We just drifted apart after that, I guess. She was really the glue that held us together, and it hasn't been the same without her. She mellowed him out, you know?

Gave him something other than work to focus on." She took a sip of her water and stared out the window. "Of course, now he's got it in his head that I should…"

"Should what?"

"Never mind." She shook her head, as if trying to shake off the melancholy of her thoughts. "Tell me more about your construction job. Or better yet, tell me what you would do if you could do anything."

This sounded a lot like the conversation from the other night, when she asked about where I'd go if I could go anywhere. It made me wonder whether she spent a lot of time dreaming about a future while stuck in a present she wasn't happy with. I wasn't really happy doing demo jobs with Ryan; it struck me that it was time to find my own dreams, a path to a future.

"Well, like I said, my buddy Ryan got me this job at his parents' construction company. Me and Ryan work as part of a crew, doing demos mostly. Every now and then, we get to do the install parts of the jobs too. The project we're doing now, we're set up for both ends of the job. I like the install better than the demo, although demo is easier—no real thinking involved. So sometimes that's better, especially when I'm in the mood to just zone out. But the installation…you have to pay attention to the details, make sure everything fits. And when it's done, there's a huge satisfaction. Not to mention the appreciation from the homeowner for their brand-new space. It's pretty cool to make that kind of transformation."

I thought about my secret project. I was itching to get started and see if my idea would turn out the way I wanted it to. Of course, what I really wanted to see was Cora's smile when she sat at the table. I could imagine her looking at me in the mirror's reflection, heat in her eyes and a promise on her smiling lips. And if I kept that train of thought up, I'd be in for a long night.

EIGHT

~Cora~

I HADN'T MEANT TO TELL him so much about my career, or my father. But at least it was out there now. I didn't have to hide everything about myself from him. Actually, I was compelled to tell him everything about myself. And I wanted to know everything about him, too.

"I can see how making something would be more satisfying than tearing it down. Although I can appreciate the freedom in just pulling shit out and throwing it around to get it out of the way. Kind of like a brutal cleansing." My smile grew. "Or like tossing some jerk on their ass."

He took another bite of his ribs. "God, this is good. It might actually be the best in the state."

"Well, it's New England...is that such a high bar to hit? I mean, it's not like you're talking Texas BBQ, where the real masters are."

"Oh? And you've been to Texas to check out that world-class grub?"

I hesitated. "Yeah. I've been there a few times. A perk of growing up in the travel industry. I've been to lots of places, from when I was a little girl. I can remember being on airplanes and the stewardess bringing me a Shirley Temple."

"So you've never been able to hold your liquor, huh?" He laughed and his eyes sparkled at me, momentarily stunning me into silence.

"Well, I was like four or five, so I doubt anyone would've given me anything stronger than that Shirley Temple. Besides, it was the whole experience of being on a plane and drinking like a grownup that stuck in my head."

"First class, huh? Must have been nice." He took a sip of his beer. "I've bummed around the country a bit since I graduated from high school about six years ago, but not too many plane rides. Met some nice people, and some not-so-nice ones, too. Traveled by train and bus, mostly."

"And where did those trains and busses take you? Or actually, where are you from originally? Was this your destination or your starting point for your grand adventures?"

"Yeah, I'm from here. Allentown, to be precise. Moved around a bit when I was a kid, but mostly different apartments and houses with my mom. And then she married Jake's dad, and we moved in with them." His focus drifted off for a moment. Then, shaking himself, he said, "But after high school, I was ready to take off. Took the Greyhound to the Midwest—the farthest I could get on the cheapest ticket out of town. I kicked around there, doing odd jobs and getting by. Worked as a convenience store clerk on the graveyard shift, a janitor for a cleaning company, a forklift driver...let's see, I think there was a short stint as a warehouse packer, but that was like for a week or something...hated that one."

"Is that why you came back home? Bad job choices? Or was it something else?" *Please don't say it was for a girlfriend...or because of a girlfriend. Shit—where did that thought come from?* It shouldn't matter to me whether he came back for a girlfriend or for a job or for any particular reason. But it did.

"Bad job choices factored into it, sure, but I was getting tired of drifting around, no real friends or roots to keep me in place. And then Jake bought that bar, fixed it up. I thought I'd check it out, and ran into Ryan there. The rest is history, as they say." Dixon licked the BBQ sauce off his fingers, and my gaze was pulled to the action.

I couldn't seem to look away, imagining his tongue licking something...someone...else. *Me.* I gulped and took a sip of my drink, trying to tear my eyes away.

"Are you checking me out again, Ms. Stetson? Tsk, tsk...can't even pretend it's the booze making you so bold and brazen. Or...that Coke isn't hiding some Jack in it, is it?" His teasing tone was cut short by the waitress coming to check on us.

"You need anything else?" The blonde bombshell leaned over Dixon, practically shoving her cleavage in his face. She totally ignored me—I was invisible as she perused Dixon like a slab of meat.

"No, thanks. Just the check when you get a chance." Dixon hardly looked at her and kept his heated gaze in my direction. "We'll get dessert at home, right, gum drop?"

"Uh, yeah, right, cuddle bear. Dessert at home sounds great." I could hardly keep my laughter to myself when I made up that ridiculous endearment for him. Served him right for calling me gum drop.

The waitress gave me a withering glare, turned on her high heels, and left without another word.

"Cuddle bear?"

My grin couldn't be contained. "What? You can dish it out, but you can't take it? If you can call me gum drop, I can call you cuddle bear." I took a last slurp of my soda. "And no, there's no Jack in my Coke. I'm perfectly sober, thank-you-very-much." God, if there had been any Jack in that Coke, I'd be calling him more than cuddle bear—more like Mr. Panty Melter or stud muffin. Hell, I'd probably be speechless if he kept that steady gaze on me and just let him do whatever felt right at the moment. Which would probably be amazing. And bad. *Don't forget...you don't need entanglements right now.* That little voice might be the voice of reason, but I was ready to tell it to shut up already.

AFTER OUR LATE LUNCH, it was only about a half-hour drive back to Jake's. And for that full thirty minutes, we played the radio, singing along to the songs and laughing at each other's off-key renditions and wrong lyrics.

"That is so not 'We built this city on sausage rolls'! Oh my God!" I laughed so hard, I was gasping for breath. "And that is the worst song ever! I can even prove it!" I grabbed my phone and searched for "Worst Song Ever." Not surprisingly, the first results were the infamous song that Dixon was belting out—with the wrong lyrics and warbling like a bird on speed. "See! The internet says so!"

Dixon grinned at me. "Nope. 'Ice Ice Baby' is the worst song ever." He whistled the tune while pulling into the parking lot and then turning off the engine.

"And should I mention that you quoted this 'worst song ever' when you were looking in the freezer for ice for my ankle? I think you like the worst songs ever—you probably even have that CD from that old music talent show—you know, the guy who couldn't sing, never made it to the actual show, but somehow got three albums produced." I pointed my finger into his chest, my mock horror in full force.

"The talented Mr. William Hung was just misunderstood by the masses. 'She Bangs' is a classic for the ages." He took my finger from his chest and wrapped his hand around it, pulling my full hand into the warmth of his palm.

The cab of the truck turned from a laughfest to dripping with anticipation. I could barely breathe, but not because I was laughing anymore. No, my heart stopped as his eyes darkened and arrested my movements. I was caught in the smoldering heat building up in the small space. I put my other hand over his hand and that same spark from our first night together popped and tingled.

Just a few inches away, and I could touch his lips. Feel that softness turn to molten heat as his mouth covered mine. Some brave part of my brain—I wasn't sure whether I'd be thanking it or cursing it later—moved my body those precious inches. And I was right there.

Dixon's breath caught and puffed out over my mouth. Then, that gentle pressure of his lips on mine had me forgetting everything but him. No work, no family, no Mark, no silly nicknames or horrible songs...just the feel of his lips, the tip of his tongue looking to dance with mine. He pulled me closer with one hand; the other wrapped around my neck, caressing the side and holding me in place. What started as a gentle kiss morphed into a more demanding, more intense...claiming.

My hands fought their way free and landed on his shoulders, trying to pull him closer...or trying to press myself against his hard chest. He tunneled his fingers into my hair, as he plumbed the depths of my mouth with his tongue. All I could do was respond in kind in a manic attempt to meld my body with his—whether that was our mouths and tongues or by eliminating any space between our bodies.

His mouth left mine, but he wasn't done.

He licked, nibbled, bit, and sucked at my neck. "You have no idea how much I've wanted to do this." His murmured words heated my blood as his actions had my heart hammering so hard, it was a wonder he couldn't hear it. "Oh, Cora." He swept my lips with another kiss before pulling back to look at my face.

I was torn between staring into his eyes and feeling his lips—and his body—pressed against mine. In an uncharacteristic move, I left my side of the cab and moved toward Dixon. I turned my body so I could straddle his lap, and he moved the seat back to make some extra room. My hands wound around his neck and I leaned in to kiss him again. A moan slipped out—but I couldn't tell whether it was me or him.

Dixon slid his hands to my ass and held on. "God, Cora."

I moved my hips and rubbed against him like a cat in heat. That was a good description of what I was feeling. All rational thought left my head as my pussy moved over his jean-covered but hardening cock. A few more minutes of that, combined with his lips on my neck, and I was sure I would explode.

"You are so amazing, Cora."

The whispered words in my ear sent shivers down my spine.

Then, without warning, he held my hips still, not allowing any movement.

"God. We've got to stop, Cora. I'm—I—oh God, this is not what I imagined when I thought about us together."

Dixon's words stopped any movement I was trying to keep going. "You thought about us together?" My heart jumped into my throat.

"Well, yeah. But dry-humping in broad daylight in front of my brother's bar, when anyone could come up and see us, was not exactly part of my scenario for getting to know you."

"I guess you have a point. It's not exactly...umm...appropriate behavior for a second date either, huh?" I climbed off his lap and sat back on my side of the cab. I pressed my hands against my cheeks.

"God, Cora. I don't want 'appropriate behavior' with you. But I thought—I hoped—our first time together would be something other than a quickie in a parking lot. Something romantic, or exotic, or heart-stopping—just like you." Dixon leaned over and his lips met mine in a passionate kiss, stoking the fire once again. "I want you—but I can wait for the right moment. And I'm thinking this isn't quite it. Not yet, anyway." He positioned himself a short distance away, but still within reach.

I brushed his hand with my fingertips and looked into his eyes. Desire and heat glowed there, and sincerity radiated in his voice. "Okay. Sounds like a third date is totally in order. I've got a busy week, but I could meet you at Jake's on Thursday. Sound good?"

"Thursday? Yeah, that's fine. Around seven?" He fiddled with my fingers and grasped my hand, twining our fingers together.

I could only nod as he pulled my hand to his lips for a gentle kiss. *So much for no entanglements.*

"OH MY GOD. YOU TOTALLY should have done it with him!" Wendy sat at the small kitchenette table later that night, staring at me.

"Wendy, I am so not the kind of girl to have sex in public! That's you—remember? What was his name? Ken? Kurt? Anyway, it's better that he put the brakes on things. I'm not looking for a relationship, remember? I haven't figured out how to get Mark to leave me alone, and I've got Dad to deal with, too. I don't think he'd be super thrilled to find out that not only I am not going to marry Mark, and not stay at Stetson Suites, and open my own B&B, but that I'm dating a construction worker. He might not be as snobby as Mark and his parents, but he's still got that kind of attitude." I brought over the teapot and filled our mugs with the steaming liquid.

"Maybe he'll be happy when you're happy. And if that means dumping Mark for Dixon and working toward your own career goals and not his—" Wendy stopped and laughed. "Yeah, right. That'll never happen. But seriously, you could have gone up to Dixon's place and then got it on. No reason to stop the action, my friend. Gotta take those opportunities when they show up—never count on second chances when it comes to amazing sex. And it sounds like it'd be amazing." She blew on the tea and waved her hand over the mug.

It was the right thing to do—stopping before we'd crossed that line—but God, I was seriously bummed about it. I don't think I'd ever felt like that before. I would have done anything he asked to keep experiencing that soaring feeling as our bodies moved together. The thought of getting naked with Dixon had my panties getting wet and my heart stuttering over itself. The anticipation high made my pulse race, right along with my imagination.

Wendy drilled her gaze at me. "So, what's the plan? I mean, after you hook up with Mr. Hot Guy. Is he going to be a night to remember fondly as you forge forward with your life plan? Or are you daydreaming about something serious with him?" She sipped from her mug, awaiting my answer.

"How do I know? I'm swimming in all these feelings and I can't tell up from down. Sometimes it feels like I've got so much going on, but really, most of it is just in my head. I haven't done much to move my plans forward. It's less than a year before my inheritance goes through, and then I can get going on the B&B, but I need to get this Mark thing taken care of. It doesn't matter whether or not it gets serious with Dixon...it's not going to happen with Mark, no matter what he or my father thinks." My hands warmed from the mug, and I glanced at the tea. "Yeah, I could see Dixon in my future...but whether it's more than a fling, who knows." My hushed words filled the room.

"Well then, get your ass in gear, girl. Time to lay down the law with your father and Mark. If you want something, you have to take it...or in this case, quit taking their assumptions about your future as fact. Time to pull up those big-girl panties...and then drop them for Mr. Hot Guy." Wendy let out a whoop and motioned as if she were cracking a whip.

Wendy's antics had me smiling in response. And daydreaming about dropping my panties for a certain construction worker with a piercing blue gaze and a heart of gold.

NINE

~Dixon~

AFTER WORK MONDAY NIGHT, I hefted the granite onto a set of sawhorses in the construction warehouse. I'd kept the legs we'd found at the Trunk in the truck's bed, and I was ready to figure out which set would look best. I didn't have much to occupy my mind or my time until Thursday night rolled around, so I figured I could start on this little project of mine. And I'd convinced Ryan to stick around after work to give me a hand. After all, if I couldn't get free labor out of my best buddy, who else was gonna help?

I lifted one of each set of legs and propped it against the granite slab. They both looked good, but the black metal ones caught my eye more. The V-shaped ones I'd save for another project. The curves reminded me of Cora—all shapely lines and contours. And I liked the contrast of the square lines in the margin mirror compared to the legs of the vanity. I more or less had my vision in front of me—minus the lovely Cora staring back at me.

I still needed a chair for her, though. And her love of chairs at the Trunk made the choice a bit more difficult than I thought it would be. I knew for sure it couldn't be the Jeweled Gem Throne of Horror, but it needed to fit in with the Arts and Crafts mirror and the curves on the base. I had snagged a card from the vendor who'd had several chairs Cora had gushed over. I didn't think any of those had fit what I was looking for, but maybe he'd be a good place to start.

I sent a quick email from my phone to Guy, the owner of Jefferson Furniture. I explained what I was searching for and gave him my contact information. That little detail taken care of, I turned back to the project. I put the V-shaped legs back in the truck bed and got out the tools I'd borrowed from work. Ryan had said it'd be fine to borrow them nights as long as they were back before the crews left for jobs.

"Lookin' good, buddy." Ryan leaned back, a beer in his hand. "I guess I can see what you were thinking of, using that granite for a personal table."

"Vanity table, dumbass."

"Whatever. You know what I mean. I'm just dying to know who it's for." Ryan smirked and took a drag from his bottle.

I looked at him. "You can just keep wondering, I guess. Until I need you to help me deliver it, anyway. This sucker is gonna be heavy—too heavy for one person to move around." A ding sounded from my phone, and I checked the email app. The furniture guy had responded; he had a chair he thought would work and included a picture.

I showed Ryan. "What do you think of this chair? It's got some straight lines like the mirror, but the front legs have a curve to them, like the table legs. Looks like a comfortable leather seat."

Ryan leaned in to look. "Yeah. Cool. Is that the same coloring as the mirror, though? Would it look better if they matched or if they were different?"

I compared the stain shade on the mirror propped up against the wall to the picture of the chair. They seemed similar, but who could tell for sure from a photo. I replied to the email, letting him know I was interested as long as it went well with another piece I had. I offered to meet up with him to see it in person.

That done, I turned back to the legs and granite, waiting to become Cora's vanity set. The cutout was a bit too deep, so I'd need to cut some of the granite back to make it look right. It'd be a straight cut, but I was going to need a wet saw to do it, and then I'd need to polish it to get that smooth surface. Then adhesive to attach the legs, and it'd be good to go.

"You gonna stand there and watch me work? Or are you gonna help out?" I set up the wet saw and got out my face mask protection. "Either way, you're gonna want to wear one of these." I held up a spare mask.

Ryan set his beer down and grabbed the mask. "I can't believe you're doing this for someone you just met. I mean, do you even know her last name?"

"You might be surprised what I know about Cora—and yes, that includes her last name. More than just details about her life, I know how she makes me feel. I can be me, you know? But the best me I've ever been. At least, she makes me want to be more than I am right now. I've never really had that." I looked at the floor, not sure what I was trying to say.

"Man, I know we don't talk about it, but none of that stuff from when you were a kid was your fault. You got dealt a shitty hand, and you and Jake did the best you could. I know Jake tried his best, but there's nothing like a parent to give a kid stability and give them a way to dream—and work toward those dreams. It just sucks that—"

"I know." I stopped Ryan before he could continue. "I'm not looking for a pity party, or a rehash of ancient history I can't change. I'm just saying Cora is more—I don't know—real than anyone I've ever met before. I've never really had real before. And I like it."

Ryan dangled the mask in his hands. "You deserve some real happiness, man. If this Cora is the one who can bring you some of that, then I'm all for it... It's been forever since anyone has shown you any kind of affection. Not just a roll in the hay, but someone who is truly interested in you as a person."

"Well, Cora seems interested, for some reason. All I can do is make sure I don't fuck it up by saying something stupid or acting like a jerk. I mean, I've never had a steady girlfriend. I don't know the first thing about being someone's boyfriend."

Ryan laughed. "Dude, just be yourself. You aren't the jerk you keep calling yourself. Let her know you care. *Show* her. If it's meant to be, everything will work out."

OVER THE NEXT FEW NIGHTS, my dreams were filled with images of midnight-black hair and green eyes—and a killer set of lips. That quick taste in my truck on Sunday did nothing but whet my appetite for Cora. She was all I thought about during the day, too, causing some good-natured ribbing from Ryan on the job.

Once everything passed George's end-of-day inspection, we were let loose, and I hightailed it back to Jake's. I had plenty of time before Cora would be at the bar at seven, but I had wild hopes she'd show up early, as eager to see me as I was to see her.

We'd been texting all week. She'd tell me a bit about her day; I'd tell her about what parts of the remodel job we were doing that day. I sent her a link to some of my favorite boy band videos, and she tried to convince me that the version of "God Must Have Spent A Little More Time on You" by Alabama was better than NSYNC's. She was wrong, of course, but it was something I could overlook. Or at least work on changing her mind about it.

I walked into the bar at six: showered, clean jeans and shirt, and ready for my next fix of Cora Stetson. Grabbing a seat at the bar, I ordered a beer from Shayla, who was covering the bar while she had Jake off doing something.

"Here you go. So, how'd you like the Trunk? Jake told me you ended up going on Sunday." Shayla pushed the longneck on the cocktail napkin across the bar. "You want to order something to eat, too?"

"Nah, not right now. I'll wait till Cora gets here, I think. Yeah, I took her to the Trunk. Cool place—lots of vendors. I ended up finding pretty much everything I wanted there." A picture of Cora in the Jeweled Gem Throne of Horror flashed in my head. *I definitely saw things there I wanted...*

"Shayla, I've got the bar. We're all stocked up for bottles, so you should be all set for the night." Jake came up behind Shayla and leaned over her, practically talking right into her ear to be heard over the jukebox.

"Thanks, Jake. See ya later, Dixon." Shayla moved out of Jake's reach and back out to the floor.

Jake looked back at me. "Now, are you behaving yourself with Cora, or am I going to have to knock some sense into you?"

There was a bit of a warning in his tone, but I could hear him busting my chops over my date with Cora. I wasn't surprised by that; he'd always been protective of women in general.

"Quit worrying about me. Maybe you need to worry more about yourself. Admit it—Shayla's kinda cute." I grinned as I grabbed the longneck and took a swallow.

"Doesn't matter how cute she is. Not interested. Not now, not ever." A steel wall slammed down over his eyes.

It was no secret to me why he shut down. Hell, I had my own issues, but he had it ten times worse. As bad as my childhood had been, it was pixie dust compared to Jake's. But now I had a glimmer of hope that not every relationship would be as fucked up as what he and I had front-row seats to when we were kids. Maybe not every person you counted on would leave. Or, more accurately, be ripped away.

"Hey. Lighten up." I spoke softly, but the message was loud.

Jake shook his head, as if trying to clear the muck out of it. "Yeah. I guess I got to get my head in the game if I'm gonna keep you in line with Cora." A small smile snuck onto his face and the cold steel in his eyes seemed to dim, letting his usual good nature come through.

"You kept me on the straight and narrow enough when we were kids. I still remember you at my back at the store, making me return that pack of gum. Damn store manager banned me for life, I think." I laughed at the memory. The old man's face had turned as red as a tomato—and had the same squished, round shape—when Jake made me fess up that I'd stolen a pack of gum from the checkout counter when we were there buying what passed for groceries: a pack of saltines, peanut butter, and Yoo-hoo. The laughter died as the rest of the memory started to creep in. I shook it off. Tonight wasn't about the past; it was about the here and now. It was about Cora.

And the next forty-five minutes were going to crawl by as I waited for her. But some higher power must have taken pity on me because the energy in the room changed; she was there. Jake's grin kind of gave it away too, but I swear I felt her heat, practically heard her heartbeat, behind me before my brother's grin finished forming on his face.

"Finally. Put this boy out of his misery, Cora. If I had to spend any more time this week looking at his sad puppy-dog face..." Jake whipped the bar towel at my arm.

I turned to see the most beautiful sight...Cora. She was all smiles, looking between me and my brother. If I was a more jealous kind of guy, I might have objected to her sending her sunshine his way, but right now, I wanted to bask in the glow myself. I could only stare at her and try to keep the drool from running down my face and my jaw from dropping. Somehow, my memories and dreams of her were nothing compared to being with her again.

"Hey." Okay, not the most original or intelligent thing to say, but my brain was getting muddled and losing its ability to work effectively.

"Hey." She sidled onto the barstool next to me and swung one leg—a long, lanky, luscious leg—over the other to settle in. Her smile was now directed straight at me, and my breath caught.

"Hey."

"You already said that, lover boy. I swear, Cora, he's only had the one drink. Must be some other reason his brain's not engaged." Jake grabbed my bottle and shook what remained in it.

His shit-eating grin grew, and I wanted to smack it off his face. I was enough of an idiot without any of his help. "Whatever happened to having your brother's back, huh? Couldn't just offer a few drinks on the house to start our date off right and then go about your business?"

"All right, you freeloader. Go grab a booth, and I'll have Shayla over there in a few. First round's on the house. Cora—nice to see you." Jake wandered to the other end of the bar to check on customers there.

"Sorry about that. Let's go grab that booth in the back corner. You look amazing, by the way." Her jeans hugged all her curves and the flowy white blouse had a V-neck collar that provided hints of her cleavage. I stood and guided her by the elbow across the room to the table I had in mind. It was out of the main area of high-top tables and you couldn't quite see all the TVs, so it was quieter and less distracting. Perfect for conversation and paying attention to your companion. Not that there'd be much that could get me to stop looking at Cora or listening to her voice.

"Sounds good. I've been looking forward to this all week. But I was sure to wear some more sensible shoes and I'm happy to report no injuries...so far." She laughed and showed off her low-heeled shoes.

Of course, I couldn't help but look again at those legs...and imagine them wrapped around me as I plunged into... *Crap.* Not the time to be thinking about sex, but it always seemed as if my brain short-circuited around Cora, and I ended up in the same daydream.

We found our way to the table and sat across from each other.

"Glad to hear you're not going to need medical attention. But now I'll have to figure out a different way to get you in my arms."

The cutest blush turned her face pink. "I'm sure we can figure out how to make that happen. I mean—"

"Hi, Dixon. What can I get for you and this pretty lady?" Shayla interrupted Cora, and damn if I didn't want Cora to finish her thought.

"Hey, Shayla. I'll have another beer. Cora, what do you want?"

Cora's blush deepened before she turned to Shayla. "I'll have the same. Thanks." She cleared her throat and looked back at me. "So, rescue any more damsels in distress this week? Conquer any other battlefields?" Her blush faded away and a smirky grin replaced it, complete with twinkling eyes.

"No, ma'am. I'm still focused on the most recent damsel. She seems to be holding all my attention. Hardly had time to do anything but think about her. And her beautiful face. Her amazing smile. Trying to figure out how I could spend some more time with her without looking like a deranged stalker." I reached my hand across the table and grasped hers, caressing the soft skin. "Remembering how soft and warm she felt in my arms when I carried her off to my secret lair."

"Secret lair, huh? Sounds kinda sinister. Not exactly knight-rescuing kind of talk." She stopped my fingers from moving and intertwined with them. "Not that I mind a little excitement with my knights in shining armor. Although, I guess there's bound to be some excitement in an adventure that lands you in a spot you need rescuing from."

"Depends on what kind of excitement you're looking for. Is it a death-defying, swash-buckling adventure you're after, or something a bit more personal?"

"Here you go."

Shayla had come back with the beers, disrupting the little world Cora and I had been weaving ourselves into. Cora released my hand and leaned back. Never had my hand felt so cold.

"Thanks." Cora glanced at Shayla, who had a funny smile on her face.

She looked between the two of us and then stared at me. "You better be good, Dixon. This one's a keeper." With that, she turned on her heel and walked back to the bar and Jake, who was watching our table.

Or was it Shayla, as she walked back toward him?

Before I could think more on that, Cora spoke up. "Why on earth would she tell you to 'be good'? Are you not the shining knight you've been showing me?" The amusement in her eyes told me she was still in a teasing mood, but there was a serious note in her tone.

Here was my chance. Confess all. Except I did not know what I could say...would say...that wouldn't guarantee she'd leave me in the dust. Who wants to hear that the person interested in them hasn't ever had a real relationship, just hookups? That they'd never had a steady girlfriend and had no idea how to be a good boyfriend. And how weird was it that I wanted to not only say I was her boyfriend, but that I couldn't get it out of my head—and some other parts of my anatomy—that we'd be good...so *right*...together. Not exactly third date material, right?

"I can be whatever you need me to be. Shining knight...biker bad boy..." *A worshiper at the altar of your body.* The words left unsaid pulsed in the surrounding air.

Her breath hitched and then whooshed out. "Wow...well then..." She glanced down, denying me the chance to see into the depths of her eyes.

I willed her to look back up so I could drown in her gaze. But I memorized the color and texture of her hair as it swung down, partly obstructing her face. The rise and fall of her chest, the way the fabric of her blouse stretched and the buttons strained had my heartbeat striking its own drum in response. My thoughts wandered to how she would look under me, the buttons freed as the shirt parted to tantalize me with her heaving breasts contained behind lacy walls. How sweet the sound would be when I nuzzled against her, bringing the nipple to a taut bud. I shifted in my chair, trying to adjust the sudden hardness trapped behind the zipper.

Cora looked back up. "We should order some food. Otherwise this beer's going to go to my head, and God only knows what could happen then." She brushed the hair back behind her ear. "Not that that would be the worst thing in the world." A shy smile slipped onto her lips. "So, seriously, I need some food. It's been a long day and a long week, and I'd love to forget all about it and have a nice meal with you."

"Sounds like a plan. Let me grab some menus from the bar." I stood and put my hand on her shoulder, unable to not touch her before I left. "Be right back."

TEN

~Cora~

I HAD A FEW MINUTES while he went to the bar for menus to catch my breath. My heart had been hammering in my chest since I saw him at the bar, his tall frame encased in jeans and a slim-cut T-shirt that showed off his biceps, talking to Jake. And everything he said seemed to be laced with innuendo. Or my overactive imagination had me thinking he wanted to lay me bare on the table and show me exactly how he'd be a knight out to save me...or a bad boy out to ravish me. I wasn't sure how one man could be both, but the promise of ravishment and safety came through his gaze and his words.

I hadn't lied earlier. It had been a long week, and I had been looking forward to tonight.

"Here you go. They have the best wings around. I especially like the dry-rub ones." Dixon slid back into his chair and handed over a menu.

Our fingers brushed and that little tingle snaked up my arm. There was no denying the attraction, and I'd made up my mind while he was at the bar chatting with Jake that there was no reason not to act on it. A fling...a short-term relationship with all the benefits...it might actually be a good thing. Maybe if I was dating someone, both my father and Mark would finally take my rejection of Mark seriously. I took a sip of my beer and glanced at the menu. "That sounds fine. And a salad, too." I looked back to see Dixon staring at me. "What? Did I spill some beer or something?" I hadn't felt any wetness—well, no beer dripping down my chin, although maybe my panties were a little damp—but checked to see whether there was something on my neck or the table. Nothing.

"Uh...no. Just watching...I mean, you watching your weight or something? A salad? Really? In a bar?"

I narrowed my eyes at him, trying to be stern. "You know, one of the quickest ways to piss off a woman is to ask if she's dieting. Yes, a salad. It's called nutrition. Woman cannot live on chicken wings alone, Mr. Shining Knight." At his look of contrition, I laughed. "Relax. I'm kidding. Sort of. I try to keep things pretty good on the food front. That way, when I indulge in decadent desserts, I can tell myself that at least I ate my veggies. Or have one too many beers." I raised my glass in a silent cheers.

He raised his glass to meet mine. "Gotcha. Here's to indulging." His heated stare was only interrupted by the waitress.

"You ready to order, Dixon?" Shayla had her order pad at the ready, glancing between the two of us.

"Yeah. An order of the Kentucky dry-rub wings and a salad. Make that two salads." He grinned at me when he added his own salad to the order. "Gotta get my veggies in so I can...indulge in dessert later on."

Shayla gave him a quizzical look, as if he'd never ordered a salad in his life. "Right. Two salads. Dry-rub wings. Any refills?" Her look bounced between the both of us.

"I'm good. But a glass of water would be good sometime." I grabbed the glass and took another sip, trying to hide my smile.

"Another beer when the food is ready." Dixon handed over the menus. "Thanks, Shayla. Now go tell Jake everything is fine here and that I'm behaving myself."

Shayla took the menus and sauntered off in the direction of the kitchen.

"No doubt he has her checking up on me to make sure I'm treating you right. He's already told me twice that I shouldn't be my usual idiot self and mess things up with you."

"I can't imagine you being an idiot. You've been nothing but a gentleman. You and Jake have that in common, I think." I glanced over at the bar, and sure enough, Jake had his eyes on our table. "So, tell me more about you and Jake growing up."

A wall seemed to come down around him, cutting off the brightness in his eyes and shrinking him into his chair. "Not much to tell, really. Just regular boys getting into regular trouble. More me than Jake, though. He was always taking care of me, trying to keep me on the straight and narrow. He pretty much raised me on his own."

"What about your mom? She married his dad, right?" I fiddled with the wrapped silverware, breaking the seal around the napkin. His eyes still had that dull look, as if he were lost in a memory.

"Yeah. When I was about ten. Jonah—Jake's dad—had dated my mom for a few years before they got married. Once we moved in, things changed. And then..." He took a gulp of his beer. "Anyway, I want to hear about this long week of yours. And how'd that presentation go? You never said in your texts."

We'd texted each night, when I was snuggled up in my covers. A very excellent way to end the day...and apparently the inspiration for the naughty dreams my imagination conjured up each night, too.

"Ugh. My boss let me do the presentation to the board, and it did not go over well. Actually, there was one person who wasn't on board—my dad." I took a sip of the beer, thinking back to that awful Monday morning meeting. "And when he wasn't happy, the rest of the board just backed him up. I swear, the man does not want to join this century, much less this decade. I just don't get it. He talks and talks about how he wants to keep the company in the family for generations but doesn't look to the future of the hotel business at all. I'm just giving him tools for advertising...I haven't even broached the subject of the actual hospitality standards we need to meet and exceed to survive." I huffed, and my beer sloshed as the glass hit the tabletop a bit harder than I meant it to.

"Do you think it's because you're the one with these ideas that he's discounting them? I mean, if he heard the same idea from your boss or someone else, would he still resist?"

"I'm not sure. He tends to talk over me, as if I'm not really there. Or a better way to put it is that he's convinced his opinion should be my opinion, and it doesn't register when I tell him something that doesn't fit into his view of things." Like about marriage and Mark, especially. But I would not let thoughts of either of those men—Mark or my father—take up any more space in my head.

Shayla walked back to us with a serving platter in her hands. "Here you go. I brought everything together...I hope that's okay." She smiled at us as she dropped off the wings, salads, Dixon's beer, and my water. "Let me know if you need anything else."

As she left, Dixon watched her. Or rather, he looked in the direction she was going, but past her...right to Jake watching Shayla.

"What is that about?" I stage-whispered to him, watching the same scene. Shayla seemed oblivious of Jake's stare as she stopped at tables to check on customers, but anybody else could see it a mile away.

"I dunno. But I think he's going to break that glass if he keeps cleaning it with his hands clenched around it." He nodded in Jake's direction, pointing out the beer mug Jake was apparently testing for durability. His smile turned devilish. "Maybe Jake's finally figured out what's right in front of him." His attention turned back to me. "God knows me and my brother might not be the brightest bulbs, but when we get our minds set on a goal, we go for it."

That smile turned into a sexy promise that had me grabbing for my beer and taking a big gulp. The thought of being the object of his full attention had my throat going dry and my panties going wet.

AS WE ATE OUR DINNER, I never wanted the night to end. His corny jokes had me laughing. His eyes sparkled, promising heated passion in their depths. His hand clasped mine as we sat at the table in the back of Jake's, watching the crowd and each other. My pulse throbbed, imagining his kisses instead of his gentle strokes on my hand.

But a ping from my phone distracted me momentarily, and the lock screen displayed the time.

"So, as much as I hate to say it, I've gotta get going. Work in the morning, you know." I put my phone in my purse, finding my car keys in the process.

Dixon stood and held his hand out to me. "Well, you can be sure I'm not going to let you leave on your own. I understand that parking lot can be hell on ladies in heels." He grinned as he pulled me up and toward his chest. "This way to your chariot, my lady." He pressed his lips to my knuckles and bowed in a bad impression of a servant.

"Thank you, kind sir." I couldn't help but giggle at his actions. Then I snuggled up into his body as we walked through the crowded bar to the door.

The heat from our bodies next to each other as we walked had my blood thrumming. The smell of Dixon—fresh, manly—enveloped me. He wrapped his hand around my waist and pulled me closer. Once outside the door, he pulled me over toward the steps to the upstairs apartment and against the wall.

I couldn't resist any longer; I had to taste him again. Had to feel his lips against mine. His body against mine.

"Oh." A breathless pant escaped as he nibbled my neck. "Dixon...oh. Yeah." I squirmed until my hands could make their way over his shoulders to draw him closer. "Yeah. Right there."

The electric pulse between us intensified but somehow he pulled back. "You know, you kind of drive me wild." He rested his forehead on mine and huffed out a breath. "Any chance I can sweep you off your feet and drive you just as wild up at my place?"

The air seemed to thicken...or maybe it was Dixon who made it hard to take in a full breath.

"I think...not. I'm tempted, believe me. God, I'm tempted."

At my words, he smoothed his hands down my sides, gripping my hips. There was a slight pressure at our joined hips, making it clear he was more than tempted. That hard bulge had my body ready to throw caution to the wind.

But my logical mind won out, and I put a firm hand on his chest. "Seriously. Tempted. But not tonight. Can I have a rain check? What about Saturday? Spend the day together?"

And the night. I left the words unsaid, but damn, the promise of them hung in the air.

Dixon let out a deep breath. "Yeah. Saturday. Saturday's good. How about I pick you up around two? We can hang out for a bit, find something to do—a movie or something—and then have dinner. And dessert." His voice went husky on the last words.

"I'd like that. Dessert's always been my favorite." I leaned forward to give him a quick parting kiss, but my tongue found his and they tangoed together, leaving me breathless once again. "Night, Dixon." I snuck out from between him and the wall, ready to head to the parking lot to get in my car...and cool off.

"Not so fast. I was serious about getting you to your car. Never know when a rogue pothole will show up and attack." He clasped my hand as we walked out to the main parking area and my car. With one last lingering kiss, he opened the car door and watched as I settled in.

"Night, Cora. Sweet dreams."

ELEVEN

~Cora~

"CORA, ARE YOU ALMOST ready? We are meeting the Franklins at the Ten Gallon in a half-hour."

My father's voice over the phone was the last straw. Any sweet dreams I'd had last night involving a certain hunk were a distant memory after the day from hell at work. And it only promised to get worse with the dinner I was expected to be at.

"Yes. I just have to finish up some emails before I shut down for the night. Do you want to wait for me, or just head over and I'll meet you there?" I could use a few minutes by myself before this dinner with Mark, his parents, my father, and a handful of others. It'd been nothing but small fires all day and the mere thought of having to go to this dinner had me on edge. So I was hoping he'd say he'd meet me there, and I'd get a small reprieve. But no such luck.

"I'll be in your office shortly, and then we'll head over." The dial tone demonstrated anything I had to say in return clearly didn't matter.

And before I could even finish more than two emails, my father's shadow crossed my desk.

"Ready yet?" A note of impatience reverberated in his words.

I counted to ten silently. "Sure, Dad. Just a sec." I saved the email as a draft and closed all the programs, ready to shut it down. The only thing worse than making him wait was having him watch my every move while he waited.

Tonight was the appreciation dinner for sponsors of the upcoming charity event for SHIELD. The Survivors of Home Invasion for Enforcement of Legal Deterrents held their annual fundraiser at the Stetson. My father not only supported the event by providing the venue and dinner, but he also brought in his fraternity alumni and business partners to contribute. The dinner would be much smaller and intimate than the actual fundraiser, but it had the effect of keeping key contributors happy and willing to keep their checkbooks open. And although I typically hated fundraising and the phony pat-yourself-on-the-back-for-supporting-a-cause bullshit that went with it, the cause was dear to my heart. Losing my mother—and the hell we went through to get justice for her—made my presence not just mandatory by my father, but helped me continue to honor my mother and others who had been taken in violence.

We walked down the hallway and into the elevator in silence, the only noise the quiet clicking of my heels on the marble. I was busy trying to clear my head of work items—the disastrous PR proposal and the aftermath was still heavy on my mind—so I didn't notice my father's stare right away. But, eventually, the weight of his eyes on me bore down.

"What? Everything okay?"

He gave me a sad smile. "I can hear you thinking from here. You are just like your mother...she always got so serious when she was thinking through a problem. Bit her lip, just like you were doing now." He moved his hand, as if he were going to caress my face, but then it dropped. "Some days are harder than others."

I hadn't heard my father's sentimental tone in far too long. It took me by surprise, and a slice of regret at our current strained relationship cut a bit deeper. Things would never be the way they were when Mom was alive, and his typical indifference toward what I wanted didn't inspire confidence he'd become the supportive father I needed.

THERE WASN'T A SOUL at the table I wanted to talk to. All I could think about was my date tomorrow with Dixon. We hadn't firmed up any particular plans, but two o'clock couldn't get here fast enough for me. But until then, I had to sit and keep my mouth shut. Which was getting more and more difficult to do.

"Cora, dear, I'll need your help with the table assignments for the event. Be at the house at one tomorrow to work with me on that." Lila Franklin's prim voice interrupted my daydreams of Dixon and what I hoped our date would be like tomorrow. Her pursed lips and pointed look completed the picture of a stuck-up socialite who'd had one too many Botox treatments.

The woman couldn't smile. I'm not sure I'd ever seen a genuine reaction on her face. Just the plastic look she currently had. And then her words penetrated my brain.

"Ah, actually, I have plans tomorrow afternoon. Can we do it early next week?"

"Mark, I thought you said Cora was going to assist this year, be more involved." Lila turned to her son, giving him the plastic look now.

"Cora, you can cancel your plans. We didn't have anything scheduled, so I told Mother you'd be available, and this needs to get done. Anything else can wait." Mark turned his attention back to his mother. "She'll be there. Don't worry. I'll send you my files with the guests who will need some extra attention from the committee." Mark sipped his Scotch.

What the hell? When had I agreed to do any of this? "Mark, I can speak for myself, thank you very much. And I can't cancel my plans." At least, I had no intention to cancel my plans. Damn if I was going to give up an afternoon—and possibly night—with Dixon to deal with Lila's back-and-forth on who needed to sit next to who, and who was cheating on who, and who was sealing a business deal with who. I cared about the fundraiser, but I didn't think I needed to sacrifice my sanity for it. "Besides, I am sure Lila can handle it. I'm not sure I know as much as she does about who belongs where, so let's leave it in her capable hands." I gave my best fake smile, as if my words didn't have some second meaning. But really, she lived for this kind of thing—like a general preparing his battlefield, this lawyer knew how to put just the right people in just the right places. And not just with her barbed words and pointed looks.

"No. You'll be there." Mark's glass thunked against the table.

"No, I won't." I stiffened and stared into his eyes, practically daring him to make a scene. "Mark, you are not in charge of my time. Or of any aspect of my life. If I said no, I mean no." My jaw started to ache from the tense clenching.

My father choked on his drink, and Lila let out a surprised gasp. Only Martin, Mark's father, was silent. But all three sets of eyes looked at me in various states of outrage and anger.

"But, Cora, don't you want to help with the fundraiser? I thought you were committed to helping more this year." My father's voice held a slight tremor, as if he couldn't believe that I'd had the nerve to stand up for myself.

I turned to him. "Dad, I'm happy to help—really, I am. I've put together the outline of events for the night, gotten significant items donated for the auction, taken care of the social media PR, and convinced the hottest radio DJ to emcee for the evening. Honestly, those are the skills I have to offer...not figuring out who needs to sit with who or who can't sit next to someone because of some life event or business deal I have no idea about. You know I don't care about that sh—" The word stopped in my mouth when his jaw opened in shock. "About that kind of thing."

"Warren, let me speak with Cora privately. I'm sure we can work something out." Mark stood and held his hand out to me, as if leading a five-year-old to her time-out corner.

Now not only was I upset he'd tried to run roughshod over my plans, he'd pissed me off with treating me like a kid. As if I were a naughty little girl who needed to listen to the grown-ups and do as they said.

I pushed up from my chair and threw my napkin on the table. "Mark, you can 'talk' all you want but I am not changing my mind." I walked out of the dining area, head held high, and made my way to the lobby area. I needed to cool off and get away from the pressure of my father and Mark's parents. And Mark.

But I wasn't going to get to do that because Mark followed me out to the lobby.

"Cora, what has gotten into you? Of course you'll help Mother with the seating. You need to learn how to do this if we are going to have any kind of entertaining when we get married. It's practice...she can help you figure out these things before you have to do it on your own. We'll have a wedding reception with hundreds of people—don't you want to be in charge of planning your own wedding?" He reached out and touched my arm.

I whirled around. "Wh—"

Startled, I froze. There, standing next to the potted ficus tree, stood Dixon and his friend from the bar. The smile on his face slid off. The next thing I knew, he'd turned around and practically ran out the lobby door.

I moved to go after Dixon, but Mark grabbed my arm.

"Cora, if he was part of your plans for tomorrow, I think it's safe to say your plans have changed." He smirked.

"The only thing that's changed is that I'm no longer interested in reasoning with you. There is nothing between us—there never really was—and the only thing I feel for you is disgust. Now, get out of my way. I have someone important to talk to."

TWELVE

~Dixon~

THIS COULD NOT BE HAPPENING. *A wedding? She was getting married?*

"Whoa—Dixon! Wait up!" Ryan's baritone got closer as I stopped at the curb outside the hotel.

We'd driven over to the hotel in Ryan's truck so he could go to a celebration dinner for little Gabby's ballet recital. The cute five-year-old had insisted that her mother, Grace, invite Ryan because he'd taken her to class sometimes when Grace had to work. I thought he had a thing for Grace, but the kid was cute. And there was no way Ryan was going to disappoint her by not showing up. He'd asked me to go with him to fend off any single mothers. It was the last place I'd expected to run into Cora, though.

I dropped into the bench for guests waiting for cars from the valet. My head was swimming. Any coherent thoughts were whisked away when I pictured the guy talking to Cora. The way he put his hand on her. How close he stood to her. His words. *Married? Just what the fuck was going on?*

"I'm guessing you had no idea she was engaged. I'm sorry, dude. That sucks." Ryan sat next to me. "You want to get out of here? Get drunk? Find some hot chick to take your mind off things?"

"Dixon! Dixon, wait!" Cora came up to the bench, practically hyperventilating. "I can explain. I swear, it's not what it looked like. Well, it was, but it wasn't." She blew out a breath and put her hands on her hips. "Please, let me explain."

I looked up at her. Her face was blotchy, and her lower lip trembled before she bit at it. Her chest heaved from her fast walking to chase me down. She looked as if she were on the verge of tears, and the plea in her voice was evident.

I wasn't sure what I'd hear, but I wasn't such an asshole that I wouldn't listen to whatever explanation Cora had for me. Maybe it wasn't as bad as it looked. My heart held onto that weak hope against the harsh voice of experience that voted to get out of there with Ryan. Somehow, hope won that battle.

I nodded at Ryan. "Go ahead and get to Gabby's celebration. You can't miss that, or she'll stomp her feet at you next time you take her to class. I'll grab a ride back to Jake's. Cora and I need a few minutes here. I'll catch up with you later."

Ryan stood and put a hand on my shoulder. "No problem. Just let me know you're all right later." He gave Cora a quick glance before he headed back to the hotel ballroom.

"Dixon, I'm so sorry. I wish you hadn't heard that—"

"I bet. Who the hell is that, anyway? And seriously—you're engaged?" My anger seeped out and each word was said in a louder voice.

Cora cringed. "Can I sit? Or, better yet, let's leave. We need to talk but I'm not sure—" She looked over her shoulder at the hotel entrance. The lurking figure in the doorway moved toward us. "Come on. I've got my keys. Let's go to your place and talk." She grabbed my arm and stood. "Please. I need to get out of here."

I looked at the approaching man. He was tall, but not particularly built. He might have a few inches on me, but I had more bulk and heft. Cora's get-me-out-of-here attitude had my defenses going up. Which was unbelievable, if any of that wedding talk was to be believed. But God knew I didn't want to believe it, so I trusted my instincts.

"Yeah. Let's get out of here. We do need to talk, and I'm thinking that's not going to happen here. But, first, tell me—are you engaged?"

Cora looked between me and the man. "No. Not really. It's...complicated. But I want to explain it all to you. Please." Her green eyes locked onto me. "Let me explain."

THE CAR RIDE TO JAKE'S was quiet. Unsettled. I was bursting at the seams to hear what Cora had to say for herself, but I wasn't ready to have some huge bombshell dropped on me while we were in the car. I wanted to look in her eyes when she told me whatever she was going to tell me. And I wanted a drink in my hand, too.

She parked by the stairs to my apartment. When she turned the car off, she turned to me. "Dixon, I meant it. I totally want to explain everything. But first, I promise, it's not as bad as you might think."

"Okay." Her earlier words about "not exactly" being engaged had circled my brain for the entire car ride. The dizzying effect was definitely getting to me. Time for that drink, and then some talk. "Let's head upstairs."

I followed her up the stairs. Her ass had my head drifting off into other trains of thought, remembering the last time she'd been in my apartment. The way she'd felt in my arms. The way she'd looked at me. How cute she'd been, getting drunk on one beer.

And then, her comment about a Mark. *Mark...* Had I just met Mark? I guess the universe wasn't done dealing me a shitty hand if she was engaged to this Mark.

After I unlocked the door and turned the lights on, I grabbed her hand, needing to hold on to any shred of hope I could find. "So, what's the deal with Mark?" The last word came out of my mouth like the knife it felt like.

She swallowed and took a small step closer.

I inhaled—almost against my will—and that sweet scent of spring filled me. Practically made me frenzied with wanting her. But I needed to hear what she had to say. Needed to hear about Mark...and this engagement.

"My father...he has some expectations of me. I kind of told you a bit about it, with the hotel stuff. But it's more than that. The past year, he's been after me to date Mark. So I did, to make him happy. But it never clicked." She looked directly at me, as if she wanted to make sure I heard her, understood what she was saying. "I told Mark months ago that it was over. It wasn't more than a handful of dates—dinners, mostly. There just wasn't a spark."

My breath caught. *A spark? Did she kiss him? Did she do more than kiss him? Did he force himself on her?* My blood boiled at the thought, which was more than ridiculous. We'd just met, for fuck's sake. I shouldn't care who she kissed—who she'd been with—before we met. God knew I wasn't in any position to throw stones on that count. But damn, it was hard to keep my temper in check when my head went off the rails at the thought of him forcing himself on her. I tried to count to ten before I spoke. *One, two—*

"Did that motherfucker hurt you?"

Cora gasped. "No. God, no. Nothing like that. I swear. We...kissed. But it was like kissing your brother. Like, absolutely no zing. Totally stomach-churning, in fact." She stepped back and sat on the couch. She dropped her head into her hands, and then she looked back up at me. "He was definitely a toad on my search for my knight in shining armor." A small smile worked its way onto her features. "My Cub Scout hero."

I dropped onto the couch next to her, itching to touch her again. But I hadn't heard about the engagement portion of the explanation yet, and I needed to before I allowed myself any more of what I was craving. "So what's the engagement thing about then? If you told him it was over, how in the hell does he think you're engaged?"

Her smile disappeared. "I'm pretty sure my father and Mark have 'discussed' the future, meaning they've planned out how they think they are going to run my life." She stood abruptly and started to pace in the small space. Two steps left; pause; two steps right. Her long legs glided over the carpet, and I was hypnotized by the sight.

"But they are wrong in just about everything they've assumed. They think I'm going to marry Mark, leave my job at the hotel, become some society wife...some kind of Stepford wife who's got no opinion, no ambition of her own. Oh, I'm going to leave the hotel, but not for their plans. I have plans of my own."

"Why haven't you told them you aren't interested? In either marrying Mark or the hotel?" I was no expert on families, but couldn't she just tell her father she didn't want to marry this guy? What was stopping her?

"Every time I try to start the conversation, there's an 'emergency.' Or I'm just dismissed out of hand." She stopped her pacing and looked out the window at the parking lot below. "Or maybe I've been putting it off because there's been no real reason to push it." She looked back at me. "Maybe I've just been a chicken shit."

She took the three steps back to the couch and dropped in front of me. "But there's a reason to push it now." Her lips touched mine.

The heat in my chest exploded, and I crushed my lips against hers. I tugged her hair, trying to get her closer. She pressed her body into mine, every luscious curve finding the hard planes of my chest. I scooted her onto my lap, straddled over my legs. The vee of her legs fit snug against my bulging cock, eager to meet that flesh.

I pulled away enough to catch my breath and look her in the eyes. Life flickered there, the spark of desire I was sure was in my eyes too. The possibility of a future. And that scared the shit out of me. I'd never really believed anyone would want to be with me, so I'd never had to live up to any expectations, any ideals. I'd never imagined someone would be willing to put their heart in my hands, and I'd never had the courage to put mine into someone else's.

I'D TOSSED AND TURNED all night. I wavered between regretting letting Cora go last night and...well, I just regretted letting her go. But I was still trying to wrap my head around this almost, kind of engagement thing with Mark and what she'd said about there being a reason to push back now. Me. I was the reason. I hoped, anyway. Had anyone ever put me first? Made me feel like I mattered? Yeah, sure, Jake had been there, but he was my brother. Stepbrother. Whatever. I'd never had a woman—and God, what a woman Cora was—put me first.

But there was the responsibility that came with her declaration. I'd need to be worthy of that. Was I? I wasn't sure, but damn, I wanted to be. I wanted a lot, suddenly.

I wanted to be Cora's. I wanted her to be mine. Would it be just for now? Or for something longer? I had no idea, but I wanted to give her everything...even though I had nothing. I wanted to protect her from Mark, from her father...from their expectations. I wanted Cora to have her dreams, not the nightmare of a loveless marriage. I wanted to be buried inside her. I wanted to watch her face as I made her come, again and again.

That was one thing I was sure I could give her. The others? Not so sure.

So I'd pulled back, not sure what to do with all that swirling in my head. God knew, all I'd needed was the slightest nudge from Cora, and I'd have taken things a lot further last night. But she seemed to sense I was all over the place and didn't push. She'd given me another kiss—lingering, tender, yearning—and stood up from my lap.

"I know it's a lot. I know I've got some things to take care of. But now...now I'm ready. It might take some time to convince them, but I will explain things to my father and Mark. They will know how I feel. And what I'm willing to do...and not do...in my future. For my future. And that future, I hope, includes you." Cora's eyes sparkled, the green dazzling and mesmerizing.

I could get lost in them if I wasn't careful. I lifted my hand and had her pull me off the couch. "You'd better think about that. Make sure it's what you really want."

She nodded decisively. "It is." Then she was out the door.

And now it was morning, and all I could do was wait. In agony. Would she tell her father—and Mark—to go pound sand? That she had her own plans for her life, ones that didn't include their agendas? And, miraculously, included me? Or would fate fuck me over again and take away any chance I had to be happy?

I trudged down the back stairs to the bar office, hoping Jake had the coffee going. I was going to need it—and some advice from him—to get my head on straight.

"Hey, brother." Jake looked up from his tidy desk. Everything had its place, and everything was in its place. Some habits were hard to break, I guess. "You look like shit. You been drinking?" He leaned back in his chair and looked me over like a man deciding whether to let a skunked dog in the house.

I wasn't sure I'd pass inspection. "Coffee. God, give me coffee." I slumped into the chair opposite his desk. "No, not drinking...just not sleeping."

"Any particular reason?" He got up and crossed the room to the coffeemaker, popping a pod in and brewing a cup.

The heavenly smell of roasted beans floated over. Enough to wake me up. "Yeah. A particular woman. And not for the fun reasons of not sleeping. I hardly know where to start."

Jake handed over the cup. "Well, you could start at the beginning, but I know the beginning. Boy meets girl; boy does something stupid, and girl tells him to drop dead. How am I doing so far?" He dropped another pod in to brew himself a cup and watched me as I stared into the coffee cup as though it held all the answers to the universe.

I looked up at him. "Not quite. I mean, I'm sure I did something stupid in the way I reacted, but nope...she's the one who did something. Well, not did exactly. More like she forgot to mention she's engaged."

Jake choked on the hot liquid going down his throat. "What? Engaged? What the hell?"

"Well, not really. It's just...her dad is pressuring her, and the guy in question has some kind of medieval betrothment ideal, where he's talking with her dad about marriage. Neither of them have listened to her when she's said she's not interested. Her dad wants to marry her off to this guy, and the guy is more than eager to make it happen."

"Um...they do realize they can't force her into marriage, don't they? I mean, you realize that, too, right? There's no way she's going to marry someone against her will." He sat back into his chair and fiddled with the cup handle. "I just can't see Cora doing that, Dixon."

I drew a deep breath. "Yeah. She tells me she's not going to do it, but that those two—Mark and her dad—just talk over her or ignore her anytime she tries to explain it's not going to happen. But she told me last night that..."

"That what?" A look of concern took over Jake's face.

"That now she's got a real reason to make sure they hear her." I dropped my gaze to my lap. "Me, I guess." The last words barely made it from my brain to my mouth. I could hardly believe it—much less begin to accept it.

"And that's what's got you sleep-deprived? The thought you'd be the one to make Cora fight to make herself be heard? Be seen?" He harrumphed. "Bullshit...whatever you've got going on in that thick head of yours is bullshit. Don't listen to that fucking man's voice in your head telling you shit that ain't true. Don't let our past steal this from you. You're stronger than that. Man up, dude."

My eyes sought his. "Man, I'm trying. But I hear it anyway. I feel it, too." I clenched the coffee cup, knuckles whitening under the tension. "I don't want to, but that fucker is in there, just taunting me."

"He was wrong. So wrong, on so many things. He was hardly worth calling a human being, much less a father or stepfather. You do deserve the good things...you do deserve someone to love you. He never should have taken that—taken anything...anybody—from you." Desperation—and guilt—came through Jake's words.

He'd always done that for me. Tried to negate what his father was...what he did. Even though it was so much worse for him. Jake never stopped encouraging me, never stopped believing in me. I tried to do the same for him, but I was never sure I succeeded.

I took a sip of the coffee, trying to get my shit together. "I know. We're not those boys anymore, but some days it's harder to leave behind. And the thought that there could be more in my life than casual hookups and drifting from place to place...it's terrifying. I mean, it could all be taken away, just like that." I snapped my fingers for effect. "It's happened before—" I stopped at the look on Jake's face. *Shit.* "It's not your fault, man."

Jake cleared his throat. "And it's not yours, either. It was a shit deal. And we shoveled that shit as best we could, together. He didn't take that from us—either of us. I'll be damned if I'll let him take any more, either. So, tell me what you said when Cora told you about this 'engagement.'"

My sleep-deprived brain was starting to work on all cylinders with the coffee hitting my system. "Well, I didn't yell or throw any glasses at a mirror. I was calm, I guess. I asked questions and let her answer. I'm not sure I've processed all her answers, but she made it clear to me that she still wants to see me. That she definitely isn't interested in her father's—or Mark's—plans for her."

I tried to remember all the details. "I think she said something about having plans to leave the hotel, but not to become some socialite wife. Not sure she said what she was going to do, come to think of it."

Jake's encouraging smile was followed by the advice I'd been hoping to get. "Well, figure out how you fit into those plans of Cora's and forget anyone else's opinion."

THIRTEEN

~Cora~

IT HAD BEEN A LONG night, but one that was a long time coming. I couldn't believe Mark had pulled that stunt at the hotel. And my father was no better. Every time I thought about that dinner—and Mark's insistence we'd be getting married—I wanted to scream. It was unbelievable how he ignored my words and what I tried to tell him.

The look on Dixon's face was etched into my memory. If there was one good thing that came out of Mark's high-handed behavior, it was that I'd told Dixon everything. Now he knew about Mark, about my father, how they had "plans" for me I had no interest in. We didn't get a chance to talk about what I wanted to do with my life, but I now had the impetus to stand up for myself.

I would not let either of them talk—or walk—over me anymore. And that started with my father. I took a deep breath in through my nose, releasing it out through my mouth. The moment of truth was here, and I was determined to be heard this time.

The door to his office was open, but I knocked on the doorframe anyway, to get his attention. Before I could chicken out, I stepped in and closed the door behind me. "Dad, we need to talk."

"Cora. Yes, I think we do." He closed out the program on the computer screen and focused his attention on me. "Last night—"

"Last night was the last time I'll be having dinner with Mark. It's done, Dad. It's more than done. I'm not interested in him. Not going to date him. Not going to marry him. Not going to start some family dynasty with him." I planted my feet in a wide stance, ignoring the swirling in my stomach but concentrating on getting the words out before he dismissed them.

"What? Young lady, you do not know what you are talking about. Mark is a good man—comes from the best family. He's in the who's-who of law in the Northeast. He'll make a fine husband...and father." His volume grew with each declaration.

"If he's such a catch, you marry him, Dad. I'm done with him. We grew up together...there's no spark...no fire. When he kissed me, it was like kissing a snake. All it did was leave me cold and wanting to run away. That's not exactly marriage material, is it?"

His expression turned from mild outrage to an uncomfortable grimace. "I don't want to hear those kinds of details about my daughter and her husband-to-be. There are just some things that should not be discussed."

My jaw dropped. He still wasn't listening. I leaned over the desk. "Dad, I love you. I do. But I will not be marrying Mark. Ever. Never. Not happening. And if you don't want to hear about my sex life, I'm totally fine with that. But know that it does not, and never will, include Mark." I straightened up. "I am seeing someone but I don't know that things are serious yet." I hesitated at what felt like a lie. "But it's clear to me that my choice will not be Mark."

"Cora, what is going on? I thought you and Mark were having a few bumps in the road, but he assured me—"

"And that's the problem, Dad. *He* told you...neither of you have listened to me over the past ten months when I've tried to tell you I'm not interested. If you wanted to make sure everything was all right, you should have talked to me. Not him. I'm your daughter. You should care about what I want, not about what your lawyer wants."

"Mark can give you a safe, stable future. The world's your oyster...there's nothing he wouldn't get for you. All you'd need to do is ask." My father's disbelieving look was only matched by his incredulous tone at the thought of taking my feelings into account.

I dropped into the chair, exhausted from the previous night and the energy it was taking to get my point across. But my father needed to hear the truth from me...all of it.

I drew in a deep breath. "I know you think a future with Mark is safe. That he can provide for me. But life is more than just money...more than financial security. At least, I want my life to be more than that. I want to spread my wings, Dad, and a life with Mark isn't going to let me do that. He's concerned with social status, with image—"

"What's wrong with a good image? Having a good social standing?" The words puffed out of his mouth so fast they seemed to knock me over.

"Dad, it's just not me. I don't care about all of that. I don't want to go to galas and dinners and charity events. I don't want to be some prop used to make a point." I stared at the carpet, mindlessly tracing the pattern in my head as I tried to say the next part diplomatically. I looked back up and stared him in the eyes. "If I care about a cause, I want to do more than have a five-hundred-dollar-per-plate dinner and pat myself on the back. I'd rather be helping people directly...see the impact of my time, my resources."

The silence stretched, with the tick of the grandfather clock marking the time.

Then he took a deep breath and exhaled. "I appreciate your stance. If I've ever made you feel like a 'prop,' it was not my intention." He looked away, his gaze softening as it landed on the photo of my mother. "She loved them, you know...the parties and galas...and I thought that—I don't know...that you did, too. That you were somehow continuing what she started." He looked at me.

"Dad, I'm not her. I loved Mom, but I can't be a replacement for her. I have different dreams. And they don't include Mark, charity events, or..." I faltered. We hadn't had a deep, honest discussion about much since Mom died. Should I keep going with more truths he might not be ready to hear, or stop and let him hear me on the Mark issue?

"I want to go out on my own. I've been waiting for the right time to talk to you about it, and this is it." I straightened in my chair and made sure I had his full attention before I kept going. "Once my inheritance is mine, I want to use Grandmother's old cottage and run my own bed-and-breakfast."

My father's eyes bulged and his jaw hung slack.

DIXON HAD TEXTED ME during the day, checking in. He asked me to meet him at Jake's, and by the time five o'clock rolled around, I was more than ready for a drink.

As I tucked my keys in my purse and made my way into the bar, it occurred to me I'd had more to drink in the last few weeks than the last six months. Not that I thought I had some kind of problem with alcohol now, but a better appreciation of taking time to relax and kick back—and how a drink or two wasn't the end of the world, no matter what my father had told me over the years. I was still a lightweight, so I'd never be one to drink much, but I could see the appeal of getting lost in the giddy feeling of actually being drunk.

Dixon was at the bar, chatting with Shayla. With his attention elsewhere, I could take my time in appreciating his physical traits. The strong back. The muscled arms. A tight butt. The rhythm of my heart did a hop-skip when I remembered being in his arms that first night we met. The way he seemed to look inside me in a way no one ever had before—where he recognized me somehow.

He must have realized I was there, because he turned around on the barstool and gave me a smile that sent tingles all the way down to my toes.

"Hey there. I was wondering when you'd be here. How'd things go with your dad?" He stood and met me halfway, leaning over to give me a kiss on the cheek. "Or did you not have time to talk to him?"

"Let's grab a table. But first," I looked over at Shayla, "can we get a couple beers? And an order of wings." I took a few steps toward the back tables.

"And two salads, Shayla." Dixon's laugh followed his order to complete our meal. "Can't forget to eat my greens, you know."

I turned back to face him. His eyes crinkled at the corners as he laughed quietly at his teasing.

"Look at you...being all responsible and all, ordering salad. I guess I'm rubbing off on you." I smiled back at him as we slid into the booth seats.

"I guess there are worse things than a salad once in a while. But at least you ordered a beer to wash it down with."

His steady gaze held me in place. I was the center of his attention, and warmth infused my body. I could say anything, and he'd let me. He'd hear me. He'd understand. Or if not understand, at least let me be me. Quite the reverse from my father, the one person who'd known me the longest and should be someone who could do that. Our conversation was still running through my head, but I didn't want to dwell on it now. I just wanted to be with Dixon.

"So, tell me about how things went with your dad. Did you get your point across to him? Is he gonna give up on the Mark thing?" Dixon glanced at the table and fidgeted with the placemat. When he looked back up, he ventured, "Did you tell him about me?"

I took a deep breath. "Yeah, we talked. I'm not sure how much good it did, though. He is stuck on setting me up with a 'good future'—whatever that is. Well, for him, it's Mark and security and high society. I told him that if he thought Mark was such a catch, he should marry him." I laughed, remembering Dad's look of confusion at that remark.

Dixon let out a huff. "Well, he's your dad. He probably thinks he has to look out for you. You could do worse, trust me. At least you still have him." His attention drifted off to the side before he looked back at me. "What did you say about me?"

The whispered question seemed important to him, like the quieter he asked it, the easier it would be to hear the answer he didn't want to hear.

"I told him I'd met somebody and that even though I didn't know him very well yet, I was more interested in pursuing something with him than anyone else...Mark included. Especially more than Mark. That Mark was like a cold snake that I couldn't get away from fast enough." I wasn't sure what Dixon needed to hear from me, but that was the truth. I couldn't stop thinking about him, and all the tingles and heart-stopping reactions to everything he did.

I reached over the table. "So, what does a girl have to do to get to know the real Dixon Reed?"

He put his hand over mine, and soon his gentle caress had those tingles running up my arm and zinging my heart.

"Well," he smiled, "I guess another date might be in order."

"Here you go, Dixon. Two salads, two beers, and wings." Shayla dropped off the order and gave me a smile. "Cora, make sure he eats all that salad, now. Every man needs a balanced diet." She winked at me before she turned away, headed back to the kitchen.

I picked up my fork. "Another date, huh? Maybe after you eat your veggies, we'll get that dessert you keep promising me. After all, dessert is my favorite." At his low groan, I looked at him.

"You drive a hard bargain, but if eating a salad means we're having dessert, I'll deal with it." He picked up his fork. "But whatever shall we talk about while we eat this balanced diet?" The twinkle in his eye belied his curious tone.

"Tell me about your week." I was more than ready to drop the subject of my father and Mark. I wanted to learn more about the man in front of me, the man who made time stop for me, and soak up his presence.

He seemed to gather his thoughts, picking up a chicken wing and pulling it apart. "Not much to tell, really. Still working the demo part of the job. The foreman is cool to work for but he's a stickler for cleanup each night before we leave. That's the only thing he's kind of a pain in the ass about. I'm looking forward to starting the remodeling part, though." He popped a piece of meat in his mouth and chewed.

Watching a guy eat should not be so engrossing, but I couldn't keep my gaze from him. His eyes seemed to focus on me, penetrating a layer I'd never realized was there and finding the real me under it. His chewing slowed, and he reached for his beer.

"You know, you keep looking at me like that, and I'm gonna think we need to skip dinner and take care of that dessert you're wanting." He swallowed some beer and set the bottle down.

"Well, maybe we should live a little and shake things up. You know...dessert before dinner."

I SHOULD HAVE BEEN ashamed about it, but walking out of Jake's—past Shayla, Jake, the bouncer, the crowd—knowing that we were headed to Dixon's place, I was excited. Eager. A little light on my feet. A little light in my head, too, I guess. And I hadn't even had any of my beer.

The walk to his apartment over the bar was a blur. The only thing I was aware of was the electric current from his fingers to mine, clasped together.

Once he had the door open, he pulled me in, shut it with his foot, and swirled me around until I was pressed up against the door. Then he pressed himself closer.

"God, I've been thinking about you all day...all night, every night." He nuzzled my neck, taking little love bites between words. The hard planes of his body found all my soft places, molding us together. He pulled back. "You still good with dessert before dinner?"

"Oh, yeah. Dessert before dinner is never a bad idea." I slid my arms around his neck, pulling him closer for a kiss. Our tongues danced together, teasing and drawing out moans. From me or from him...I couldn't tell. Maybe both.

My heart beat so fast, it should have jumped out of my chest. I took a steadying breath. It was all I could do to keep upright. That lightheaded feeling mixed with the zip and zing of Dixon's touch, with my knees going weak. Thank goodness I was against the door, or else I'd've fallen over. As it was, my eyes couldn't focus and fluttered closed in surrender.

"You are sweeter than any dessert I've ever tasted."

Dixon came back in for another kiss, seeming to steal my breath with every word he spoke and every motion of his hands. Those tingling touches roamed from my hips up my torso, whispering right over the swell of my breasts.

My shirt and bra weren't enough to hide the strength...the gentleness...of his fingers as they rubbed my nipples through the fabric. They pebbled in response, eager to rise to the caress. I pressed my chest closer to the source of the incoming pleasure, lost in the sensation. All too soon, the heavenly fervor faded when his hands stopped and the kiss ended.

"As much as I'm enjoying this, maybe we could move this to a bed." His husky voice washed over me as he waited for my response. His hand held mine, ready to bring me with him once I agreed.

"Yes."

The soft response galvanized Dixon. Quicker than I could say another word, he led me the few steps to that bed I'd spent the night in hardly more than a week ago. But this time, I wouldn't be in that bed alone.

He moved to turn the light on, but I stopped his hand. Taking a few steps to the window, I adjusted the blinds to let in some light from the full moon. When I turned back to him, his eyes were focused on me, full of desire and something else I couldn't quite figure out. But whatever it was, I wanted to see more of it.

"I don't do this often, but I am on the Pill. Still..." I took a quick breath. "Do you have some protection? I don't mean to imply anything—"

"It's not a big deal. Yeah, I've got some condoms in the nightstand. We can use that, too, if that makes you feel better. It's fine by me." Dixon tilted his head toward the table, reaching out to open up the drawer and fishing out a foil package.

I wasn't going to think too much about why he had a stash of condoms close by. I was going to concentrate on feeling those zips and tingles everywhere Dixon touched me, and let everything else go.

I lifted my shirt and pulled it over my head. His nostrils flared, but not a word came out of him. I put my hands on the snap of my jeans and popped it. The clicking of the zipper was the only sound in the room. Although I couldn't imagine how he couldn't hear my heart pulsing under his full attention. Once I shimmied out of the jeans, I took a step toward him.

Before my feet hit the ground, he was right there. Arms enveloped me and held me close. Now I heard his heart beat, and the wild sound matched my own. A hand moved up and cradled my head, bringing it into perfect alignment for another scorching kiss. The heat was still there, setting all my girly parts on fire, but a possessive tenderness came through too.

"Damn."

The word glided near my ear, tickling me. Then I made some demands of my own. My fingers fumbled as I tried to find the edge of his T-shirt. Well, fumble...feel the six-pack abs...same thing, right? The chiseled chest came into view when he took a hand off me and helped get that pesky shirt off. I traced over the contours of his chest, with a little tweak of his nipple. I smiled at his tiny inhale.

Dixon's eyes closed as I continued to roll my hand over his body.

A quiet hum filled the space between us as I felt over his muscled pecs. My fingers caught an old scar on his left shoulder. I rubbed it and looked at him.

He opened his eyes. "Not important. It was a long time ago." He moved his hands behind my back, searching for the clasp of my bra. It was like butter under his hot touch and melted away, and he brushed the sides of my breasts as he fully removed the bra from my shoulders. "This is what is important. Now."

Dixon returned the favor and plucked at my nipples. At my sigh, he turned up the heat and pinched. The slight sting and pressure had me leaning into him, asking for more. And more he delivered.

While he teased my breasts with one hand, the other wandered to the edge of my panties. The panties I couldn't wait to be out of. The panties that proved no match for Dixon's insistent hand. He slid a finger toward my wet folds, and then his hot mouth covered mine. His tongue demanded entry and then began its assault. Each move of his tongue was echoed in the action of his fingers: twisting, turning, teasing; faster, slower, faster again; wet and wild.

He turned us around so the backs of my legs hit the edge of the bed. He stepped between my legs and guided me back onto the comforter, fanning out my hair and running his hands down my body. Dixon grabbed the waistband of my panties and pulled them all the way down, carefully disentangling them from my feet.

"So beautiful." A kiss landed on the side of my ankle. "So soft." A kiss whispered against my calf. "So strong." A little love bite on my thigh. "So much...more." A breath blew over my mound, sending a shiver through my body. He gazed at the apex of my legs, taking a reverent inhalation.

"Oh God." I wanted to burn under his touch, but right now I was consumed with his hands-off worship of my body. Such an intense stare would usually make me uncomfortable, but I was fascinated with his fierce stance. "I need you to touch me, Dixon."

He ran his hands down from their position on my thigh, closing in on my center.

A flutter of a touch had me aching for more, seeking more than a tease. I needed those strong fingers, those strong hands, to find the key to opening the vault of heaven I was sure awaited us both. I thrust forward, looking for contact.

"Like this?" He plunged his fingers into my wet heat, and he bent his head.

After the sensation of being opened to his touch, the gentle lap of his tongue acted as a soothing contrast. But that balm was soon converted to a storm I couldn't tame—didn't even try to. The pressure, the suction, the swirl of his tongue had me clutching the bedspread under me. Each moment that passed drew me closer to a bliss I was begging him to deliver.

"Please...more...Dixon..." The words were incoherent, but the meaning clear.

He moved his tongue and fingers in unison, with a rhythm I found myself following. My hips bucked, until that final crescendo broke over me.

"Oh my God..." Breathless, I looked at Dixon.

His face, silhouetted between my legs, was still focused on my pussy. "Definitely sweeter than any dessert I've ever had." He looked up at me, all intense and all-consuming. "Something I can't seem to get enough of."

Before I had a chance to respond, he dipped his head again, dropping little bites and smoothing licks. His attentions moved up my body, with special regard to my breasts. He cupped the fullness of each, with fingers dancing over my nipples, teasing them to hardness. After a moment of suckling, he blew a hot breath over them, causing them to harden further.

"But there's more to dessert than just sweetness. There's the decadent richness..." Dixon kissed the shell of my ear.

I swear, the man purred into my ear. The vibration had me shivering, with goose bumps forming all over my body. I couldn't move, held hostage not just by his words but by the delicious feeling flowing through me.

"The gorgeous presentation..."

He stared at me, his eyes inviting me into their depths. I couldn't have said a word, so mesmerized by his devotion to making me the center of his world.

"The temptation..." His mouth claimed mine, and all I wanted to do was take what he was offering.

"The sublime experience..."

After a crinkle of foil, and an eternity as I watched him sheathe himself, his rock-hard length found its home as he entered me.

His next kiss left me gasping for air. Our sweat-slicked bodies moved in unison, the only sound in the room our heavy breathing. He cradled my head, his strong fingers splayed at the base of my ear.

"Oh God!"

I wasn't sure who let out the exclamation, but all I could do was drag him closer as he rocked in and out. Each thrust brought us closer...not just to each other, but to a climax that left both of us shuddering.

FOURTEEN

~Dixon~

AFTER MY NIGHT WITH Cora, I found myself in a strange place: wanting more—more time with Cora, more of her attention, more of all those light feelings she gave me. I'd never been one for a relationship—probably still wasn't—but this was the first time I'd wanted to see a woman after we'd spent a night together. The unfamiliar sensation was unsettling, and it showed. I was screwing up on the job, and Ryan had had just about enough of me this week.

"Jesus, dude. Watch what the fuck you are doing!" Ryan ducked as I turned around with a two-by-four on my shoulder. "You almost went through the window with that thing." He glared at me. "You keep that shit up, and George is gonna fire your ass."

"I know. I know," I grumbled. Try as I might, I could not get my head in the game. If I wasn't thinking about this foreign feeling, I was daydreaming about Cora. About our night together—I couldn't get the memory of her face as she called out my name out of my head—but also about the way she looked at me. The way she wanted to know about that old scar. The way her eyes lit up when she laughed at something I said.

"Hey, you going to Jake's tonight? We can have a beer and watch the baseball game while you tell me what the hell is going on." Ryan had a shit-eating grin. "Of course, I want the details. You spent the night with that Cora chick, right? How was it?"

Any brain fog cleared up at Ryan's tone. Fuck if I was going to let him talk about Cora as if she were some piece of meat. "You want to be able to have your own night with someone in the future, you'd better shut up and mind your own business. Or else you're gonna feel the pain when I dick-punch you. Anything between me and Cora is just that...between me and her." I dropped the two-by-four at his feet.

"Okay then. You're clearly in it for more than a piece of ass. So quit being an asshole and fucking get on with it then. Call her. Go spend time with her. Anything but this miserable, distracted funk you're dragging yourself into." He put his hand on my shoulder. "You know, now that you know more than her last name, go find out if what she's making you feel is gonna make you happy. Because, seriously, dude, you need some happiness. And you need to not get fired."

I stared at Ryan. The fucker had been pulling my chain...and I fell for it. "Fine. I'll call her. But later, after we get this all squared away. Probably shouldn't be making personal calls on the job, right?" I looked around for George, who'd be bound to show up the second I pulled my cell phone out.

"Right. Anyway, how's that project you've been working on going? I've seen the light on in the warehouse the past few nights." Ryan picked up the two-by-four I'd dropped at his feet and moved it over to the workhorses.

I joined him there, tape measure in hand and ready to mark off the correct measurement. After lining up the square, I drew the line and motioned for him to make the cut. "It's going. I've got the right dimensions for the cutout, and the legs are fastened now. I'm still waiting on the chair, though."

"I thought you'd bought that one online." Ryan cut the wood and then unplugged the saw. "Didn't you talk to that guy?"

"Yeah. But it's a custom piece, so it's taking some time for the details."

We lifted the wood, and I held it steady while Ryan screwed it into place.

"Custom? Man, where are you getting the dough for all this? I mean, I know what this job pays, and I don't see any custom woodwork in my budget." Ryan fixed a penetrating stare in my direction.

"I worked out a deal with him. I showed him what I was working on, and we're bartering services. He wants some showroom tables, and I agreed to make them. I've already got that extra set of table legs, and I'm going to head back to the Trunk and find some more materials. And I was hoping I'd pick up some more demo'd stuff from our jobs, too." I gave him a quick grin, hoping to press my luck and keep using his family's space for my new projects.

"And what if you don't find what you're looking for at the Trunk? You're gonna be up shit creek then, bud. And I ain't got any paddles for you." Ryan shook his head. "And next, you're gonna ask to keep using the warehouse, right? It's a good thing my parents like you. I'll make sure it's okay, but consider it done. You can keep using the space."

"Thanks, Ryan. I appreciate it. And I'll find something to make for your parents...a kind of thank-you thing. I mean, I never thought about it, but I'm actually pretty good at this. Taking something that's been thrown out and finding a new life for it...combining it with something you'd never really think of...it's pretty satisfying."

The only thing more satisfying was time spent with Cora.

THE PHONE RANG THREE times before she picked up. "Hello?"

Her quiet voice through the line sent a little thrill through me. I could tell she was at work and shouldn't have picked up...but she did. For me. As if I mattered enough to bend the rules for. God knew I'd bend any rule for her, even though I'd never been much for rules.

"Hey. Sorry to bother you at work. But I was hoping you'd stop by Jake's tonight. I wanted to see you." That was not what I expected to say. Not what I planned to say. It was the truth, but I didn't think I was going to blurt it out like that.

The immediate response was silence.

A breath whooshed over the line. "Yeah. I can do that. I'd like to do that."

I couldn't hold in my grin or my little-kid excitement. "Awesome. I'll be waiting."

"'Kay. See you soon, Dixon." She paused, and then said, "I'm looking forward to seeing you, too."

After I pressed the button to end the call, I turned around and came face-to-face with Jake. With a shit-eating grin on his face and his hands clasped in front of him like a schoolgirl.

"Oh, Cora, I can't wait to see you!" he singsonged, ducking out of my reach when I moved to push him away. He burst into laughter. "Now maybe you'll stop being a grouch. Seems I remember you were a happy dude for a day or two after the last time you two were together, and then you got all cranky by the end of the week. You must need a dose of Cora every other day or something."

"Yeah, yeah. Keep it up. Just remember, turnabout is fair play. I seem to recall you acting like an idiot last week whenever Shayla was around." I looked around for the redhead. "Maybe you need a little TLC so you're not so cranky, too."

"I don't know what you're talking about." Jake stepped back. "Anyway, we're talking about you, not me. You deserve a little happiness, and I'm glad you're trying to find it. What are you and Cora going to do tonight?"

"Not much. At least, I don't have any plans. I just want to see her. Hang out. I was going to ask her to go with me to the Trunk again next weekend. I've got some projects I'm working on, and I need some more reclaimed material."

"Well, I'm sure she'll be happy to spend time with you, but geez, make an effort, man. 'Hang out' is the best you can do? Maybe you should consider a real date...you know, picking her up, flowers, a nice restaurant..."

"What? Your place isn't nice enough?" I laughed. "Cora isn't fancy. She doesn't care about restaurants where there's a waiter for each course or a wine snob who tells you what to drink with your meal."

"You sure?" Jake gave me a skeptical look. "She kinda is from money, you know. Maybe a beer here is fine once in a while, but maybe she likes her high-end life, too."

"I'll think about it. But a beer here tonight is fine. We're still getting to know each other." Jake had a point. Maybe a guy who had itchy feet like mine, with no bankroll behind him, had no right to get involved with someone from her world. I snorted. If I had money, I'd be called eccentric for having lived in so many places, always wandering around the country. But without money? Just another broke-ass working-class guy.

My mind wandered back to how well we were getting to know each other...in the personal, physical sense. And that trumped any thoughts of her bank balance compared to mine. Now I could only count the minutes until she walked through the door.

Until then, I scrolled through my phone and checked out some sites I'd found earlier in the week. I was coming up with new ideas for projects every day: tables, mantels, bookshelves, cabinets. Everywhere I looked, I found something I could re-use, re-purpose, and create a whole new, cool item. I lacked space to store any real supply of materials, though...not to mention money. But little things, not quite as big as my secret project for Cora, might be achievable. I'd found a local sawmill that had odds and ends pieces. If I had some slabs of tree trunks, they'd be perfect for creating unique wall clocks. I could have assorted sizes and tree species, ready to be hung on someone's wall. Hell, I'd even seen projects that used scrap wood pieces, like plant stands or shadow boxes.

I was engrossed in looking at specs on a project when the scent of spring floated near. My heart sped up, and I looked up into gorgeous green eyes.

"Hey, Dixon. What's got you so intrigued? I almost thought you wouldn't notice me." Cora dropped her purse on the bar and leaned over to give me a kiss on the cheek.

"Oh, I'm pretty sure I'd notice you, no matter what's on the screen." I smiled. I liked that she'd kissed me hello, but I wanted to taste her lips, feel her in my arms. A little peck on the cheek was a tease. I stood from my chair and put my arms around her. That electric charge zinged, and I pulled her closer. My soul seemed to settle and when our lips met, the sweetness that was all Cora flowed over me.

"That's a nice hello." Cora pulled back and beamed. "And just what I needed. That, and maybe some dinner. Or dessert." She gave me a wink and sat.

If I hadn't been distracted by thoughts of Cora earlier, I sure as hell was now. But that growing urge had to wait—at least a little while. Jake's words about taking Cora somewhere nicer than his bar had sunk in. Where could I take her on my limited budget that would still be somewhere amazing? I couldn't do a champagne-and-caviar kind of place, but there might be an option for some dazzling views.

"Well, what do you think about a change in venue? Jake can pack us up some dinner and we'll take it on the road." There was still some daylight left, and it wasn't too cold. The perfect place for a dinner and alone time with Cora had popped into my head. It'd been forever since I'd been there, but I couldn't think of a better place to do a little stargazing later on.

"Am I dressed okay for this adventure?" Cora glanced at her pinstripe skirt and pumps.

I couldn't help but admire the view as I looked her over. "Well, it's definitely not a dressy place. But I think we can make it work." I'd need to grab a blanket or two from my room upstairs, but the bed of my truck would be the perfect place for this impromptu picnic dinner. No wet or cold ground, and no hiking out on a trail. There was a turnout on the country road that looked out over the valley.

"Then let's do it." Cora flagged down Jake behind the bar. "Looks like your brother here is taking me on an adventure tonight. Can we get an order to go, and I'll have a water while we're waiting for everything to be ready."

Jake's eyebrows rose. "Adventure, huh? Wonder where he got that idea." Jake's grin grew with every word. "Yeah. Give me about ten minutes and I'll have the to-go boxes ready for you." He slid a glass out to her and filled it from the bar spritzer with water before he turned to me. "How 'bout you? Something to drink?"

"Nah. I'm good. Listen, Cora, why don't you stay here for a few minutes while I head up and get some supplies? Once I get everything in the truck and the food's ready, we'll head out." I pushed the barstool back and stood. I leaned over and was surrounded by her spring scent once again. "Be right back." After a quick kiss, I headed up to my apartment.

ONCE WE GOT SETTLED in the truck, I headed out of the parking lot. I was more than ready to have some time with Cora, with no distractions. It sounded like a pure slice of heaven to me, something I'd never expected I'd get.

"So, really, what was so engrossing on your phone that I almost snuck up on you?"

Cora's inquisitive tone pulled my attention from the road for a moment. She was looking right at me, green eyes focused on me, while she waited for my answer.

"Well, actually, I've been getting interested in some woodworking projects. And using some of the stuff I've seen at those remodeling jobs Ryan and I have been working at in some new ways." I tapped my fingers along with the song playing on the radio. I tried to shove my nervousness away. I'd told Jake and Ryan about my projects, but Cora's opinion seemed to matter more to me. Like if she thought it was a stupid idea, then maybe it was.

"Really? Like reclaimed wood and stuff like that? That's what you needed those legs for at the Trunk, huh? What kind of project was that for? A table?"

If she only knew... "Yeah. That was my first project. It's still not quite done...just some finishing details left. But that was a big project, and I had to borrow some space at Ryan's parents' warehouse to get it done. I have some smaller projects in mind, but I still need a place to store materials and tools. But I think I can keep using their space for a while longer. Besides, I don't know what I'd do with them...how to sell them or whatever."

"I could help you with that. Get you set up with a website or social media site, where you could list your items online and get sales or even custom requests." Cora turned toward me. "It'd be easy to do. You might need to learn a bit about the program, but once it's set up, you can add new items pretty quickly. Even take online payments, too."

Her growing enthusiasm was infectious. "Yeah. That'd be great...if you had the time. I mean, I don't know anything about it, but a website is a good idea." And if it meant spending some more time with Cora, all the better.

I slowed the truck as we approached the turnoff for the scenic route that ran parallel to the highway. The two-lane country road had curves and turns that required more focus than the highway. But it was pretty, with the fields of spring flowers blooming and nothing but the scattered old farms along the way.

"Wow. It's been forever since I've been on this road. Are we going to Rock Bridge?" The curiosity in Cora's voice was equaled by her excitement. "We used to go here all the time when I was little. Mom would pack a lunch, and we'd find this little creek and picnic there." Her voice turned wistful. "But we never did get Dad out here. He'd always be too busy at work. So it'd be girl time for the two of us."

She fell silent, and I could practically hear the memories take her back to when she was a kid, spending time with her mom.

"You're lucky you got that time with her. My mom was a single mom. I never knew my dad. She had to work two jobs and there never seemed to be time for picnics. She got to quit working when she met Jonah, but there still wasn't time for us to just hang out. He pretty much monopolized her time." The last words were bitter on my tongue. It'd been much worse than that. He'd been a bastard, and the reason I'd lost my mother.

Cora's hand found mine across the seats. "I'm sorry. That must have been hard. But you got Jake as a brother when they got married, right? That had to help some."

If it hadn't had been for Jake, my life would have been so different. But that was hardly a terrific date-night conversation. Maybe someday I'd tell her. But not tonight.

"Yeah." I drew a breath in and let it out in a whoosh. "Yeah, without Jake, things would have really sucked. He must have really wanted a little brother, because he put up with my shit and looked out for me, even when I was a whiny ten-year-old brat. Most thirteen-year-olds wouldn't have put up with me and my crap." I thought back to the times he'd defend me against his own dad, and how he'd been so considerate and helpful for my mom. "He's a good guy." I looked back over at Cora. "I'd tell you how awesome he is, but he's got a big enough ego. Besides, I'd hate to pale in comparison." I winked.

"Oh, I don't think you'd come out too bad compared to Jake. He's been super nice to me and Wendy, and he runs a great bar. But you've got the title of Cub Scout Hero, saving ladies from broken heels and twisted ankles. I'm not sure he even compares." She waved her hand dismissively before she dropped it back in her lap.

Man, I missed that feel of her hand on mine. I thought about tugging it back, but I really did need two hands on the wheel for this last bit of the ride. Last thing I'd want to do was lose control of the truck. Losing control of a different sort popped into my head, and I pressed on the gas pedal to hurry and get to the lookout spot so I could get closer to Cora without worrying about anything.

I smiled at her. "Good to know. Anyway, we're almost there. Did you and your mom ever use that little pullout area at the top of the hill here as a picnic spot? It's got great views of the valley, and with the sun going down soon, we'll get to see the stars pop out."

"No, it was always down by the river. She liked the bubbling sound, she said. And it was always daytime. So this will be my first time at night."

Her smile lit up her face, and it was all I could do to not get lost in the radiance.

"Well, I hope you have as much fun tonight as you did with your mom."

She reached out and settled her hand on my leg. "I'm sure it'll be even more special."

FIFTEEN

~Cora~

THE VIEW FROM THE LOOKOUT was amazing. But nothing compared to the intense look Dixon gave me as we finished up our dinner, sitting in the bed of the truck on the blankets he'd brought from his place.

"What? Do I have something on my face?" I wiped my lips, checking for stray crumbs.

He reached out and brushed some hair behind my ear. He cradled my head, and his stare had me holding my breath. "No. Just looking at the prettiest woman I've ever seen." He bent toward me.

It might have only been seconds before his lips touched mine, but the timespan was an eternity. A torturous, agonizing eternity. I was desperate—to feel his warmth, to feel cherished, to feel like I'd found a home in his arms.

And when we connected, the heat combusted, and we were a tangle of arms, grabbing and pulling but never getting quite close enough. He left trails of warmth as his hands caressed my back. His mouth was just as hot and possessive, urging me to return the passion with some fire of my own. I ran my hands over the bulge in his jeans and then broke away from his kiss. "Maybe we should find somewhere more comfortable."

"Soon enough. I'm liking the feel of you in my arms too much to want to leave right this second. Come here. Snuggle up and let's enjoy watching the sky change." He moved so his back was against the truck cab and widened his legs to let me in.

I changed position so my back was against his front, and then pulled the blanket over us. The length of his hardness pressed at my back as I wiggled my way into his lap. I dropped my head back, and soon the touch of his lips at my neck had me shivering. "Mmmmm...that...feels..."

"Feels what?" he whispered.

"Good." The words escaped in a whoosh, and I closed my eyes. "Too good for you to stop."

"I had no intention of stopping." The wicked intent came through his chuckled words.

I could get used to this. I'd never had any relationship with a man where I was turned on not just by his touch, but by his words. I wasn't sure I could even say Dixon and I were in a relationship, but every time we were together, I found more and more of myself...and found I couldn't get enough of him. Gone was the spineless girl who let other people determine her future; gone was the woman just dreaming of her own bed-and-breakfast. Instead, there was the confident girl; the woman who paid attention to what she needed. And right now, I needed Dixon.

"Please."

"Please, what, sugar plum?" He ran his tongue up a path on my neck, ending with a quick bite on my earlobe. "What do you want?" His breath tickled me as he exhaled.

I turned my head to look at him, and I flushed under his intense gaze. I wanted more—more of Dixon. And not just in my bed, but in my head. In my heart. "I'd like to show you my place. I've loved our little picnic, but I think it's about time to find a softer bed than your truck bed."

"I think I can handle that. You sure about going to your place? Actually, I don't think I even know where that is." He scrunched his face, as if he just realized how much he didn't know about me.

"Well, I never really said. It's unusual, but I live in a hotel. You know the Stetson Suites main hotel downtown? It's the original hotel the chain was built on. Anyway, I have the penthouse there." I bit my lip, waiting for the inevitable response. Nobody ever thought it was a normal thing to live in a penthouse—and reactions were either amazement or jealousy.

"A penthouse, huh? I've never been in a penthouse before. What's it like?"

"If you take me home, you'll see for yourself." I laughed to myself and smiled. I couldn't wait to show him my home. I couldn't wait to show him more of me...and see myself the way he did.

"Then let's go." He picked up our joined hands and kissed my knuckles. "I'm dying to see where my little gum drop lays her head at night when I'm not lucky enough to be with her."

ANY WHIFF OF ANXIETY at bringing Dixon to my place was squashed by my excitement. I'd never had any man come home to my hotel penthouse. Mark hardly counted; he'd known me all my life. Those couple of dates were the only reason he'd even shown up at my door. And although he'd seen the entire apartment, including the bedroom, he hadn't been impressed. I guess when you lived in a mansion, it was difficult to be impressed with what was essentially a hotel room. But it was home for me, and now I'd be sharing it with Dixon.

As long as we got through the lobby with minimal interaction, I might be able to avoid whoever it was who reported back to my father. Then again, I was an adult, living my own life. After declaring to my father that my personal life was my own—and his insistence about not hearing about my sex life—he'd only have himself to blame if word got back to him about Dixon spending the night. And that's what I wanted: for him to spend the night. No wham-bam-thank-you-ma'am. No gotta-get-up-early excuses. Although we'd have to pick up my car from Jake's at some point. But that was hardly important right now.

Dixon parked the truck in the lower level of the garage. When he pulled the key out of the ignition, he looked at me. "You still good? I swear, I won't hold it against you if you wanted to change your mind."

"Change my mind? No. No chance of that, Dixon." I unbuckled my seat belt and slid over to him. I put my hands on the sides of his face and pulled him down for a hot kiss. "Unless...have you changed your mind? I know it might be weird to be here—"

"Fuck, no. I'd go wherever I had to just to be with you. I don't care where...here, my place, the truck. Anyplace you are is where I want to be." He rubbed my arms. "I don't know much about much, but I know that much."

I laughed. A bubble of happiness percolated and spilled over. "I think you do know much about much." I slid back over to my side and gathered up my purse. "At least, the much that matters." I winked. "Come on. Let me show you my place."

As we walked toward the elevator, I reached out for his hand. It was right there, clasping mine tight. The bits of lightning prickled up my arm, and I swayed closer to him. His body heat generated a field that I couldn't pull out of...not that I wanted to.

The ride up to the lobby was quick, and I steadied myself. There'd be at least one counter person watching the elevator. I hoped we'd be lucky and there'd be a large group checking in to mask our arrival. But even if there wasn't, I was determined not to care. Not to worry. Because as much as I loved my father, I was done answering to him.

The elevator door opened. As we stepped out, hand in hand, it became clear luck would not be on my side. The hulking figure of Mark stood next to the check-in counter, involved in a conversation with someone I didn't recognize. The woman barely came up to his shoulder, but her attitude made up for any height difference. Her face was turning red, and she pointed her finger at Mark. The clerk behind the counter was flustered and looked as though he wanted to be anywhere but there.

I couldn't let the situation escalate. Even though the last thing I wanted was to bring Dixon anywhere near Mark again, I had to defuse the situation before any customers witnessed whatever was about to go down.

"Hey." I half turned to Dixon. "I'm sorry. I think I need to see what's going on there. You want to hang back? It should only take a second."

He tightened his grip around my hands. "Nah. I'll stick with you. I'm sure it's nothing and we can get back to our night." He kissed my cheek. "I'll do my best to keep my mouth shut, but if he gives you shit..."

"He won't. We're out in the middle of the lobby. I'm sure he'll behave." I smiled at him, even though I wasn't sure I believed the words coming out of my mouth. "And if he doesn't, well...let's not borrow trouble quite yet. Let's go get this over with."

As we approached, the movement must have caught his eye. Mark looked up at us, and his diverted attention didn't go unnoticed by the petite woman.

"This isn't over." The woman had daggers in her eyes when she walked by us, and she looked at me. "Not by a long shot."

I stopped in front of Mark. "What was going on? It looked like that woman was about to let loose and let you have it in the middle of the lobby here." Dixon pulled me closer to him, and I leaned into him—not an embrace, but a steadying presence I was thankful for.

"Cora. Good evening. I apologize if Marcy seemed upset. It's nothing. Now then, who is this? Aren't you the person Cora ran after the other night?" Mark went from cordial to stern disapproval. "Really, Cora?" He looked back at me, a frown on his face. "Slumming a bit, are we?"

Dixon tensed beside me, and I reached for his hand to keep him from lunging forward. Not that I would have minded too much if Dixon were to put Mark in his place, but any action in the lobby of the flagship hotel was bound to reach my father's notice.

"Mark, who I spend time with is not your concern. But yes, this is Dixon. And if you won't treat either of us with respect, then it's clear we don't need to spend any time together...in any capacity. I only stopped to make sure there wasn't an issue with you and that young woman. She looked pissed off, and I don't think a big blowout is a good image for the hotel, whoever it might be who's causing trouble." I turned to leave, my hand still in Dixon's.

As we walked away, Mark couldn't help but get the last word in.

"We'll see about that, Cora. We'll just see." His arrogant laugh echoed at our backs.

THE ELEVATOR RIDE UP to my apartment was just as quiet as the ride to the lobby, but this time my tension wasn't about excitement. Rather, it was borderline anger. And I didn't think I was the only one feeling that way.

When the door opened, I moved to exit but Dixon didn't match my steps. I turned to face him. "You okay?"

Shoulders slumped, he looked at me. "You sure you still want me to come up? I mean, Mark..." He gulped. "He didn't seem too happy about me and you being together. If that's gonna—"

"I don't care about Mark. I don't care about what he thinks." I stepped back toward him and rested my hand on his arm. "I care about you. You are who I choose to be with. You are the one I think about first thing in the morning and last thing at night. And you're the one I want to see next to me when I wake up tomorrow." I brushed my lips over his, and then closed the space between us for a deeper, longer kiss.

"That's something I want, too."

The elevator doors closed, but it didn't move. But he pulled me closer, bringing me tight against his chest. I put my arms over his shoulders and molded my body into his. His hard bulge met my soft curves, and I couldn't help the moan that escaped my lips at the contact.

I whispered in his ear, "So, are you going to worry about him all night, or are you ready to see a penthouse bedroom?" I teased. At his sharp intake of breath, I stepped back, hit the button to open the door, and drew him with me across the threshold of the elevator and toward my door. After a quick search for my key, I opened the door and let him in. "Or do you want the full tour first?" I gestured at the space beyond the doorway.

He looked over my shoulder at the floor-to-ceiling window and the skyline beyond. The lights of the city illuminated the vista, obscuring the stars we had started to see out on our picnic. To one side was a kitchenette with a breakfast bar and three stools. On the other was the couch, a loveseat, a high-def television mounted on the wall, and an unorganized desk full of papers. Beyond that was the short hallway to the bedroom and bathroom. It had all the clean lines of a hotel penthouse suite, but that was just the main living area. The bedroom was my personal space, where those royal-purple walls welcomed me home every night and I kept the photos of my childhood displayed.

"I think I've seen enough of your living space. But I need to inspect your sleeping area..." His eyebrows rose suggestively, and his tone was once again that of the self-assured and sexy Dixon. "You know, to see if it meets all my fantasies about penthouses..."

He crushed his lips to mine, and all rational thought disappeared. I couldn't get close enough with all these clothes on—his and mine. I fumbled for his T-shirt hem, trying to pull it over his head while somehow not breaking our kiss. The fraction of a second our lips were apart was just enough time to complete that task, and for him to fuss with his belt. But before much more could be removed, we were pressed together again, stumbling back toward the promised land of my bedroom.

Within moments, the back of my legs hit the edge of my bed. Our tangled tongues paused, and I caught my breath. My hands roamed over his muscled chest, working their way to the zipper of his jeans.

He stopped my hands from going much further than popping the top button. "Wait. I haven't had a chance to return the favor." His fingers found their way to my blouse, releasing each button and gently pushing the fabric to the side. At the sight of the lacy black bra, he inhaled. He bent his head and kissed the tops of my breasts, cupping each with his skilled hands.

My head fell back, and my nipples hardened under his touch. When he gently bit through the material, I let out a gasp.

"Hmmm...as sweet as ever, Cora." Dixon finished the job of taking off my blouse, and the clasp of my bra was undone. As he slid the straps down, he stared, his gaze piercing me. "How did I ever get so lucky?" He captured my lips again, stealing any answer I might have had for him.

Because it was me who was lucky, not him. Meeting him that night at Jake's had jumpstarted something that had lain dormant. Something inside me that I never believed I had. He was the spark that made my world light up, filling my heart and igniting my passions. All my passions...and right now, that meant making him the center of my attention.

"Speaking of returning the favor..." I dropped onto the bed and reached for that zipper once again. Each clack of the zipper teeth opening seemed to echo in the silent room. I looked up at his face, my smile growing at the sight of him: head leaned back, eyes closed. His chest rose and fell quicker than normal, and I slid a hand up to feel the coarse hair of his happy trail. Using both my hands now, I slid them between his warm skin and the briefs under his jeans. I tugged the offending clothing down, getting about halfway down his legs before I realized my mistake. He still had his sneakers on.

"Damn." I stopped and laughed softly.

"What?" Dixon snapped his head back up, and he looked down. "Oh. Well, that's easy enough to fix." He stepped back, toed off his shoes, and wiggled the rest of the way out of his pants. He moved forward, and he cupped my cheek. "Now then, as much as I'm liking this, it seems a bit one-sided." He pulled me up to standing and reached for my waistband. After his nimble fingers worked their magic, my pants puddled at my feet.

I slipped out of my low heels and stepped out of the pile of fabric on the floor. Once freed of the material, I sat on the edge of the bed and scooted back toward the headboard. I looked him over from head to foot, and back, and smiled. A naked Dixon was a sight I don't think I could ever tire of.

"You keep looking at me like that, and I can't be held responsible for your lack of sleep tonight." He dropped onto the bed next to me, lying on his side, and he ran his fingers up and down my stomach.

The light touch had me shivering in anticipation. "Sleep is overrated." I cupped his cheek, and my thumb stroked along his jawline. "Kiss me, Dixon."

His eyes held mine as he inched his way down to my waiting lips. His breath fanned over my face with his next words. "Damn, Cora. There's nothing hotter than you wanting me." His mouth covered mine, and the heat turned up.

Thank God I was naked, because my clothes would have burst into flames from the fire we'd started.

He reached for the nightstand, grabbed a condom, and tore the wrapper off. After rolling it down his hard length, he positioned himself at my entrance.

The blue of his eyes deepened to cobalt. Desire flared there, and I wet my lips. I lifted my hips, ready for the heat those eyes promised me. With each inch his cock traveled inside me, I surrendered to my own need.

All I wanted—all I could do—was hang on to him tighter, kiss him harder, and throw myself into the volcano that exploded as we came together as one.

ONE PERK OF HOTEL LIVING was the room service. But I didn't want anyone to intrude on the private world Dixon and I were in. So I hoped I had something in my fridge and cabinets to nibble on.

"Hey. Where you going?" The mumbled words came from under the pillow. A hand clasped over my arm as I made to get out of the bed.

"Just a little sustenance. A girl might need her salad, but after all that activity, it's time for a re-fuel." I dipped down and pushed the pillow off his face to place a kiss on his cheek. "Be right back. You need a water?"

By the time I got to the doorway, Dixon was propped up on one arm, a little blurry-eyed but a smile on his face. "Sure. But be quick. I might get lost and lonely in this big bed all by myself."

I laughed on my way to the kitchenette. I would hurry...not because he'd get lost and lonely, but because I didn't want to be apart from him. I found a couple of bottles of water in the fridge, and some cheese. I had some grapes, too, and then scrambled to find some crackers. I put the little snack plate on a tray, with enough room for the bottled waters.

When I got to the bedroom, I paused, taking in the sight before me. Like the first morning I'd seen him sleeping on the couch, the six-pack abs had my mouth watering. Now from firsthand knowledge, not just dreaming. My cheeks heated at the thought of feeling that rock-hard body at my fingertips, and I moved quicker, getting back to where I wanted to be.

"Hey, sugar bear. What did you find on your foraging expedition?" He took the water bottle, twisted the top off, and took a large gulp. "Man, that hits the spot. Although..." His grin grew. "I could think of another spot or two I'd like to hit." He lifted the tray from my hands and put it on the floor on his side of the bed. Then he reached for my hands and pulled me on top of him.

I was captured in his gaze. The blue shifted from a brighter shade to something darker, and his teasing morphed into a scorching heat. "Oh yeah?" My breath puffed between us. "Does X mark the spot?" I danced my fingers on that old scar he glossed over our first night. "Dixon, what happened here? More Cub Scout misadventures?"

I could feel him withdraw even before his hands left my body.

SIXTEEN

~Dixon~

I DROPPED MY HANDS to my side, no longer holding onto Cora's tempting body. But Cora still traced that damn scar. The tingling touch was just as electrifying as it always was, but it left me uncomfortable.

And not for some unknown reason. I knew damn well why I was pulling back. Not just physically but from that emotional connection, that passionate response to being with Cora. It was always lurking there, ready to jump out and fuck up my life. As if it hadn't done a good enough job when I was a kid.

"Dixon?" Cora whispered.

Her soft tone was full of questions. Questions I'd spent my life avoiding.

"Dixon...you don't have to tell me. But, you know, I can tell it's eating you up. I know. I had the same look in my eye after my mother...was killed. I mean, she was in a coma for a long time after the assault. There wasn't anything we could do. The nurses couldn't do anything. The doctors couldn't do anything. Everyone was helpless. And when all you have is helpless, sometimes it turns into anger. Or fear." She moved herself off me and sat on the edge of the bed.

Cora looked down for a moment, and then her eyes focused on me again. "For about a month after my mother was attacked, I couldn't sleep by myself. I was afraid all the time, afraid if I was alone that someone would break in and hurt me. I stayed with Wendy, and the only reason I got through that was because she'd sit with me every night, until two or three in the morning, when I couldn't fight the sleeping pills anymore and I'd finally sleep. She'd let me talk—gibberish, mostly, I think—and cry and scream and yell until I couldn't anymore."

She held my hand, and the heat of her touch warmed me, took some of the chill off my heart. When she stroked my hand with her thumb, the little pinpricks of electricity popped.

"I'm glad she was there to help you. I can't imag—" I took a deep breath. "Actually, I don't have to imagine what you went through. I know it, too. My mother didn't just get sick and die. No. It was much, much worse than that."

Cora inched closer to me, and the silky skin of her leg brushed mine. The gesture spoke of support, care...things I didn't have any idea how to react to.

"Do you want to tell me?"

I only had one answer to her question: yes. I wanted to tell her. But if I did, it would change everything. I'd be opening myself up, and that was something I never did. Very few got close—Ryan, for example. The biggest exception was Jake, and that was because he was with me and knew it all. Hell, it was worse for him. In the grand scheme of things, I got off easy in comparison.

"Do you really want to know? It's not...a happy fairy tale. It's not fun. It's mean, and cruel, and most important, it's in the past. It doesn't have anything to do with you and me." I closed my eyes, not ready to see compassion—or worse, pity—in her beautiful green eyes.

"I want to know all about you, Dixon." Cora touched my cheek, and her breath warmed my face when she leaned over. "Not just the good bits, but the terrible, dark, bad, no good stuff that you've been through, too. All of it made you who you are right now, and that's a pretty incredible guy."

She brushed her lips against mine, and that spark made my heart leap in response. Before I knew it, my hands were tangled in her silky hair, pulling her closer to me as I claimed her mouth. Damn, this woman knew how to make me feel secure and strong at the same time.

"I think you're pretty incredible too, Cora. And if you want to hear the terrible parts..."

She nodded.

"Okay." I sat up in the bed, rearranged some pillows, and pulled back the blankets to invite her in. "Snuggle up, buttercup. It's going to be a long, sad tale."

Cora snuggled up to my chest, hands on my abs and her torso tucked under my arm. Her fingers roamed over my chest in a slow-moving motion that settled my nerves.

"So, you already know that my mom raised me herself until I was about ten. That's when she met Jonah, Jake's dad. I never knew my real dad, and Mom never said much about him. But she fell in love with Jonah and married him a few years after they started dating. While they were dating, everything was fine. Jonah treated me good, and he encouraged Jake to hang out with me...act like a big brother. We had family time with the four of us—camping, bowling, hiking, playing board games.

"After they got married, things started to...change. I was too involved in my own life—I mean, I was a teenager—but sometimes I'd find broken things in the garbage when it was my turn to take it out. Like glasses or picture frames. And my mom started to 'trip' over things...at least, that's what she'd say if someone asked about a bruise or a cut. I never saw Jonah raise a hand to her, but it became clear even to me that something was going on.

"Then, one day, Jake and I came home from school. Mom was on the couch. She'd been crying, we could tell. She told us she had cancer. Mom tried to soften the news, but the doctors said the outlook wasn't good." My wooden words covered my fifteen-year-old self's confusion and pain.

Soft hands clasped around mine, grounding me to the moment.

I cleared my throat. "Well, anyway, after that, Jonah's behavior was more...erratic. Sometimes he'd be all loving with her, but I saw him hit her when he'd be frustrated over something. Small things, like helping her dress. She still tried to hide it, but her body was getting weaker and weaker. She didn't have the strength to lie like she used to." I stopped, not sure I wanted to go further. There was still more, but I wasn't sure how to say the words.

"I'm so sorry, Dixon. I remember you said things changed after you and your mom moved in with Jonah and Jake. No kid should see their parent hurt like that, but when she's suffering from cancer..." Cora placed a soft kiss on my arm and snuggled back in. "I can't imagine."

"Well, it wasn't long before his frustrations spilled out to Jake and me. Before Jonah met my mom, he'd been 'frustrated' with Jake, too. He never told me those first years, but after Mom's diagnosis and Jonah's temper flaring up, Jake promised he'd keep his father away from me as much as he could. And he did. He'd always step between us whenever Jonah raised his fist at me. Got a few nasty punches and black eyes from his own dad." I sucked in a deep breath, still amazed at how Jake had stood up for me, how he'd put himself between his own father and a kid he was no real brother with. God knew what would have happened if he wasn't there. The few times Jonah cornered me by myself were difficult to think about.

The times Jake took the pain were sometimes harder to deal with. Because I felt like a coward for hiding behind him. He was older than me, but it was his own father hurting him. But he kept on standing there in front of his father, protecting me...and my mother, when he could.

"After my mother died...I was scared...I didn't know whether Jonah was going to kick me out or send me off to foster care, or what. And even if I stayed there, I was sure he was gonna make every day miserable. The only person who cared about me was Jake. But the first year or so after her death was...tolerable. His frustrations must have settled down when she was gone, even if I was a reminder of her.

"But something happened. I have no real idea what. He started drinking...Jake said he'd been a drinker before he met my mom...and the beatings started up again. Jake was getting ready to leave the house. He was almost twenty and was ready to leave his father behind. But he didn't want to leave me alone with him. So he stuck it out, just to keep an eye out for me.

"One night, Jonah started yelling at me about my mother. Said she betrayed him. Had treated him like a fool. He came at me with a knife." I pointed at my left shoulder. "I'm not sure what he was aiming at, but that's where he got me. I probably needed stitches, but I didn't want to go to the hospital. Didn't want people asking questions. Jake bandaged me up as best he could when he got home and saw it. Jake had enough at that point. He packed up his stuff, packed up my stuff. Then he told me we were getting out of there for good."

Cora looked up at me. "Sounds like Jake came to his senses and got you two out of there. Where did you end up going?"

"Not far, really. We spend that first night in some crappy no-name motel, but the next day, Jake was out looking for apartments. I was still in school, so he didn't want to leave town...just get me out of that house and away from his dad. He figured he was already working and could support both of us with a small one-bedroom apartment. He'd been saving up, so that was good. I got to stay in school, and he kept his job, and we both stayed as far from Jonah as we could. He never seemed to care that we were gone, although once in a while he'd call Jake when he was drunk and threaten to beat him up for something or other. His drunken ramblings never made much sense to me."

If I stopped here, it'd be enough for Cora to go through in her mind. After all, the death of a mother and having an abusive stepdad was bad enough. Who needed to pile more on the fire? Apparently, I did. In for a penny, in for a pound, right? Getting all this putrid crap out of my system was freeing, clearing out the nooks and crannies in my busted-up soul. All that new space was filling up with the feeling of Cora in my arms, the scent of her flooding over and calming my soul.

"That...that wasn't the worst thing."

Cora stopped her caresses. "Not the worst thing? There's more? Oh, Dixon." Her breath whooshed over my chest.

"Yeah, there's more. I had to go back to Jonah's for some paperwork I needed to apply for a job. I needed my Social Security card, and it was with some things of my mother's. When we first left, it wasn't high on the priority list. But I eventually needed it, and I knew she'd kept it in her nightstand. So I went back there during the day when Jonah'd be working.

"I found it easy enough, right where it was supposed to be. But I also found a journal...my mother's journal. I probably shouldn't have, but I read it. I wanted to see her handwriting...imagine her voice as I read her words. Now...now I almost wish I'd never seen it, because what she wrote, I did hear in my head in her voice." My voice cracked as my heart sped up at the mere memory.

"She wrote about how she was feeling, how the cancer was stealing her away from her boys. She'd loved Jake like her own, always called us 'her boys' when she introduced us to people." I smiled, thinking about how proud she was of both of us. "But there were things she wrote about Jonah that weren't so nice. I found out how much he'd done to her, and for how long. It broke my heart to realize how much she'd protected me from..." I got caught up in the memory of those words, and hot tears threatened to spill. Gravity won, and several tears dripped down my cheek.

I sniffed, trying to keep going without stopping now. This would be the hardest part. The part I never talked about. "Anyway, that wasn't the only thing she put in that journal. She—she talked about how Jonah seemed to change over their marriage, not just with being abusive but...how secretive he'd be about things. He'd hide things in this little spot in the attic. She caught him once up there, looking at some necklace. It wasn't hers, and he told her it wasn't any of her business and not to tell anyone about it. Right after that, she seemed to go downhill real quick, and there weren't many more entries in the journal.

"But it was the last one that freaked me out. She wrote that she'd confronted him about the necklace after she went up there again. Not only was there that one necklace, but several of them. He tried to brush it off, telling her she was making things up and her medicine had her all confused. But she wrote that one necklace matched one that a friend of hers had...a friend who had gone missing. She was afraid that Jonah had done something to her.

"Once I read that, I hauled ass out of there. I took my Social Security card, and the journal, and hightailed it back to Jake's. By the time he got home from work, I'd worked myself into a frenzy. And once he saw the journal, Jake was right there with me. There'd been a string of missing women—not just one of my mom's friends, but like half a dozen women the police couldn't account for. Both me and Jake were convinced Jonah had something to do with it, and the journal was, well, not proof...but a damn good start.

"We took it down to the police, and, well, it turned out my mother had been right. Jake and I were right. Jonah was brought in for questioning, and ended up confessing to kidnapping and killing those women. He'd stashed his little 'mementos' in a box in the attic, and a few days after my mom found him with them..." I took what felt like my last breath. "He confessed that he killed her, too. It wasn't enough that she was already dying...he snuffed out any chance she had to pass peacefully, with me and Jake by her side."

AFTER TELLING CORA about my childhood and the abuse we'd all suffered under Jonah, I should have felt like hell. Reliving that shit never felt good. Even with a couple of Jack and Cokes in hand. But all I had was lightness. Lightness of soul. Lightness of heart.

Or maybe it was more that by releasing all that pent-up sorrow and fear, I had room for something better. Something like Cora.

"I...I don't know what to say." Cora bit her lip, staring deep into my face. "To say that what you went through was awful just seems so...inadequate. So small in comparison to what it really must have been like for you." She lifted her hand to rest on my jaw. "But I know your mother must have been proud that you and Jake did the right thing by turning that journal over to the police. It would have been so much worse if he'd been able to keep on hurting people."

"I guess. But still, sometimes I feel guilty that I turned him in. Or that I didn't find that journal earlier. Maybe there'd be a family or two who wouldn't have had to go through all that pain if he'd been in jail earlier. If I'd thought to take my Social Security card the night we left, I might have taken that journal then, too. Who knows?" I shrugged, but did my best to keep Cora tight against me.

"But you might not have been ready to look at your mother's journal right then, anyway. Maybe you would have put it away and not looked at it for a long time. So when you did read it, you might have saved countless women and their families by going to the police right then." Cora gave me a quick kiss. "There's no reason to beat yourself up on what-ifs. You'll drive yourself up a wall like that." Her fingers intertwined with mine.

That contact, that connection, was like a long-lost memory, fighting its way to be remembered. Fighting to be front and center. It'd been the thing I'd lost when my mother died, when she was ripped from my life. But here it was again: different, but the same. Security. Acceptance. Peace.

And this amazing woman in front of me was working a miracle, bringing my heart back to life, along with ideas of a future...one where I could be happy and loved.

THE NEXT MORNING, CORA grabbed her laptop out of the purple carrying case.

"Damn. It looks like you could pack an entire office in that thing." It was professional, but huge.

"Yeah, pretty much." She pulled out a power cord and a mouse. "But I've got a larger laptop, with a big screen, so I need this size bag." She finished getting set up and powered up the computer. "So, did you have any ideas on what you want to showcase to sell? Did you think of a business name? I assume you have a bank account that we can link up to your online store, right? Do you have any social media sites already where you can start posting?" Cora looked at me.

Each question hit me like a hammer. I hadn't thought of any of that. Shit. Maybe this was going to be more difficult than I thought. I must have had the look of the Roadrunner after he'd just figured out he'd run out of road and was about to plummet off the cliff.

Cora reached out, caressing my hand. "Nobody ever really thinks about that at first. Don't freak out." She patted my hand. "So let's concentrate on one thing at a time. Do you have any projects we can take pictures of and put up online?"

Immediately, I thought of the vanity table. It was complete; I just hadn't found the right time to show it to Cora, much less figure out how to give it to her. "Well...yes, I do have one completed project. It's down at the warehouse...Ryan's parents are letting me use the space there. I guess we could go down and take some pictures. Would that work?" I shifted in my chair and pulled at my shirt collar.

"That would be great. Let's work through some more details, and then we can head out."

Cora's mega-watt smile settled my nerves.

"Next. Let's see...how about social media? You post anywhere?"

I shrugged. "Not a big social guy. I've got a few accounts."

She typed a note on her computer. "Okay. You'll have to get in the habit of posting regularly, but you should use whatever site you like best. You should focus on photos and descriptions of your projects, maybe some 'works in progress' posts...that kind of thing." She paused. "Do you think you want to get all official with a company name, or do you just want to sell under your personal profiles?"

I definitely hadn't come up with a company name. "Just under my name, I guess. I'm not great with words or coming up with clever stuff like that, so let's skip that." I swallowed hard. "Not off to a great start, huh?"

"Nonsense. This is your business, so you get to make your own rules, do what you want. Nobody gets to dictate what works for you. Plenty of small businesses start off pretty informally and do just fine." Cora smiled reassuringly.

"Let's go take some shots of that project, and then we can get it up online and start putting your name out there." Cora shut down her computer and closed it. "And once we start doing that, like I said, you need to keep interest up by posting often. Make sure you take tons of photos while you are working so you'll have in-progress shots to share with your fans." She stood and pulled me up with her. "And yes, I am sure you'll have fans." She kissed me, lingering as the kiss heated. "You've already got one in me."

I PULLED UP TO THE warehouse. My palms had started to sweat on the drive over. As I put the truck in park, I took a deep breath through my nose. "So, this first project...well, I had a specific idea in mind. I started thinking about it a day or so after we first met at Jake's."

Cora smiled. "Really? I mean, I figured that our trip to the Trunk and you picking up those metal legs was part of a plan, but I didn't realize you'd just thought of it that recently." She tilted her head to the side, appraising me. "Wait...do you mean that I was part of what put this idea in your head?" She smiled even wider at the thought.

"Well, yeah. In fact, it's not just inspired by you...it's for you." I looked her straight in the eyes, looking for her reaction.

She leaned over and kissed me, hard. Our tongues met and their dance had me almost forgetting about getting out of the truck. I'd be a happy camper to stay there, wrapped in Cora's web, for as long as she'd let me.

She pulled back. "Well, I can't wait to see it." Cora got out of the truck and was by the warehouse door practically before I had my hand on the door handle.

Her enthusiasm swiped away any uncertainty that lurked in the back of my mind. "All right then, let me show it to you," I said as I climbed out of my seat and found the keys for the warehouse door.

"Just remember—this is my first project. I've got a few more ideas percolating, especially after our trip to the Trunk. I've got that other set of legs that I need to use...just need to find the right table top—"

"Oooh...a table. That means I need a chair for it, right?" She laughed at my expression. "I probably have a chair already, don't worry."

"Actually, I've got plans for a chair, too. So don't go thinking I was going to give you an incomplete present." I reached for her hand as we walked toward the back of the warehouse, where I had the vanity table set up, just waiting for the right moment to show it to Cora.

Cora slowed her stride. "Oh my. Dixon..." She turned to me. "It's beautiful! I love it." She leaned in to give me a kiss. "The black is so deep...and there's green sparkles in there, too..." She bent over the table, checking out the detail work. "And those legs...it looks so awesome all together." She turned back to me. "You really have a talent here, Dixon. Everyone is going to be so jealous when I show them the picture of this vanity...I hope you are ready to make some more projects."

I watched Cora's expressions, and her tone matched her excitement. I put a finger in my belt loop and rocked back on my heels. "I'm glad you like it. I was a little worried that maybe it wouldn't be your style, or that maybe you just wouldn't like it. And like I said, I've got a line on a chair that I think will work with it." I pulled my phone out of my back pocket and scrolled to find the email with the picture of the chair from Jefferson Furniture. "What do you think?"

She came closer, and her clean spring scent filled my head. Damn, I just could not get enough of that aroma.

"That looks perfect. I see how it fits in just right with the lines of the table legs—a complementary contrast." She held onto my arm, leaning in for another kiss.

One I was ready for. Cora had my body revving with excitement and anticipation. It wasn't only the way she responded to my touch; it was the way she lit up when we talked, the way she wanted me to succeed...and believed I could.

My chest puffed with pride...and hope. The act of creating something new from discarded, what some would consider worthless, scraps—and the way Cora appreciated it—filled me with the courage to do the same in my life. I'd take the pieces of my past, and forge them into a new life...one where I was worth something...worth Cora's love.

SEVENTEEN

~Cora~

"SO, DO YOU WANT TO go on an adventure today?" I looked at Dixon at the breakfast bar, after he'd spent the night at my place again. His hair was mussed but his smile filled me with joy.

"Well, what kind of adventure? Will I need to be prepared to save you from broken heels and twisted ankles? Or are we going really wild and doing some bungee-jumping?" He winked and pulled me in closer.

The warmth of his palms seeped through my T-shirt, and I liked the way it felt to be in his arms once more. Memories of last night had me heating up, and a blush must have landed on my face.

"Hmm...maybe you're talking a sexy-time adventure, by the way your face is turning a pretty shade of red, my little cinnamon fireball." He leaned over and gave me what might have been a quick kiss...until I turned up the heat and gave his bottom lip a little suck.

I pulled back and looked at him. "Well, I'm not ruling out some sexy-time adventures later, but right now I was talking about a country drive. There's something I want to show you." I dropped my hands and made to turn around, but Dixon kept a tight hold on me.

"A little show-and-tell? A little bit of 'show me yours and I'll show you mine'? Didn't we do some of that last night?"

His wide grin and teasing tone made me laugh.

I rubbed his arms. "Yeah, I'll show you mine. And by 'mine,' I mean my plan for the future."

Immediately, Dixon's eyes narrowed. Normally, I'd love to have my hands all over his hard muscles, but the tension in his face wasn't what I had expected.

"Hey, it's not a big deal. I just thought you'd like to take a ride and see someplace special to me. I'm not inviting you to a bridal boutique or somewhere to taste-test menus." I slapped him playfully on the arm. "Not yet, anyway." Then I burst into laughter. "Seriously, Dixon. Not a proposal or some kind of trap. Just wanted to show you what I'm planning for next year. It's a nice ride out to the cottage."

He drew in a breath and let it out. "Yeah. Sure. I could go for a nice ride. And maybe some breakfast...no taste-testing menus needed." He grabbed his keys from his pockets. "You want to take the truck? Or do you want to drive?"

I got my purse. "Nah, let's take the truck. More of a country ride feel in that instead of my little Nissan. As long as you don't mind me giving you directions and telling you where to go?" I turned and headed for the door.

Dixon's quick steps had him right behind me. Right as we got to the door, he leaned over and rumbled in my ear, "I appreciate a woman telling me where to go...as long as she's willing to let me enjoy the ride there."

His words ended with a love bite at the junction of my shoulder and neck. With just a little suction, my knees wobbled, and I leaned back into his strong frame. "Hmmm..."

"Let's hit the road." With a quick kiss to my earlobe, he reached around me and opened the door. "After you, milady. Adventure awaits."

Now I wasn't sure whether I wanted to show Dixon the cottage or have some sexy-time adventures instead. But at the gentle push at my lower back, the decision was out of my hands and I stepped forward, ready to share my plans for my future with this man who was quickly finding his way into the depths of my heart.

I HAD DIXON DRIVE THE longer, more scenic route. We'd stopped at another small diner for breakfast on the way. I wasn't in any hurry to have our day be over. We kept teasing each other over our favorite songs—and my off-key singing—and I pointed out some landmarks as we made our way to my grandmother's cottage in Atwater Falls. The small town had the typical New England main street, with the locals offering services like high-end skin and beauty care, to hipster coffee joints, to a no-nonsense hardware store—complete with the owner's dog at the door to greet every customer.

But down one two-lane road, about five miles from the center of town, was the heart of my dreams and goals. Grandmother Stetson had used this as a summer home, so it'd always been "the cottage" to me. But it was a sprawling farm mansion. The driveway led to a porte cochere—the fancy name my grandmother used to describe the covered area that connected to the house and kept visitors out of the elements—but continued beyond the front of the house to the side, where there was direct access to the kitchen. But the welcoming double door was made of stained glass that had never failed to fascinate me as a child.

When you entered, there was a staircase that split to either side, with wide stairs made of hickory. The chandelier wasn't one of those fussy multi-light monsters, but one of simple elegance. The design of the reflected light always captured my attention more than the actual fixture. Multiple rooms had fireplaces in them; others had the old-fashioned radiators for heat. The four bathrooms upstairs each had porcelain clawfoot tubs and princess sinks. Several rooms also had built-in cabinets and drawers. There were huge rooms downstairs that would connect and form a ballroom. There was a front porch, a side porch, and a sunroom.

But my absolute favorite place as a young girl was the attic. Grandmother had it converted to a bedroom for me, and every time I visited, I had my own castle in the cottage up there. The center brick fireplace below meant the room had a brick chimney right in the middle of the room. Wide windows looked over the expansive backyard. The row of narrow stained-glass windows let me see the activity in the front. Wide-beam floors were covered in plush Oriental carpets, and there was even a bookcase the full length of one wall.

Every summer, I got to spend two weeks with Grandmother at the cottage. It was two weeks of pure heaven, as far as I was concerned. Between being able to be with my grandmother and having the run of the country estate, there was no better way to spend a summer vacation.

The barn out back was large enough to hold a dozen horses, but because Grandmother didn't spend all her time at the cottage, the building was used more for storage and projects. She had her husband's Model T in there—something he'd tinkered with for fun. And the maintenance crew had their supplies and tools stored in there, too.

Because of that connection with my grandmother and our time together, she'd always told me that someday the cottage would be mine. As much as I didn't want to imagine her death, the thought of owning such a wonderful place thrilled me. I'd dream about being married and having a dozen children, and raising them all in the house where I felt safe and loved.

I outgrew the dream of a dozen babies—thank goodness!—and finding Mr. Right was a challenge, but my love of the cottage never wavered. And instead of sharing it with a large family, I thought about sharing it with people who needed to feel that same safety and care it had provided to me. With a family of hoteliers behind me, a bed-and-breakfast seemed like a natural choice. After my Cornell courses, I had an even greater interest in pursuing it, although I'd kept that to myself while I got some practical experience at my family's hotel. Only Wendy knew about my goals.

My Grandmother Stetson had died several years earlier, before my mother. Both my parents had assured me Grandmother's will had indeed specified that I was to be given the deed to the cottage—as well as a substantial dollar figure—when I turned twenty-six. Until then, they were the trustees of the property and account. I had no idea why Grandmother thought twenty-six was such a magical number, but that was her decision. And now I was less than a year away from that milestone.

Less than a year away from taking charge of my life—including leaving the family business...and Mark...behind.

THE CHATTER DIED AS Dixon pulled up the driveway toward the porte cochere. He stopped under the overhang and put the truck in park. Then, he turned and looked at me. "Wow. 'Cottage'? You mean 'mansion,' right? This place is as big as the governor's mansion!" His wide eyes held a look of disbelief.

It was all I could do to not laugh at his reaction. "Are you sure? When's the last time he invited you over for a beer?" I nudged his arm. "But, yeah, this is the cottage. I know it's not really an accurate description, but that's what Grandmother Stetson called it, so that's what I call it." I unbuckled my seat belt. "Come on. Do you want to see the house or the land first?"

Dixon followed suit and met me at my side of the truck. "I dunno. How much land are we talking? And do we need some kind of ATV or a horse to see it all? Maybe we should start with the house." He grabbed my hand and squeezed. "After you." He swept his other hand out to the side.

I found my keys at the bottom of my bag and opened the front door. An unwelcome waft of stale air billowed out. "Umm...let's leave the door open and let it air out. Or find some windows to open. It's been a few months since I've been here last. I try to come every other month to make sure the property maintenance company is taking care of the upkeep and there aren't any unaddressed issues." I moved into the foyer and paused at the staircase. "Well, here's the grand entrance. I'm thinking there's enough room between these two staircases to set up a check-in desk."

"A check-in desk? Wait, aren't you planning to live here? Why would you need a check-in desk?" His face scrunched up, and he dropped my hand as he looked around.

"Did I not mention that detail? Yes, I plan to live here...but I want to open up a bed-and-breakfast. I'll have a living space up in the attic—it's bigger than it sounds—and refurbish the space for three or four guestrooms. The space downstairs will be the common areas, like the dining room and a special sitting room. The kitchen needs some updating, but it's already large and has plenty of pantry space. I'm hoping to fix up the barn out back, and have horses or ponies for guests to ride the property. A garden for people to enjoy. There's a fountain out back already, but as you can guess, it hasn't been used in ages." I waved my hands, gesturing toward each area. Words rushed out, overflowing with enthusiasm. "And there are fireplaces in the bedrooms. Or old-fashioned radiators. And each bathroom has a clawfoot tub, perfect for soaking after a day of relaxing.

"I'll decorate for each season—spring, summer, fall, and winter. And have special cocktail hours, too. Live music, if I can find some locals who want to play for a small audience. Who knows, maybe I'll branch out as a wedding venue for small, intimate nuptials." I looked around the space, envisioning guests enjoying themselves.

"That...that sounds like a lot of work." Dixon's tone was cautious. "You seriously want to do that? Have people around, coming in and out at all hours, no privacy, and dealing with food and housekeeping and marketing and promotions?"

I laughed. "Yeah, I think I do. I want this place to feel as special to everyone as it did to me when I was little. I want to share that feeling with everyone. I want to make everyone as happy as I was here. To experience the magic of a summer bonfire, chasing fireflies, breathing the country air. Anything seems possible then, don't you think?"

"I know I'd like to think so." Dixon moved in closer, putting a hand on my arm. "But anything seems possible when I'm with you." He brushed his lips against mine. Lightly at first, and then with more passion.

I leaned into him, savoring the heat and desire in his touch. My senses lit up and all I could feel, all I could taste, all I could recognize was this man with me. There was nothing and no one but the two of us.

"Meow."

At the feel of something brushing against my leg and the plaintive cry, I jumped out of Dixon's embrace.

"What is this? How'd a cat get in here?" Dixon looked at the tabby cat currently weaving between our legs, a slight purr starting up as it did so.

I bent to pick the stray up. "Hello, sweet thing. Who do you belong to?"

The only answer was a headbutt and an increase in purring volume.

Dixon laughed. "If you're not careful, the answer to that question will be you." He petted the cat, rewarded with the creature leaning into the motion.

"Well, I'm sure it's somebody's barn cat, or an outside cat wandering around. We left the front door open...it must have just walked in." I shifted the cat in my arms. "Let's show you both the rest of the place."

Room by room, I walked through the home. I pointed out the inlaid flooring in one room, the clawfoot tub in another. All the while, the cat snuggled in my arms and Dixon was at my side.

"Wow. Those cabinets look amazing." Dixon went to the corner of the bedroom to investigate the workmanship. "Who built these? Do you know?" He turned to me.

"Like I said, my grandfather liked to tinker, and woodworking was one of his hobbies. I wouldn't be surprised if some of the woodwork was his, but I don't know for sure." I joined him at the wall and pulled out a drawer. "But yeah, it's held up well over the years."

The cat was less impressed with the craftsmanship and was more intrigued with the view out the window.

The second story overlooked the vast garden, which, sadly, had seen much better days. But the last time there'd been a maintenance review of the property, the fountain had still worked, and the irrigation was still in working order. All it would take would be some TLC, and the garden would attract the birds and bees once again.

I grabbed Dixon's hand. "Come on. I want to show you the attic."

"Hmmm...your secret lair? Sounds good to me. I'd love to see where little Cora spent her summer nights." He squeezed my hand and grinned. "Who knows what I'll discover about you up there?"

I laughed. "Can't be letting you find out all about me quite yet. But I'm sure we'll have fun learning each other's secrets." I pulled him in for a quick kiss and then spun out of his arms, leading him to the hidden door at the end of the hallway. "But here's the first secret...a secret doorway. You have to know it's even there before you try to open it." The natural design of the woodwork made the shape of the door fade into the overall pattern of the wall. I pushed on the correct square, and the door swung inward. "Come on."

He took a step into the new space. There were about three paces before the steps up to the third floor; his long legs devoured the space, and we headed up the staircase. "This is so cool. I can see why you'd love to spend time here every year. If I had a place to hide away from everybody when I was a kid, I don't think I'd ever leave it."

The wistful smile had a hint of melancholy. Before it could set on his face, I teased him, "But there's no TV up here...so no video games, just books. And you can be sure that my grandmother would never have let me have any boys up here. Although, it is pretty removed from the first floor and she could never hear me blasting the radio and dancing away. It was my own little world up here. Not even the maid—"

"Wait a minute...maid? You had a maid?" Dixon shook his head. "So outta my league." The last words were under his breath, followed by a light chuckle.

"Well, not me...my grandmother. But yes, she had household help. There's no way she could run the hotel business and take care of this property. Both are full-time jobs, and like I said, her father insisted on her being part of the business."

We'd gotten to the top of the stairs and the wide-open space of the attic stopped our conversation. Memories washed over me, warming me and making me miss my grandmother. I turned to Dixon to see his reaction.

He swiveled his head from left to right, taking in the view. He stopped at the window and walked toward it. "I can see to the next state from here! Wow. I can imagine you sitting here and playing with your dolls and reading...doing your girly stuff." Dixon dropped onto the window seat, even though the cushion was no longer there.

I sat next to him and looked out the window. "See? There's the fountain. It used to run twenty-four hours a day, and I pretended it was the ocean or a rainstorm or a waterfall. I'd imagine all sorts of things, looking out this window." I turned to look at him. "But you're better than anything I ever imagined." I closed the space between us. My lips met his, softly at first, and then with more pressure. I put my arms around his shoulders, and Dixon pulled me into his embrace. I melted into his warmth, and the zips and zings from our first night together rushed over me.

"Meow."

Dixon pulled away and laughed. "Man, you are really cramping my style, kitty." He looked up at me. "Maybe your grandmother was reincarnated as this cat, and she's keeping you from any hanky-panky." His chuckle grew louder, and I joined in.

"Well, Grandmother Stetson was never shy about her opinions, that's for sure. But I have a feeling that she'd like you. She'd make an exception in your case." I gave him a quick peck.

"You know, it just occurred to me. If you and your father are Stetsons, and your grandmother was a Stetson, but took over the business from her father, wouldn't she have a different last name after she got married?" Dixon looked curiously at me.

I laughed. "Well, my grandmother was a little ahead of her time—not just in business but in her personal life. She was married and had taken his last name. But when he died shortly after my father was born, she decided she was going to go back to using her family name, for both her and her son. As you point out, the hotel was already named after the family, and she needed all the aura of authority she could get to even out the playing field in the business. She figured if she had the 'wrong' last name, people would take her less seriously. With the 'right' last name, it was clear she was in charge."

I stood and walked around the room, checking the drawers and tops of dusty bureaus. "Even with the 'right' last name, it feels like I'm still not taken seriously at work. It's one more reason I want to leave and open up this bed-and-breakfast. Make something of my own. Be my own boss. No more kowtowing or putting up with egotists who think they know more than me, or better than me."

Dixon followed me around the room, watching me trace patterns in the dust and adding his own swirls after me. "I can see some of your grandmother's strength in you. I mean, she had to be a force to be reckoned with if she kept the hotel chain going for her family when it wasn't the thing she wanted to do. And to hand down that kind of legacy to her son, and then to you...doesn't sound like someone who wasn't in charge."

"You know, maybe that's partly why I haven't rushed out the door. I mean, I'm not happy with the way I'm treated by some people...especially my father...but it is my family name on the business. I know how much my grandmother put into it, and the thought of turning my back on that and all she did to give me this heritage... I feel a bit guilty about walking away from that." I'd walked the perimeter and was back at the window. I dropped onto the window seat and sighed. "But it's just not the thing that makes me excited to get up in the morning." I looked up at Dixon standing next to me. "And I should do what makes me happy, right?"

"If you are lucky enough to know what's going to make you happy, you should definitely go after it. You're in a good spot if you know that...I'm not sure what I want to be doing long-term, but like I said before, it ain't tearing out kitchens and basements." He reached out his hand and pulled me up. "But right now, I'm happy here with you."

I smiled and squeezed his hand. "And I'm happy here with you, too. Come on. Let's go finish this tour and then grab a bite in town before we head back."

WE WENT OUT THE BACK porch door and walked the gravel path to the barn. The tabby had followed us out, and was now crouched in the tall grass, interested in some movement. I had the keys in hand, ready to unlock the regular door to the side of the sliding barn doors.

"I haven't been in here for a long time, so hopefully we don't walk into a bunch of spiderwebs." I shuddered, thinking about the possibility.

"What...some little ol' spiders make you nervous? Don't worry, m'lady...your knight in shining armor remains vigilant to all dangers, whether they be potholes, broken heels, or furry, eight-legged creatures in the dark." With exaggerated motions, Dixon took the key, unlocked the door, and peered inside the dark space. "All clear."

"Why, thank you, kind sir." I gave a little curtsey and laughed when Dixon bowed in return. "Maybe a little light will help us out." I reached to the side of the door and flipped the switch.

Once the space was lit, Dixon whistled. "Wow. This is awesome." He stepped forward and then he wiped at his face. "Ugh. Okay, I have now cleared the way through the spiderwebs for you." He spluttered, still moving his arms to clear the space in front of him.

I tried not to laugh too much.

He turned to look at me and stuck his tongue out.

But once he started walking around the barn, he was caught up in the discovery of everything left behind. "A tinkerer, you said? More like a professional craftsman. Your grandfather had just about every kind of tool available, it looks like."

He glanced at the pegboard filled with tools covered in dust and cobwebs. There was a table, six or seven feet long, with more tools and equipment that I had no idea about. Across the aisle, there was another table with even more stuff, although this looked more like my grandfather's antique car section of the barn.

Former horse stalls had been converted into sections, each with its own focus. Dixon had found the hand tools and car stuff, but other stalls had actual farm equipment, farrier items, and old cans of unknown products. You could spend days out here without finding the bottom of all the collected items.

But Dixon was ready to catalog it all. He moved from table to table, stall to stall, and wall to wall, all the while murmuring words I either couldn't understand or didn't know. He was mesmerized by the sheer volume of items that called the barn home.

He brushed his fingers over tools and gadgets, and I wished I was lucky enough to feel his soft caress again. Was I getting jealous of a damn hammer? Talk about pathetic.

Determined to get out of that mindset, I invited him to see what I considered the best part of the barn.

"Hey, want to see the loft? The stairs are back here." I pulled him away from some woodworking tools. With my hand firmly in his, we walked to the front of the barn and tromped up the wide planks. "I loved this almost as much as the attic."

When we got to the top of the stairs, Dixon stopped, as if his feet were made of cement.

EIGHTEEN

~Dixon~

CORA HAD TO DRAG ME away from the hand tools I was drooling over. I could have checked out everything in those old horse stalls for hours. But she wanted to show me more. I couldn't believe there was more of anything...this place was already so magical. Or impressive, overwhelming, amazing. Unfortunately, it was reinforcing the feeling that Cora was out of my reach...that there was no way I was good enough for her. What would I possibly offer her? And what the fuck was I doing, even worrying about that kind of shit? It'd never happened before. Before Cora, anyway.

All of that was running through my head as she led me up the stairs.

If only I'd known what she was pulling me toward.

Once we hit the landing, I stopped. Cora's gentle grasp of my hand let go as she kept walking and I stayed still. All I could imagine in the space before us was something out of that old Patrick Swayze movie, where he lived in a hayloft of some old man's barn.

The room was open in every direction: no doors, no separate rooms. There was a double door on one wall that I was sure would open up and expose the view over the valley, just like the view from the attic. The flooring was wide wooden beams, and there was a door there, too. I guessed for throwing hay down. After all, it was a hayloft.

But I imagined it more like that movie scene...more like a place to live. Build a kitchenette along one wall; add in a simple bathroom; a table for two in the corner; the bed in front of that double door, which would be switched out from wooden to glass to let in the sun. I was picturing myself in this space when Cora's words registered in my brain.

"What do you think?"

"I...I mean..." I tripped over any coherent words. When I turned toward where her voice came from, the last bits of logical thought dripped through the sieve of my brain. "It's amazing, just like you." Even though it was a pipe dream that I could be worthy of her, I couldn't resist the pull to Cora. With a few steps, I had her in my arms, and I kissed her. The warmth and passion as our tongues danced encouraged that prior vision of a bed in this space. I envisioned Cora laid out on that bed, the sunshine of the day nothing compared to the burning-hot desire I felt for her.

Cora put a hand to my chest and gave a gentle push. "Wow. I never would have guessed that haylofts were your thing, Dixon." She splayed her fingers against the fabric of my shirt, and her green eyes peered up at me. A teasing smile accompanied her next words. "But if you've never had a roll in the hay, you don't know what you're missing." She snaked her hand back up to my neck and pulled me closer for another scorching kiss.

I couldn't respond with anything more than encouraging moans and molded her body to mine. I was willing to find out how much fun a roll in the hay could be. But fate—in the sound of a lonely wail—had other plans.

"Meeeeooooowwww...meeeeooooowwww." The mewl echoed in the high ceilings and stopped us both cold.

Cora stepped back and looked around. "Where is that darn cat? I thought it was hunting little insects or a field mouse. I didn't realize it followed us in here."

As much as I didn't want her to leave my arms, I couldn't let that cat just be miserable, wherever it was. We searched the loft for any sign of the creature, but all we were rewarded with were occasional sounds of distress. There wasn't much to go through—the space was pretty bare—but several old hay bales were pushed against one wall, and some boxes on the other. After looking in those spots, we decided the cat must have gotten into trouble in the main barn, not the loft.

As we headed back down the stairs, I looked back at the loft. The improbable thoughts jelling in my head were interrupted when Cora got to the bottom before me.

"Hey, Dixon...I think I can hear it better down here. It must have gotten trapped in something or behind something in one of the stalls we were in." Cora moved farther down the center of the barn, looking in each of the stalls. She'd pause now and then to listen for the cat's wails.

"Meow." The tabby cat wound itself around my legs as I followed Cora down the length of the barn.

"Here he is." I picked up the cat and it offered another headbutt in appreciation.

"Meeeeoooowww."

The sound definitely did not come from the critter in my arms, and Cora looked back at me, her eyes widening.

"Well, looks like we have a second cat somewhere." Cora grinned. "Unless you are a secret ventriloquist and you're just pulling my leg...and showing off your animal impressions."

"Nope. Can't say I've ever even tried to throw my voice around like that. It's definitely another cat." I moved closer to Cora, the tabby still in my arms. "Trust me, if I had to choose between kissing you or pretending to be a missing cat in distress, there's no contest..."

The mewling got louder, and the tabby wiggled out of my arms. He trotted over to a closed door and scratched at it.

"I guess his lady friend is in there. I wonder how either of them would have gotten in here." Cora twisted the door handle. "This was the old office space. The maintenance crew had a desk and phone in here, and I think a small refrigerator, too." Dust danced in the light as she opened the door wider and walked in.

Sure enough, in the bare-bones room, there was a desk, two chairs, and a bookshelf full of cobwebs and old books. I moved to the wall to see what was buried under the layers of dust. I wiped a finger down the book spines. *The Gentleman and Cabinet-Maker's Director*, some *Future Farmers of America* pamphlets, a *Chilton's Auto Repair Manual*, and *Shrubs in Colour*.

Cora ignored the mess and zeroed in on a pile underneath the desk. There, in a handful of rags, was our crying culprit. The calico tried to stand, but its paw was clearly giving it trouble. Cora inched forward, making reassuring noises, with her hand outstretched. The tabby stood guard between Cora and the calico, watching warily.

"Come on, sweetie. There's a good kitty." Cora dropped to her knees, closer to the calico but not so close that the tabby would get cranky about it.

"Cora, let me grab that cat while you get the calico. He doesn't look like he's too thrilled with you getting closer to her yet." I scooped up the cat again and pet him, hoping to either distract him or soothe him. I didn't get any purring for my trouble, but he stayed calm and didn't wiggle out of my grasp.

"Hi there, kitty. Aren't you so sweet? There we go." Cora stroked the calico for a minute before moving closer. Then she picked up the cat, resulting in a quieter meow out of the poor thing. She moved the front paw gently, and the cat tensed up and rumbled out a low warning.

Cora turned to me, cat still in her arms. "I think she broke her paw somehow. I think the next part of our day together is going to include a trip to the vet's. Nothing but fun with me, huh? First you have to rescue me from a broken heel, and now we've got a broken paw to deal with."

"Do you even know where the vet is? Or if they're open on a Sunday?" I walked over to Cora and freed a hand to pet the calico. "Hi there, sweetie. We'll get you taken care of soon." The cat in my arms purred again and leaned over to headbutt his companion.

Cora shifted her hold on the cat so she could grab her cell out of her back pocket. "Damn. No signal in here. Let's get out of here. Once I've got signal, I'll do a quick search for the closest vet and see if they're open."

Each holding a cat, we walked out of the barn, following the path to the house. I thought we would walk through the house and lock it up as we left, but a banging noise stopped us in our tracks.

"What the hell is that?" Cora muttered. "It sounds like it's coming from the road...or the front yard."

I followed her around the house to investigate. The pounding noise became louder as we got closer to the front, taking on a rhythmic quality: bang, pause, bang, pause.

"Son of a bitch!"

A man had just closed his pickup truck door and started the engine. The bed was full of For Sale signposts. Minus one...the one that had been driven into the ground at the front of the cottage's property line.

CORA STARED OUT THE window, silent. I had turned on the radio, but she was too distracted to tease me about my boy band favorites playing. "So...the vet is going to call you in a few days with an update, right? We were pretty lucky he was there, catching him right before he left for the afternoon. And especially lucky he said he'd board the tabby, too, while the calico rests up. Can't imagine what she could have done to break her leg. I mean, cats are always supposed to land on their feet, right? I guess she must have landed wrong or something." I rambled on, waiting for some kind of acknowledgment or sign of life from the other side of the vehicle.

Silence.

I tapped the steering wheel, too fast for the beat of the song playing. I'd never seen Cora closed up like this, and it was unsettling. In my nervousness, I was hyperaware of every clench and unclench of her hands, every breath she exhaled through her flaring nostrils—all while I tried not to move and held my breath.

I was more apprehensive the closer we got to the cottage. Still couldn't believe Cora owned a mansion, had some huge inheritance, and wanted to leave the family business to run a bed-and-breakfast. But I suspected those plans were now up in the air.

The house was in sight, up the road a bit, when Cora finally spoke.

"Can you pull into the driveway for a minute?"

I couldn't decide whether she sounded mad, sad, or something else. It was the same attitude she'd had since we left the vet's: flat, dull, almost robotic. But hell if I was going to say no to her. At this point, I'd do practically anything to get a genuine response out of her. Even anger would be an improvement.

"Sure. Did you want to get out and show me more of the house?" I cringed at the question. I shouldn't have asked it. There'd be no more showing off the house for Cora.

We pulled into the driveway, and I parked. Silently, Cora opened the door and walked toward the sign. The one the real estate agency had just installed. She stared at it.

She balled up her fists, and she straightened her spine.

"Those motherfuckers. They will not take this from me."

Cora spun around to face me. "I can't decide whether I am more mad at my father or at Mark. There's a small chance one of them did this without the other, but I'm betting they are both in on it. They don't want to see me succeed as anything that's not in their little pea brains as 'my place'—or, more accurately, they don't want me to be a person of my own, just an extension of them, like a third arm or something. Well, fuck that and fuck them!"

She whipped back around, pulled out her cell phone, and took a picture of the sign. Then she marched right past me, back to the truck.

Impressed—and grateful that anger wasn't directed at me—I followed her to the truck and got in. "Where to now? You want to go back home? Or Jake's for a drink?" I turned the ignition and headed back for the road. I wasn't sure Cora's burst of anger was complete, but at least now she was talking. I mean, she'd spoken when we were at the vet's, but once the cats were taken care of, she'd withdrawn and been hard to engage. Now I wasn't sure how much to push.

"You know what? A drink might be a good idea. And would you mind...I want Wendy to come, too. I need to talk to her about this."

"Oh. Yeah. Sure. I understand. I'll drop you off, and you and Wendy can huddle up and figure it out. No problem. I'll—"

"What? No, Dixon." Cora put her hand on my arm and lightly massaged it. "Please...I didn't mean that I didn't need you there too. I really could use someone's opinion who isn't so close to the situation."

All I could think, other than I would do anything she asked, was that I really, truly wanted to be close to her and the situation, and that really, truly freaked me out. Never before had my opinion been important to anyone—except Jake—and no one had ever said they needed me.

❦

WENDY WAS AT JAKE'S by the time we got there. Cora made a beeline for the table, but I swung over to the bar to say hi to Jake.

"Hey there, little brother. I see you've got your hands full over there." Jake nodded toward the two women, heads bent together.

I assumed Cora was telling her about the For Sale sign and her suspicions about Mark and her father. "Yeah. I think we'll need a round of beers over there. And keep 'em coming. Any chance we can get some wings and loaded tots with that?" The last thing Cora needed was to get plastered and make some bad decisions. Hopefully some food with the beer would take the edge off her irritability. Plus, I had no idea how Wendy was going to factor in Cora's next moves.

"Sure thing. I'll have Shayla drop off the beers and place the order in the kitchen. What happened, anyway? Wendy came in, looking nervous and anxious, but she wouldn't tell me a thing." Jake caught Shayla's eye, and she wove through the tables to the bar.

"I don't know all the details or back story, but it looks like either her father or that guy Mark—or maybe both—screwed her over. She was planning on one thing, and they pulled the rug out from under her. She's pissed. And let me say, although it's pretty impressive to see, I never want to be on the receiving end of that." My laugh might have warbled a bit at the thought, but I pitied anyone who stood in the path of Cora's fury.

I slapped the bar and turned toward the two ladies. Their voices became clearer as I got closer.

"I can't believe....well, shit, yeah, I can believe Mark would pull this kind of stunt. But your dad? I dunno, kiddo. Doesn't quite seem..." Wendy looked up at me, her expression changing. She smiled. "Well, if it isn't Cora's rescuing knight in shining armor. Hello, Dixon. Nice to see you again." She winked at Cora as she stuck her hand out for me to shake.

"You, too, Wendy." As I quickly shook her hand, Cora was moving over on the bench seat, and I settled in beside her, moving my arm over the back of the seat. "I've got beers coming, and ordered some apps, too." I looked to Cora. "I hope that's okay. I figured this conversation was going to last awhile, and it's been a long day."

"Sounds good. I'm probably hungrier than I think I am. I'm so pissed I can barely remember the last time we ate today." Cora put her hand on mine, and the tiny circles she drew with her finger sent those zings up my arm.

The sensation had me thinking about that kiss in the hayloft and my fantasy of her and me in a bed up there. If any of that were to have even the slightest snowball's chance in hell of happening, Cora needed to figure out what to do next...and I needed to figure out where I wanted to fit in in that future.

"I agree. Beer and food will help us solve this problem." Wendy looked at both me and Cora, but she glanced at Cora's hand over mine. Her lips quirked up. "Of course, some problems aren't really problems at all."

I had no idea what she was talking about, but the arrival of the beers stopped Wendy from saying more and meant I didn't have to reply, either.

"Here you go. Three beers. Jake said the first round is on him." Shayla handed out the glasses and then the beer bottles. "And your food will be ready in a few." She left us to check on some of her other tables.

I raised my bottle. "Here's to giving that rat bastard, whoever he ends up being, a shit time and getting Cora's house back to her."

The girls raised their bottles and clinked them with mine.

"Rat bastard, huh? I am starting to like you, Dixon. Yes, to the downfall of the rat bastard!" Wendy took a generous gulp of her beer before pouring the rest into her glass.

"To the downfall of the rat bastard," Cora echoed as she raised the bottle and drank.

"So, what's the plan?" I leaned back and looked between the two of them. "Or is that still up for discussion?"

Cora scowled, her face tightening, and I couldn't tell whether it'd be more ranting or a brilliant idea. I hoped she'd calmed down some after talking to Wendy and was ready to figure out her next steps.

"Well, that rat bastard—or rat bastards, as the case may be—are going to hear about it from me. I'm not standing by while they take away my dream. I mean, I just told my dad about my plans, and I'm not sure Mark ever bothered to ask me about any thoughts I had for the future...he's always assumed whatever he said would be the end of discussion. I need to talk to my dad first and ask if he knows about the sale of the property. If he knows..." Cora gulped. "If he knows, whether it was his idea or Mark's, I'm going to have to draw a line in the sand. Either he stops it before it goes any further, or I'll quit."

"I don't see how that's much of a threat. I mean, you're gonna be quitting anyway, right, if—I mean, when—you open up this B&B. Will it matter to him that you leave now instead of in a few months from now?"

If Wendy could have thrown daggers at me, it would have hurt less than the glare she threw my way. "I take it back. I am not liking you, Mr. Negativity."

And the hurt in Cora's beautiful eyes made it all the worse.

"Hey, I'm trying to make sure you think of all the angles before you head off and do something rash you can't take back. Maybe it's enough of a threat to get your dad to back off...I don't know." I tried to backtrack, but I wasn't sure I'd be getting away with it. Damn mouth...just another instance of my own dumb speaking before thinking. Only this time, it wasn't charming the socks off anyone, much less Cora.

Cora looked at Wendy. "He might be right. I mean, whether I leave now or in a few months still means I'm leaving...and he's not going to take that lightly. But..." Cora had a devilish grin. "I just need to find the right leverage. I could tell him I'm moving out, but again, that's going to happen when I start my bed-and-breakfast. So that's not enough. I could bow out of the charity thing...that might motivate him to back off."

Wendy blew out a breath. "But didn't you tell me you've gotten pretty much all of that taken care of? There's not much left, so you wouldn't be leaving him in a big jam. And besides, I know you support that to help with home invasion victims. You wouldn't want anything to impact the fundraiser..." Her sympathetic tone reaffirmed how important the event was to Cora.

"Crap. Yeah. Okay, not much of an impact there, except maybe to the overall fundraiser. And you're right...it's important enough to me personally that I don't want to see any issues with it. Damn... Well, what else can I do?"

I had an idea, but it seemed extreme. I wasn't sure it'd be something Cora would do, but if we were spitballing ideas, I figured I could offer it up. "What if—and I mean, it's just an idea—what if you sued him? Tell him you'd get a lawyer and stop the sale. Maybe even sue for damages...like, emotional distress or something. I mean, this was your inheritance from your grandmother, who you loved and cherished, and now he's trying to take it away from you, when it was her intention that you get to have the property."

Wendy's smile came back. "That sounds perfect...tell your father to back off the sale, or not only will you quit in protest, you'll sue him to stop the sale and ask for a gazillion dollars in damages."

"A gazillion? That sounds like a bit much. But yeah, the thought of lawyers and lawsuits might make him reconsider. And if it wasn't his idea, he can tell Mark not to move forward with the sale because

I'd sue him, too. I'm not sure it's enough to convince him, but if I don't at least try, the sale will go through anyway, and then where will I be?" Cora gave me a cautious smile.

I reached out and grabbed her free hand. "Whatever you need me to do, I will. I mean, it's not like I can afford a lawyer...or even know one...but you need a sounding board or a shoulder to cry on or someone to vent to, I'm your guy." Once the words were out of my mouth, I couldn't take them back. Nor could I take back the next thought: I *wanted* to be her guy. The one she turned to when she was down or in trouble; the one she sought to support her when things were tough. It was a bit of a mystery how I'd come to have those feelings, and I could only marvel at the sensation.

Cora's eyes sparkled, and I was drawn into their emerald depths. I could have stared into those glittering jewels forever, but we were interrupted when Shayla showed up with the food.

"Here you go, guys. Tots and wings. Enjoy!" After setting down the platters and some plates and utensils, Shayla flitted away to check on her next tables.

"Oh my God. This smells awesome. Now that I've got some idea of what I'm going to do next, I think I can breathe a bit now." Cora picked up a wing and took a bite. "Definitely needed this. Thanks, Dixon." She leaned over and gave me a kiss on the cheek.

I'd been hoping for something more intimate than that, but with Wendy watching our every move and Jake vigilant at the bar, the innocent gesture would have to do. For now. There'd be time enough later to bring some of those earlier barn loft fantasies to life.

NINETEEN

~Cora~

NO TIME LIKE THE PRESENT. I repeated that mantra as I headed into the office the next day. I'd had time to think about my plan, and I was confident about it. First, I had to find out whether it was my father or Mark who'd put the sale into motion. If it was my father, I'd draw that line in the sand: either stop the sale, or I'd be quitting immediately and starting legal action of my own. If it was Mark's doing, my father was going to have to insist that Mark stop the sale, or face the same consequences. And it wouldn't hurt to state once again that I had no intention of marrying Mark—to the both of them. Because apparently they both still needed to accept it.

I would not be pigeon-holed into a role either of those two thought I should be in, and I wasn't going to marry someone I didn't love. Hell, marriage was the last thing on my mind.

Although, that wasn't strictly true. I had some deep feelings for Dixon, and it went beyond our physical attraction. Spending a lifetime with someone like Dixon would be something to consider. Okay, not *like* Dixon...but actually Dixon. I'd had daydreams about the two of us making a life together. I mean, yeah, our physical relationship was intense—I'd never had such a strong response to a man before—but the honesty in what we talked about and shared...that was special.

I could remember my mother looking at my father that way, as if he were the only person in the room, or even in the world. She adored him, and he her. That was the kind of love I wanted, too. I never figured I'd find it. But maybe I had...or at least the beginnings of it. I couldn't wait to be with Dixon, to talk to him about my day, to hear about his, to make his eyes light up, and to feel that zing each time he touched me.

"Hey, Cora. You're in early today." Maeve stopped in the hallway, a folder in one hand and a coffee in the other. "Trying to get a jumpstart on the social media campaign?"

Her commiserating tone was enough to keep my kick-ass-and-take-no-shit attitude firmly in place. I was invested in the success of the family business...but I needed my family to be just as invested in me. Show me the respect I'd worked for in the hotel business and deserved as someone they loved. I might have had that with my mother and grandmother, but my father certainly hadn't been giving me any support lately.

I straightened my skirt. "Not exactly. I need to check in with my father, but not about the campaign. There's a...personal discussion I need to have with him."

She smiled back at me. "Good for you. I don't know exactly what's going on, but I've been getting the sense that your frustration with his responses to your social media efforts is about at its limits. Maybe if you tackle it head-on with him, you'll make some headway and you'll be able to drag him into this century."

I laughed. *If only she knew.* My father needed to be dragged into this century if he was still harboring thoughts that he could arrange my marriage to a man I didn't love, just for the optics of our families being this grand force in the business world. And if he thought he could run roughshod all over my plans for my future, he was about to be disabused of that notion.

"I guess we'll see if I can make an impression that sticks this time. I've tried before, but he clearly wasn't listening." I took a step toward his office and gave Maeve a little wave. "Wish me luck!"

"Go get 'em, girl!" Maeve lifted her coffee cup in salute and turned down the other hallway to her office.

Little butterflies circled in my stomach. Despite my determination, I wasn't looking forward to my next conversation. Visions of Dixon's intense gaze and the echoes of his encouragements kept me on track, though, and before I knew it, I was at my father's office door.

I knocked, waited two seconds, knocked again, and then pushed the door open. My father sat at his desk, reading the morning paper with a coffee mug on his desk. His gaze was stuck on the newsprint; my knock hadn't registered.

"Dad?" I moved forward and into the office. "Hey, do you have a minute?"

He looked up, a confused look on his face. "Cora...I wasn't expecting you in the office so early today. What's going on? Is everything okay with Mark? Have you finally said yes to him?" He stood, a smile on his face now. "Should I congratulate you on your engagement?"

"Dad. No. This has nothing to do with that. Well, not nothing, but I needed to ask you about something I saw yesterday." I sat in the chair across the desk from him, dropping into the leather seat.

The grin was wiped away, and he sat back down. "Well, that's disappointing. I was hoping you'd come to your senses and said yes. I can't imagine why you'd even hesitate for a moment to accept his proposal. He's a fine man, with a fine—"

"Dad—enough," I snapped. "I told you before, and you need to hear it again. I am not now, not ever, going to marry Mark. I am not in love with him. I am not even 'in like' with him. I think he is pretentious, snotty, pompous, and...and...a real jerk." I stuttered over my words, but I was trying to make my point clear without swearing in front of my father. I had some strong words about Mark, but I didn't think swearing like a sailor—no matter how satisfying to say—would win me points with my father.

"Dad, what I wanted to ask you was about Grandmother's estate. You know, the cottage. My birthday is months away still, and I know her will said it was in trust for me until I turned twenty-six. But I was there this weekend, and I saw a real estate truck there, with a guy putting up a For Sale sign. Did...did you authorize selling the cottage?"

He leaned back in his chair. "Yes, I did. It's time to let the past go, Cora. That house hasn't been lived in for years, and there's no way you and Mark—"

I pushed the chair back as I stood. "Dad, I told you. Mark is not in the picture. There is no future of mine where we are together. I had plans for that house, and you have no right to sell it out from under me!" My heart beat rapidly and a sinking feeling settled in my gut. My father—not only was he not listening to me, but he was trying to run my life as though I had no say in it. My hands shook at my sides.

Through clenched teeth, I delivered my ultimatum. "Either you stop the sale, or I quit."

The shocking words had some effect—just not what I hoped for.

He pushed back his own chair when he stood and leaned over his desk. His eyes were cold and his mouth downturned. "I will not stop the sale. You will continue to work here, or you can leave. And by that, I mean the hotel penthouse suite too. Either you live by my rules, under my roof, or you are out. No home, no job, and no inheritance. Unless you marry Mark. Then you'll be living with him, and he can figure out whether he'll let you keep your job or not." He waved his hand in dismissal.

I was too shocked to speak. He couldn't deny me my inheritance, could he? And what, did he think I was sixteen and was throwing a hissy fit because he instituted some curfew that I'd broken? And what was that bullshit about Mark "letting" me keep my job?

"Dad, I don't know what is going on with you lately, but I am asking you, as your only daughter...your only child...don't push me like this. I won't live under your dictatorship, and if that's all you have to offer..." I straightened my shoulders, doing my best to hide my shaking legs and limp arms. I gave him a moment to respond, but all he gave me was that dead-eyed look he'd had since my mother's death.

"I see. Well then, I will spend the day closing up any projects and handing them off to Maeve. And I'll be out of the penthouse by the weekend." I turned and headed for the door.

"That's a move you'll regret, Cora."

I stopped and drew a deep breath. When I turned, I deliberately looked him in the eyes. "The only thing I regret is letting you think you have any say in my life. And I think Mom would have told you that you can't keep me under your thumb forever."

THE REST OF THE DAY at the office was a blur. I'd given a surprised Maeve my notice, made notes on various projects, cleared the office of any personal items, and then, at the end of the day, broke down in the ladies' room. After a major crying jag, I cleaned up as best I could and made my way back to my small office. My former office. Whatever.

What a damn mess I was in.

And it was only going to get worse. Now I had to pack my apartment and move...somewhere. I did not know where that somewhere was, but it was time to talk to my rock and get some advice.

My finger hovered over Wendy's contact on my cell.

Then I picked Dixon's number instead. My heartbeat increased, but my anxiety dialed down. His deep baritone caused a sense of calm to rush over me.

"Hey, gum drop. What's up?"

"I...I...I can't believe it. My dad...he was the one behind the sale of my grandmother's cottage." More tears escaped, and the hurt began to swell again at my father's betrayal.

"Oh, Cora. I'm sorry. So sorry. You want to meet up and have a drink or something? Go for a drive? What can I do?" Dixon's quiet strength came through his words.

"I don't know what to do. I have to pack my apartment...if I can find a place to live, even. I mean, I don't know..." I took a quick breath. "And I'm done at the hotel, too. No more fighting over social media ads versus traditional ads. I guess I don't have to worry about that battle anymore." My laugh morphed into another sob. "I just..."

"Where are you? Are you still at the office? Or at the penthouse? Let me come get you. I can be there in fifteen minutes, tops."

I grasped at the offer of help. "I'm just finishing up my final notes for my boss...my former boss, I mean. I can meet you in the hotel lobby in twenty minutes."

"See you soon, gummy bear. We'll figure it out...I promise."

When I hung up the phone, I picked up the box of mementos, turned off the light, and shut the door. The walk to the elevator was quiet—no one was left at the end of the day—but my father's office door was open. There were murmuring voices but I was determined to ignore them. Until I caught my name.

"Cora never used to be this difficult, Mark. I have no idea what's gotten into her lately."

Mark harrumphed. "I think it's a who, not a what. Ever since she met that construction worker, she's been unmanageable. She continues to ignore my calls, and that last dinner... I couldn't believe she spoke to my mother that way. But I am sure that with the sale of the house, she'll settle down. It might take a day or two, but she'll be back. She won't have anywhere to go and no job...it will be the perfect time to announce our engagement."

If I'd had any kind of control left, I would have kept walking. But my nerves were frayed, and the attitude on display was the last straw. I marched right into that private conversation and dropped my box at their feet.

"Fuck you both. I cannot believe my own father would not only put me down, but he'd basically steal my inheritance by selling the place I loved to spend time with my grandmother, and try to barter me off in marriage to someone I don't love. I am not a 'thing' to be handled. I am not a possession the two of you get to shuffle between you. I am not 'difficult.' I am a grown woman who can run her own business, or contribute to an existing business—I don't lean on my family name to get by. I earned my degree, and I earned my position here at Stetson Suites. And anyone who says otherwise is a damn liar. If you don't want me here, that's fine. I'll leave. There's more to life than this family business. But you can be damn sure I won't be coming back with my hand out for help." I turned toward Mark. "I will not 'settle down' and be the Stepford wife you clearly want."

I picked up my box and headed for the elevator, leaving my father and Mark speechless.

BUT APPARENTLY MY LUCK wasn't going to hold out. Just as the elevator door was about to close, Mark clasped the edge and kept it from fully shutting. He put pressure on the frame, and the door re-opened.

"We are not done, Cora. There's a discussion you and I need to have about your grandmother's property." Mark's face was a stone façade, his eyes burning a hole through any bravado I'd had in my father's office.

"What kind of discussion? My father is selling it...against my grandmother's wishes, I might add. I don't think there is much more to say."

"I believe there is room for...negotiation. If the property is so important to you, that is. Let's go to my office and discuss the options." He stepped into the elevator and hit the button for the third level, where his law firm had the full floor for offices. "If you are willing to be reasonable, I am sure there is a solution." He looked at me with an expressionless face.

My first impulse was to tell him to fuck off...again. But if there was a way out of this mess, I wanted to make sure I'd at least considered all the angles. Besides, anything he told me might help any legal case I might end up pursuing.

The brimming silence filled the space. The ride down four floors was as fast as a sloth climbing Mt. Everest. I couldn't stand to be so close to Mark, so I stepped back into the corner, away from his towering height and cloying cologne scent that started to overpower my senses. The two steps wasn't nearly enough to provide any relief, and my jaw tightened as I tried to maintain my silence. Anything I said would just come out in a rapid-fire staccato, and I'd be tempted to give in to the urge to slap the bastard.

Finally the elevator dinged and the doors slid open. Mark marched out, not bothering to look behind him to make sure I was going to follow him.

A moment of indecision had me hanging back. What could he possibly offer that would be worth my time? I'd just told him and my father I wasn't going to dance to their tune, and here I was, ready to follow Mark into his office. Maybe I should just leave and not even entertain anything he had to say.

But knowledge was power. If I knew what he wanted in exchange, maybe I could figure something out.

I followed Mark down the hall, past his secretary's desk and into his private corner office. I stood just inside the doorway. "All right, I'm listening. What exactly do we have to discuss about my grandmother's property?" I ignored the plush office and concentrated my stare at Mark's back. I put the box on the floor, never taking my eyes off Mark.

He approached his desk and sat in the leather chair. He folded his hands, the pointer fingers meeting at a point. "I have a proposition for you. Before you say no, you should be aware that I can make these silly dreams of yours happen, or I can make sure they never happen. And I will not hesitate to do so." He leaned back, his hands now going to the armrests.

"If you agree to marry me, your father will agree to stop his efforts to sell the mansion. You and I will live there. If you insist on pursuing a career in hospitality, you may convert the barn structure into an exclusive boutique hotel, with a maximum of two guest suites. I don't want you to be a maid, so you'll have a staff under your direction to take care of the day-to-day details. I think that will satisfy your father, and I am agreeable to letting you work in this type of environment. Of course, I will expect you to be available for any social gatherings we need to host...you can put that hotel management experience to good use in managing our social calendar and obligations."

I would have laughed out loud, if my breath wasn't stuck in my chest. Anger and indignation warred for my attention, but Mark's next words sucked away any coherent response.

"If you do not agree to marry me, I will purchase the property from your father. I will tear down every stick, brick, and stone." He leaned forward. "I will plow down the field. I will bulldoze the barn and rip up the concrete floor. Then, I will build a house more suited to my tastes." His smirk only grew. "The choice is yours, my dear. But only for a short time. You have one week—until the night of the fundraiser—to make up your mind. After that, I will move forward with my architect and my renovation plans."

I couldn't believe Mark would be so mean-spirited, so vindictive. Sure, he was a snob and a spoiled brat, but this was way beyond a normal response to being turned down. He was serious...and my father would back this asinine plan. I could recover from the loss of my dream of running my own bed-and-breakfast at the cottage. It'd be difficult, but I could. The thought of my grandmother's home being demolished...that wasn't something I could just let happen.

I picked up the box. "Then I will call you within the week." With as much dignity as I could muster while my heart grew heavier and tears clouded my sight, I turned and walked out of the building—and the world—I had always considered my own.

TWENTY

~Dixon~

MY HAND WARMED CORA'S back as we walked into Jake's. She was still in a daze from whatever happened at the office. I'd found her in the lobby of the corporate offices, taking shaky breaths and swaying on her heels.

"Come on. Wendy's waiting." My words rumbled in her ear, and I directed her to the back wall.

"I—wait—what? I didn't call her, did I?" She looked back at me.

"No. I figured you needed some extra support, so I checked with Wendy to see if we could all meet up and figure out what's going on. Or at least hear from you what's going on."

Wendy was waving and getting out of the booth as we were talking. She grabbed Cora in a big hug. "What the hell is going on? Dixon called and said your father is selling your grandmother's house? Is that right?" She pulled back and looked her in the eye.

"Yeah. It's been a hell of a day." Cora dropped her head and sighed. "I still can't believe it. I mean, he's been overprotective since Mom died, but this...I don't know. I can't get through to him. He insists that I either live by his rules, under his roof, or I was out—out of the apartment and out of the business. Oh, he'd 'let' me marry Mark, but other than that, it's his way or the highway. So now I have no job and no apartment."

She looked up. "Oh God. I have no apartment! Where am I going to go?"

Wendy answered immediately. "My place. It's small, but we'll make it work. When do you want to pack up your stuff? How quick is your father going to shut you out?" She nibbled on a fingertip. "And what should we do with your stuff? It won't all fit in my apartment—we'll need to get a storage unit. First thing tomorrow. And I'll take the day off—help you get out of the penthouse and settled at my place."

She looked at me. "Time for those muscles to be of use, Dixon. You can help, right?"

Wendy's question circled in my brain. Of course I'd help Cora any way I could: lifting boxes, moving furniture, a shoulder to cry on...arms to hold her with...lips to kiss.

I shook myself out of my daydream. There'd be time for that later. Right now, Cora needed reassurance that everything would work out. Even though I had no idea how. But first steps included a beer, some wings...a salad...and hearing what Cora's father said to her. Maybe it wasn't as bad as she thought. Maybe there was some way to stop the sale of the house.

"Of course. So let's get started with some strategy. Tell us what your father said and let's figure this thing out."

We all sat at the table and listened to Cora's retelling of her conversation with her father. It was as awful as she made it out to be. Not only had he shattered her dream by selling her grandmother's house out from under her, he'd also shut her out of the family business when she tried to stand up for herself. When he kicked her out of the penthouse, too, he put the final nail in the coffin in his relationship with Cora. Damn.

I could relate to getting shut down by someone who should have been on your side. When I was a kid, I had Jake to prop me up whenever his father cut me down. Cora didn't have that kind of support. Except from Wendy—and now me, too.

"Well, I can't say I'm too surprised, Cora. Your dad has always been domineering whenever it comes to you. But now we'll get to be roomies, like back in college. Although this time, no third roommate." Wendy smiled at Cora, and the two let out a small laugh.

Cora turned to me. "When Wendy and I roomed together at Cornell, we had a third roommate who played the tuba for the marching band. A wild Friday night for her was practicing her field maneuvers with a few other marching band geeks...marching every square inch of the dorm room and then up and down the hall, tooting her horn. Needless to say, we tried to be anywhere but our room on Friday nights."

"Sounds like a fun time. Does that mean that I shouldn't break out my accordion and bust out a polka for you?" I grinned back at Cora, happy to see the smile on her face at my teasing.

"Accordion? Yeah, that's a hard pass, Dixon." Wendy laughed.

"Okay, no accordion serenades outside your window. Noted. But, now, seriously...what's the plan? You need to move out right away, right? You'll need to find a storage place, and then we'll need to get your essentials to Wendy's. How far away are you from the hotel, Wendy?" I took a sip of the beer that had arrived, although we were still waiting on the food to show up.

Right then, Shayla came over with the wings and another round of drinks. "Jake says you guys look like you need another round. Here you go." She looked at Cora. "You all right, honey? When you first came in, you looked so upset. I see that Dixon here has worked his magic and you're looking better. He wasn't the reason you were unhappy in the first place, was he? Men can be idiots." Shayla moved her gaze to me, a sharp-eyed look to put me in my place—and then one in Jake's direction.

Cora jumped in. "No, it wasn't Dixon. I'm having some issues with my dad, and plans I thought I had are kind of up in the air right now. Dixon and Wendy are helping me figure things out. I don't know where I'd be without them right now."

A warmth of satisfaction flowed over me, and I reached out to grab hers. "Anytime, jelly bean. Anything to help." Without a second thought, I leaned over to give her a kiss. It was supposed to be a quick peck on the lips, but when we touched, that zipping-zapping spark shot off and I couldn't resist taking the kiss deeper, wilder.

Wendy cleared her throat. "You know, there are other people here."

The teasing in her tone was enough to have me pulling back. "Sorry. Not sorry. But I'll try to contain myself in public...just for you, Wendy." I teased her right back, grateful Cora had such a friend in Wendy. "And yes, Shayla, you can tell Jake that I'm behaving myself...mostly. And thanks for the drinks." I raised the glass in her direction.

"Sure thing. But, Cora, you let me know if this guy treats you bad. Between me and Jake, we'll straighten him out. Don't you worry about that."

Cora leaned over to look more directly at Shayla. "Thanks, but I don't think Dixon needs any straightening out. He's just fine the way he is." She winked.

Shayla headed back to the bar—either to pick up her next round of drinks or to report to Jake...maybe both—and we got back to our conversation.

By the time we finished the food, we had a plan. We'd get a storage place in the morning, spend the late morning and afternoon packing Cora's place up, get everything over to Wendy's that Cora needed for the immediate future, and anything left—including furniture—would go over to the storage unit. I texted Ryan, and he agreed to help move the heavy stuff with me, so neither of the women would need to worry about that. He also said he'd work it out with George to take the day off, so that was all set, too.

Wendy left, winding her way through the bar until she got to the door. She looked back at us and waved once more. We waved back and then stared at each other.

"Well, you ready to head back to your place for your last night there?" I intertwined my fingers with hers, lightly rubbing her palm with my thumb.

"Yeah, I guess so. It's so weird to think about. I mean, I've been there since college and it's really become my home. On the bright side, though, I won't have to worry about who's watching me come and go and then reporting it to my father." She tightened her grip. "And my overnight guests will no longer be subject to scrutiny from afar, either."

"Wait—what? Someone tells your father every time someone spends the night?" I was consumed with the thoughts of other men in her apartment overnight, and I wasn't liking the road that was taking me down. I wasn't one to be jealous, but that nasty green-eyed monster was taunting me with the idea of a rotating circle of men going through her door.

Not that I had any room to point fingers. I'd never been much for relationships, and my door had plenty of action over the years. The steadiest relationship I'd ever had—outside of Jake—was with Ryan, not a romantic one.

"No. Well, maybe. It's not like there's ever been a line of men going in and out. It's just that he always seemed to know when anyone came by my place, even if it was Wendy spending the night after we'd gone out for drinks and then came home to commiserate about the lack of men in our lives. And now I won't hear those 'what were you doing' comments from him." She sobered. "I'm not sure I'll be hearing anything at all from him. He's never been one to just call and chat. We mostly talked at work, and it was almost always about work. Unless he was bothering me about Mark. And trust me, I'll be happy not to have to have those conversations anymore."

I lifted her chin. "Well, I'm happy you won't have to have those conversations, either. And I hope I'll be the only man coming in and out of your door." The words flew out of my mouth before my brain could stop them. I meant them, but I sure didn't mean to say them out loud.

Cora leaned into me, a breath away. "It's just you, Dixon. Just you." And then there was no space between us. Her kiss was fierce, and there was no way I wasn't going to respond the same way.

We stood there...could have been a minute, could have been an hour...lost in each other. Someone jostled into my back, disrupting the moment and bringing me back to reality.

"Sorry, dude." The guy who'd bumped into me offered his apology and continued on his way to the table behind ours.

"Well, I guess we should get going. My apartment won't pack itself, and if I get a head start tonight, it won't be so much for tomorrow. And I feel like tomorrow is going to be a long day."

WE GOT TO CORA'S PLACE. By the look on her face, the reality of the situation was sinking in. In the space of hours, she'd lost her business dream, the connection to her grandmother, any chance for a relationship with her father, her home, and her job. If I'd been in her shoes, I don't think I would have been holding it together as well as she was.

"Well, might as well start thinking about what's going and what stays as company property. Don't want to have my father after me for illegally taking the TV or something." Cora choked out a sad, gasping laugh.

"Where do you want to start? Maybe the main rooms will be easier to go through. Most of the big stuff isn't yours, is it?" I walked toward the kitchenette area. "Did it come furnished with the pots and pans and stuff? Or did you buy some on your own?" I opened the cabinets to inspect the quantity of items hiding in them. It didn't seem too packed, so if she had bought them, it shouldn't take more than a few boxes for it all.

"It's a bit of both, I guess. I found some stuff I liked at some tag sales and added to what was already here, so there's not a lot in the kitchenette. But definitely the teapot." She picked up the ceramic pot decorated with blue flowers of some sort.

We worked quickly, sorting between hotel and personal equipment. Eventually we had a small pile on the counter—about four boxes' worth of stuff, I figured.

"Hey, where are you thinking you'll even find boxes at the last minute? I know this isn't much, but there's bound to be more in the next few rooms you need to box up, right?" I watched Cora as she stared at the pile.

Absentmindedly, she said, "Oh, they have plenty of boxes down in housekeeping. I'm sure I can get some there. Or maybe Benny in maintenance. He's always been pretty helpful when I need something like that." She nibbled on a fingertip, and I was riveted by the way her lips wrapped around her finger.

If I didn't get my mind out of the gutter, there'd be no more packing tonight. Although, a little distraction wouldn't hurt. I stepped closer to her. "I am so sorry, Cora. I know this isn't how you wanted things to go." I wrapped my arms around her, drawing her in closer. I could smell that beautiful spring scent of hers, and I wanted to get lost in the promise of that spring day, with the sun of her smiling face warming my heart. Somehow, my dirty mind and hurting heart joined forces, and the gentle kiss I'd planned on morphed into the over-the-top, passion-filled kiss that had my heart ready to burst from my chest.

Cora put her hands on my chest, burning through the thin fabric of my shirt. As the kiss intensified, they tangled in my hair. Her chest heaved against mine, and I tightened my hold on her, savoring every taste of her in our kiss. My hard cock pressed into her, ready to go at a moment's notice. Hell, all of me was ready for Cora.

She pulled back from my embrace. Cora lifted the hem of her shirt, and I was faced with the bounty of her bra, holding back her luscious breasts. Then she was right back up against me, kissing me with a fervor about to set me on fire. With gentle nibbles and hot breaths, she worked her way from the base of my neck to my ear. "Dixon, I need you."

I'd never heard anything sweeter...or hotter. "I need you, too." I reached for the edge of my T-shirt and tossed it to the floor.

Cora kissed me again, walking backward toward the bedroom and pulling me along.

As if I'd let her go now...

Once the backs of her legs hit the bed and stopped her momentum, our kiss broke off and she met my gaze. A soft smile came over her face. "You're on my turf now, Cub Scout." She sat on the edge of the bed and unbuckled my belt. She sank her hands between my underwear and skin, and shimmied them to free my rock-hard cock from the confines of the fabric. Cora lowered her head; her silky lips covered the head and her sweet tongue lapped up the drop of pre-cum.

"Oh..." Not the most intelligent response, but it was all my brain could manage as all the blood rushed to that one point of my body. "Oh, God, Cora." The suction of her lips over my length overwhelmed me, and I sagged toward her. "So good. So, so good." I reached for her head and guided her as she continued to suck and lick.

Cora hummed her response, and the vibration was pure ecstasy. Much more, and I was gonna burst, right into her mouth. The thought alone almost had me at that edge, but I wanted more. More of Cora. More of us, together. I found some strength and pulled away. "Cora. I need to be inside you." With a slight push on her shoulder, I pressed her down to the bed. I worked at the button of her pants while I toed out of my shoes, and tossed her pants and panties on the floor.

Cora opened her nightstand and pulled out a foil packet. Then she scooted back, giving me room to join her.

I tore open the package and rolled the condom down my length before getting on the bed. I held myself up on my arms, staring into her beautiful eyes. Her black hair fanned out around her, just like in my dreams. I couldn't resist the vision in front of me and swooped in for another kiss. One that turned into a full-fledged inferno as our bodies rubbed against each other. The movement had my cock right at the edge of her entrance, teasing her with light pressure.

"Oh, Dixon."

The whisper escaped when I pulled back to look at her again. I couldn't wait any longer to feel the heat of her pussy, and I notched myself at her opening. With one forceful thrust, I was enveloped in the wet warmth. Heaven could not have felt any better. With a rock of my hips, I had Cora join in my rhythm. We stared at each other, just feeling our bodies move together. Every motion drew me in further, losing myself in that emerald lake of her eyes. A man could drown in them... I willingly would.

Sooner than I expected, her back arched and a low moan tore from her throat. She clenched, and it was more than I could handle. Not able to hold back, I called out, "Cora! Oh God, Cora!" and exploded inside her.

I was careful not to collapse on top of her and rolled off to the side. I grabbed a tissue and wrapped the used condom in it. I pulled her close, her back to my front, and nuzzled her neck. "Cora, baby, that was...I'm not sure there are words. The things you do to me..." I nibbled her earlobe. "I mean, I've been with plenty—"

"I'm not looking for your number, Dixon." Cora interrupted what was probably going to be some stupid shit spilling from my mouth.

Thank God. No need to go there. But...she needed to know that this was unusual for me. More than unusual...unheard of. I'd never been in a monogamous relationship before. It was new territory, and I was sure I'd fuck it up somehow. I didn't know the rules of how to do this. I knew the rules of one-night stands and hookups.

"Oh, okay. Anyway, I've never had a serious relationship with a girl...a woman." I wet my lips and debated how honest to be. "And...well...I kind of like how this feels."

Cora brushed her hand over my arm. "I do too, Dixon. More than kind of. I really, really like it." She climbed into my lap and the heat from her body had my dick thickening.

"I've never felt this way before." My heart was still thundering, but now it wasn't because of any physical exertion. Nope—it was the feeling of my heart opening after being closed off for so long. "What I mean is—"

Cora stiffened against me.

Shit. Did I fuck this up?

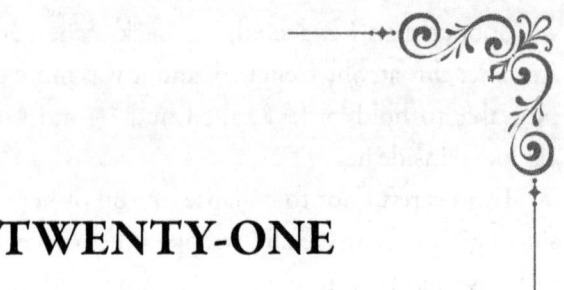

TWENTY-ONE

~Cora~

I TENSED. *He couldn't be thinking...* After Mark's ultimatum, I wasn't sure I could take any more declarations...even positive ones. I put a hand on his chest and pushed off him. "Dixon, I don't think I've ever felt this way before, either. Actually, I know I haven't. I never connected with someone like I do with you. But things are so messed up right now...I'm messed up right now. I don't want you to say something that you might...I don't know...not regret—but maybe it's too soon to say anything serious. I know it feels right to be with you, to be in your arms. No one else has ever turned me on like you do. I can't imagine anyone else in my life but you. And I hope you feel that way too." I looked at him, trying to gauge how my words were hitting him.

"I do feel that way. Nothing has ever felt so natural and right as being with you. I've never had that. I've never done relationships before...not real ones, where someone is a part of my life, a part of my heart. And part of that scares the hell out of me, but then I see you and all that goes away. Then it's nothing but the need to be with you—just you. To be your sun and your moon." He pulled my hand to his lips and gave it a soft kiss. "I'll take whatever you're willing to give, and give you everything I have." He grinned. "Of course, I hope that includes a whole lot of what we just did."

I laughed. Happy little bubbles percolated throughout my body. "Yeah. Definitely lots of that." I kissed him quickly. "But we'd better get some sleep. It's gonna be a busy day tomorrow, and I need you rested up to provide all the muscle needed to move me to Wendy's place." I wrapped a hand around one of his biceps.

He flexed. "Oh, gum drop, I've got plenty of energy for you and the move. Don't you worry about that at all." His grin only grew as he shimmied down, dipping his head between my legs.

And then he proceeded to prove his point.

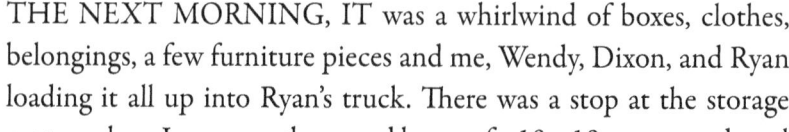

THE NEXT MORNING, IT was a whirlwind of boxes, clothes, belongings, a few furniture pieces and me, Wendy, Dixon, and Ryan loading it all up into Ryan's truck. There was a stop at the storage center, where I was now the proud lessee of a 10 x 10 corrugated steel locker. After leaving the big items and not-needed items there, we headed to Wendy's apartment.

I could never repay Wendy for her help. Only a true friend would let you move into your apartment on a day's notice and never ask for rent or demand something in return.

"Wendy, thanks again. I know this is a big inconvenience." We were in Wendy's car, leading Dixon and Ryan in the truck. I looked over at her in the driver's seat. "And I promise to not have gentlemen callers stay overnight."

Wendy glanced at me and wiggled her eyebrows. "So, how is that going, anyway? I'm guessing that you might not be staying overnight at our place that much, if a certain 'gentleman caller' has his way." She stopped at the light and gave me a longer look. "Give me the short version before we get to the apartment. Is it serious? Should I start prepping my maid of honor speech?" She hummed the Wedding March and then switched to Darth Vader's theme. "Or am I going to have to go all Jedi on Dixon's ass and squeeze the life out of him?"

I laughed. "No, no Jedi mind tricks or powers needed. And no maid of honor speeches. Not yet anyway. I've got a lot going on, sure, but Dixon and I are good. Better than good. But I've got some things to figure out." I sobered up. "And top of the list is finding out if my father can really sell my grandmother's house. It doesn't seem right that he could do that, but he's the trustee of the estate until my birthday. It's less than a year from now, but if he can do anything until I take control of the estate, then I'm pretty much fucked." I blew out a breath. And there was Mark's marriage demand to figure out, too. How could I prevent him from buying the house and making good on his threat to tear it down if I didn't marry him?

"And the other thing I've got to get under control is the fundraiser. The last thing I want to do is sit at the same table with my father, Mark, and his parents. I can fake a broken leg. What do you think?" I looked at Wendy, only half joking. The words about Mark hovered on the tip of my tongue, but I couldn't force them out.

She looked back at the light and hit the gas when the light turned green. "I'm sorry to say that I don't think that solves your problem. Broken legs don't heal overnight...you know, like twisted ankles do." She laughed. "A-ha! That's it. Bring Dixon with you. He can distract you from anything your father or Mark tries at the dinner. And you'd have the satisfaction of making your point that neither of them are in charge of your life—you are."

She had a point. Dixon would be a good distraction, and a definite move forward in living my own life on my own terms...if I told Mark a wedding definitely wasn't going to happen. Mixing Dixon and Mark at the same function would only spell trouble, with Mark thinking he had the upper hand on my future. But the charity was important to me; the people it helped were people like me—people who'd lost loved ones to senseless violence.

"If I asked Dixon to go, it might be uncomfortable for him. I mean, I love my father and even I don't want to be at his table...imagine how Dixon'd feel sitting there with him and Mark making snide comments. Or Mark's parents...God knows how cruel they would be."

"Could you just make an appearance? You know, show up, get a drink, mingle, and then get the hell out of there before the dinner?" Wendy glanced over at me and then turned in to the driveway to her apartment complex. "Home sweet home."

"Well, I guess I could. I'm supposed to help out for the silent auction, but most of that is before the event opens up. I could excuse myself after that gets going...there are some other committee members who could cover for me." I straightened up in my seat and took off the seat belt as Wendy parked. "Yeah, that could work."

As we got out of the car, Dixon and Ryan pulled up next to us.

"Alrighty, let's get this done!" Ryan slammed his door closed and walked to the truck bed to lower the tailgate. "Hopefully it'll only take a few trips to get this last stuff taken care of."

Once everyone had something in hand, we followed Wendy into the building and to my new living space.

After we'd gotten everything out of the truck and the boxes in my new room, along with minimal furniture in the space, I offered to take the group out for lunch. It seemed like the least I could do.

"Well, I wouldn't turn down a beer and a burger at Jake's." Ryan clapped Dixon on the back. "And a little friendly bet on the game this afternoon." He grinned at his friend.

Dixon laughed. "Yeah, right. A beer and a burger...but no bet. I'm tired of losing to you, bud."

"I can't help it if your team sucks." Ryan pushed Dixon out the door. "But at least your taste in the ladies is improving!" He looked back at me and winked. "And she's offering to pay for the beers, so let's get a move on before she changes her mind."

AFTER AN AFTERNOON hanging out at the bar with Ryan, Dixon, and Wendy, I stopped worrying about my father, Mark, the inheritance...there was only room for happiness. And love.

If I'd been toying with the idea earlier, it was no longer just an idea. I had fallen—head over heels, like the sun into the sunset, like a feather to the ground, and like a drop from the tallest roller coaster—in love with Dixon. All those feelings surrounded me. The tumbling, stumbling excitement of finding him. The sinking into his welcoming arms. The softness of his touch. The pounding heartbeat just being near him.

"Hey there, gum drop. Where'd you go?" Dixon danced his fingers over my shoulder as we sat next to each other. Ryan and Wendy had left earlier, and it was just us two in the booth.

I looked at the mesmerizing eyes focused on my face. I traced his jawline. "I...well, I guess you caught me daydreaming." My cheeks heated.

"Oh really? Daydreaming? Is there anything I can do to make those dreams come true?" He leaned in closer, brushing against the side of my neck. "Are those daydreams about night things?" A light growl seemed to echo, and I shivered against it. "In the middle of the afternoon?"

I laughed, recognizing the old country song lyrics. "Busted. But now I've got a roommate, so it'll have to wait, I guess. Or..." I swallowed. "Maybe we could go to your place." Suddenly, that was the only thing I wanted: to be alone with him, to cocoon with him in a bubble, and keep the world at bay. Reality would knock on the door soon enough; grabbing this magical time together was a luxury I wouldn't turn down...and one I was becoming determined to chase after, regardless of the roadblocks.

"Best offer I've had all day. 'Course, any offer from you would be the best offer of the day." He kissed me.

What was supposed to be a light, teasing kiss turned fiery-hot, burning up any anchor to the reality that we were in the middle of his brother's bar. I couldn't get close enough, and all these damn clothes were in the way.

I broke the kiss. "Then we'd better get out of here before Jake kicks us out for causing a disturbance. I'm pretty sure me peeling off your shirt is bound to get noticed not only by him, but by every woman in this place." I scooted out of the bench seat and held out my hand. "I am a bit of a spoiled brat...I don't like to share what's mine."

He took my hand as he stood and pulled me closer. His intense stare looked deep into my soul. "I like the sound of that...as long as you remember you're mine, too."

The rest of the world blurred away. All I could see was his face; all I could feel was his hand in mine. "I like the sound of that, too." Happiness that couldn't be contained spread across my face, and mirrored in his.

"Then let's get outta here."

LIFE AS AN UNEMPLOYED person with no direction was a startling change. No office hours to get up for. No errands to squeeze into the day or spill over into the night. And even though we'd never spent time together at the office, just knowing my father was down the hall was reassuring in a way.

Of all the things I missed that first week, that was the biggest surprise. Maybe it shouldn't have been. After all, he was my father. But then I'd think about how he and Mark talked about me that last day in the office, as though I were a mirror or some other inanimate object they were deciding how to showcase to make themselves look better. Maybe what I missed was my delusion that my father cared about me, not the reality that he apparently was fine with marrying me off for a business deal.

And there's nothing like a day of no responsibilities to let your mind wander. By the third day, I'd cleaned every inch of Wendy's apartment, organized every cupboard and closet, tossed all the old cosmetics in the bathroom, and perfected my vacuuming technique so I could leave those directional marks the hotel maids did in my old place.

Wendy humored me. After all, now she had a maid, she joked. But worry lurked behind her eyes when she looked at me.

"Okay, spill. I can't tell if you are trying to plot your revenge against your father and Mark, or whether you've suddenly become the queen of organizing, ready to be the next Martha Stewart or Marie Kondo." Wendy bumped my hip while we stared at each other in the bathroom mirror, her getting ready for work and me getting ready for...nothing.

"I don't know either. I mean, there's an appeal to being the next Martha Stewart...I can buddy up with Luke Combs like she did with Snoop Dogg, and we'll get a show on cable." I laugh-snorted. "Of course, I'd skip the jail time that Martha did."

Wendy laughed. "Yeah, you can totally skip that. Although, maybe there'd be a cute prison guard I could, you know, distract when I came up to visit you at the minimum-security lockup. I could promise him all sorts of things so he'd make sure you had an easier time in jail." She wiggled her eyebrows and swiveled her hips.

I sighed. "I don't think I'm cut out for Martha's life, even with famous singer friends. I guess I'll have to start figuring out how to make sure my father and Mark don't get their way." I blew out a breath and my hair fluttered in my exasperation. "I just have no idea where to start."

"Well, you need to figure out whether the trustee of your grandmother's estate can sell the property. If the answer's no, then you are good to go. If the answer's yes..." She turned to face me directly. "Well, you could buy it, right? I mean, I know that's not what you planned, but it's an option, right?"

I chewed my lip. "It's worse than that. There's something I haven't told anyone yet."

Wendy stared at me. "Now what? What could be worse than you having to buy the house you were supposed to inherit?"

"Mark...he told me that if I don't agree to marry him, he will buy the property from my father, and then tear everything down. Everything. Not a stick left of my grandmother's home." A tear slid down my face. "And I have until the night of the fundraiser to give him my answer."

"Who the fuck does he think he is? I can't believe he'd actually think you'd agree." At my garbled gasp, Wendy calmed down a bit. "What are you going to do?" Wendy rubbed my arm. "And what about Dixon? Haven't you told him yet?"

"Nope. I couldn't bring myself to say the words out loud to anyone, especially Dixon. He'd tell me that I shouldn't give up my dream for him. He'd expect me to kick him to the curb and marry Mark." I looked down at the floor. "If I married him, Mark promised he'd 'let' me renovate the barn and run it as an exclusive guest house. We'd live in the main house, and I'd be in charge of his social calendar. He thinks that's some kind of compromise *he* can live with."

When I looked at Wendy, her eyes were narrowed, her eyebrows pulled down.

"Well, I think you need to find out exactly what your rights are as the beneficiary of the trust. Maybe you can find a lawyer who'll find a loophole or something. 'Cause I think the last thing you want to do,

Cora, is marry Mark to only have half of your dream, especially when anyone can see it's Dixon you belong with." Wendy puckered her lips and fixed her lipstick.

With a final adjustment to her hair, she walked out of the bathroom. Over her shoulder, she said, "But first, take a damn shower and put on some real clothes. No house chores for you today. Today, you conquer the first step to your future...whatever the hell that step is."

I stared in the mirror. Wendy was right. Today was the day to stop wondering and to start doing.

"THANKS, GAIL. I APPRECIATE you following up." I hung up the phone and stared out the window. Any slight hopes I had of the law being on my side disappeared like the petals of a flower in the wind. Submitted to the cruel winds of nature in her glory. My high school friend Gail worked for a firm in town and she'd made a few inquiries with her law firm's trust lawyers, and the trustee of an inheritance had authority to sell property, without any input from the beneficiary. The only thing a trustee couldn't do was sell to a company they owned, or benefit from the sale of property. Considering it didn't seem like my father was trying to sell the house to the hotel or any of its subsidiaries, he was within his rights to sell. And selling to Mark didn't qualify as benefiting, even though it was exactly what my father wanted.

He'd just not be honoring the intent of my grandmother. Or keeping faith with me.

I hung my head. A single tear welled up in the corner of my eye, and I let it hang there. If I could control that one tear, I could control them all. Gravity won, and it slid down my cheek. And another, and another. Like my dreams, my tears slipped away. With each tear, a fire started to burn. It was unfair. It was mean-spirited. It was petty.

It was controlling. What started as a small flame grew into a bonfire, fed by the last remnants of love I had for my father, and contempt for Mark. These two men thought they could mold me into what they wanted, but the energy of that growing inferno would only make me stronger.

And more determined to find a life and a love of my own.

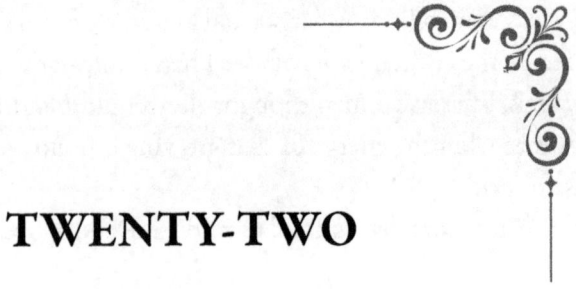

TWENTY-TWO

~Dixon~

I PULLED MY CELL OUT of my back pocket. I didn't recognize the number, but because I was now selling items from my web page, I answered. Maybe it'd be another custom order, or a sale on something already listed.

"Hello?"

"I am looking for Dixon Reed."

The answering voice was male, smooth, confident, and set me right on edge. "This is Dixon. How can I help you?"

"Well, Mr. Reed, you can help me by staying away from my fiancée."

My stomach dropped. *Mark.* It had to be. I'd never spoken directly to him, but the sound of his voice dinged my memory of that night in the hotel when he'd dismissed me and Cora.

But damn if I was going to let this asshole run this conversation. I had a few choice words for him and his smarmy lawyer attitude. He might think he owned the world, but he sure as hell didn't own me...or Cora.

"Since I don't know who you are engaged to, buddy, you'll have to be more specific. But, if this is Mark, and you're talking about Cora, you are sadly mistaken. She's not engaged to you, despite any pressure from you or her father."

"I believe you know exactly who this is. And yes, we may not be engaged at this moment, but it's only a matter of time."

The smirk could be heard through the phone, and I tightened my fist in response. The loser was lucky he wasn't in front of me, because I'd gladly punch his face in for even thinking Cora was going to be with him, much less marry the jerk.

"Well, until I hear differently from Cora, I'm going to keep seeing her. Nothing you say is gonna change that." I plopped on the bench in front of the warehouse, my legs unwilling to be as strong as my words.

"I'd think again, Mr. Reed. Cora indeed will be my wife. I expect by the end of the week, you'll be singing a different tune." His voice hardened. "And you will stay out of my way. I can make your life very...unpleasant, Mr. Reed, if you insert yourself where you don't belong. My private investigator gave me quite the dossier on you and your family...what little is left of it now."

I sucked in a breath. Even though I'd told Cora all about me and my past, it cast a long shadow over everything I did. Everything I thought. And now it was going to push Cora into Mark's arms...or at least let him pull her into his world.

"You know I can give Cora everything she needs. You have nothing. Not a college degree, not a home, no prospects for a career. How did you think you would ever fit into Cora's world? She has money, class, intellect... Surely you understand, even with your limited mind, that you don't belong with someone so superior to you in every way?"

I could hardly breathe at his harsh words. Unfortunately, they were the same words that had swirled in my head, mostly in the negative voice of Jonah. If I wasn't sitting down, I would have fallen over at the impact. As it was, I couldn't come up with a coherent response.

"Your silence confirms we are on the same page. Leave Cora to me. Stay out of her life. Or I will be sure to make yours a living hell."

The phone went dead, and my clenched fist went slack. I might have sat there for ten minutes or ten hours for all I knew. The damn phone rang in my hand again, shocking me back to reality. This time the caller ID showed a picture of Cora's face, from the picture we'd taken in that god-awful chair at the Trunk.

"Dixon?"

"Hey. Everything okay?" It was all I could do to keep an even tone. I couldn't bear to use any of the nicknames I usually did. My head was hardening my heart against disappointment.

"Hi, Dixon. Yes...no...I don't know. I know you're working, but I really wanted to see you. Can I stop by your jobsite?"

She didn't quite sound like herself. Something had to be up. Maybe she was calling to tell me we were over. That she was going to marry Mark. That anything we'd had was just a fling before she moved on to what she really wanted.

"I'm at the warehouse to get some equipment." I swallowed. "It's not a good time."

"How about I pick up some sandwiches and meet you at the warehouse? Would that okay? I really need to talk to you."

The sunshine in her voice was gone. I could feel the rainclouds swelling, ready to rain on me and turn my life into that fog-filled, misty place where I was alone.

"I need to say something to you, too. But let's just get this done now, all right? It's been fun, Cora, but I don't see this going anywhere."

"What—"

"Like I said before, I've never been one for relationships, and it's clear you're too much for me. Too good. Too kind. Too—"

"Dixon, that's bullshit. Nothing could be further from the truth."

"Listen. I'm sorry, but it's over. Good luck with your bed-and-breakfast. I'm sure Mark will make your every dream come true." I disconnected the call and turned off the phone.

A DAY LATER, I STARED at the walls. The beige, lifeless walls. If there was a better metaphor for my life without Cora, I wasn't sure what it would be. It'd only been one day, but all the color had been sucked out of existence. I tried to scroll through my social media feed—I had a few comments on some posts of the projects I had in progress—but I couldn't concentrate. My mind drifted back to Cora...and the conversation I'd had with Mark. All I'd do is pull Cora down...Mark could give her everything she deserved.

My head told me that I'd done the right thing by breaking up with Cora, but my heart was miserable. Maybe I could drown my sorrows like every other clown with a broken heart. I was starting to understand all those sad country songs where the guy is crying in his whiskey.

Definitely time to head downstairs for a drink and maybe some big-brother advice. Then again, he'd told me not to fuck things up with Cora, so maybe Jake wouldn't be a source of comfort...just more recriminations. And damn if I wasn't doing a good enough job on my own on that front.

So no drink. Maybe a ride out on the back roads would help me clear my head. Except...all I was thinking about now was our date overlooking the valley. And the visit to her grandmother's cottage. Which just led me back to how much Mark could offer her...and how little I could.

Fuck.

This was getting me nowhere. Maybe I could bang out some of this frustration on a project. That sounded like a better idea, so instead of heading into the bar or out for a road trip, I drove over to the warehouse. At least there, I could be alone in my misery.

I flipped the lights on and walked to the workbench. I had a few projects in different stages. I was almost finished with the tables for Guy. The website—thanks to Cora's input—was getting attention. A few interior designers interested in upcycling had found me online, and now recommended me to their clientele. It wasn't enough to quit the construction job yet, but it was getting close.

Instead of paying attention to any projects, I sat my sorry ass down in front of the vanity. We hadn't been able to get it into Cora's hotel penthouse suite before her father kicked her out, and then it was too big for the apartment she was now sharing with Wendy. So here it was, getting covered with dust and practically forgotten. The glow that had penetrated my life was as muted as the dulled sparkle on the table top.

THAT NIGHT, I'D PLANNED to bring a special thank-you present to Ryan's parents. Greg and Wilma had always been kind to me, and letting me use the warehouse space and scrounge from the demo'd materials had really helped get me started.

I had chosen a barn wood box as a gift for Greg and Wilma. It'd been in the warehouse for a few days, just waiting for the night they'd invited me to dinner. Ryan told me I always had a standing invitation, but I hated to butt in on family dinners...even if I really wanted to be a part of a family like that.

Wilma opened the door. "Dixon, honey, it's so good to see you! Come on in and tell us all about what's going on with your business." She pulled me through the doorway and had the door closed before she kept going. "And that girl...Ryan says you are getting serious with someone. When do we get to meet her?" She smiled expectantly, looking between me and her husband.

Greg reached over and shook my free hand. "Dixon. Good to see you. Now, Wilma, let the boy get a breath in before you start grilling him on his love life." He smiled at me and winked. "The G-rated version, of course."

"Ha. Yeah. Right." I swallowed and tried to redirect Wilma's attention. I thrust out the barn wood box. "This is for you. Both of you." I looked over at Greg to include him. "Thanks for letting me use the warehouse. It's been a great spot to make my projects and store them until I get them sold."

Ryan came into the living room, little Gabby in his arms. "See, I told you Dixon was coming." He tickled her belly, and she laughed and squirmed in his arms.

"Hi, Dix." The freckle-faced five-year-old put her palm to her lips, made a loud smacking sound, and flung her hand in my direction.

The munchkin was the only one I'd let call me Dix. She was too cute to say no to...which was how she'd wrapped Ryan around her little finger. Or maybe that was Gabby's mother Grace who had him wrapped up.

Either way, I grabbed the kiss and blew her a kiss back. "Hey, kiddo. Is Mom here?" I looked at Ryan. "Or is she on a date?" The state of my love life might be in shambles, but Ryan had been in love with Grace for years without ever saying anything to her about it. I broke up with Cora to make sure she had the good life she deserved; Ryan kept himself in Grace's life and made himself miserable over every date she had. At least I planned to stay far away from Cora and spare myself the agony of watching her bloom without me.

Just then, Grace came out from the kitchen. "Did I hear my name? Come here, baby. Ryan must be tired of holding you so long. Hey there, Dixon." She brushed up against Ryan as she reached for Gabby.

Maybe no one else noticed, but Ryan's eyes followed Grace's every move as she took Gabby back to the kitchen.

"Hey, Grace." I nudged Ryan. "Looks like her date is with you tonight, buddy," I whispered in his direction.

"Shut up." Annoyed, Ryan shoved my arm and then followed Grace into the kitchen. "Last one in has to wash dishes!"

"Oh, boys!" Wilma laughed and gave me a smile. "Maybe someday that boy will get serious about telling her how he feels. Can't be soon enough for me. I'd love to say that cutie is my granddaughter."

Greg put his arm around his wife. "Now, Wilma, let the boy move at his own pace. Can't hurry love and all that..." With that, he swung her around and started to hum as he danced her into the kitchen.

I PUSHED THE FORK ACROSS the plate one last time. If food could heal a broken heart, Wilma's apple pie was the thing to do it. "That was delicious. Thanks, Mrs. Chatfield. Awesome as always."

"Thank you, Dixon. Now tell us more about your business. This centerpiece is so beautiful." Wilma pointed to the barn wood box centerpiece I'd given her when I arrived. "And lilacs are my favorite."

"Well, like I said before, I wanted to thank you both"—I looked over at Greg—"for letting me use the space in the warehouse, and thought this would be a small gesture to show my appreciation. I had some smaller wood pieces hanging around, and found those cool milk jugs at a tag sale. Just painted them up, put together the box, added some twine handles, and grabbed some lilacs from the bush at the corner of Jake's property line." Never figured Jake for a gardener, but he must have kept the bushes for some reason. Just my luck to be able to add them to the present for Ryan's parents.

"And what about this online stuff? I didn't know you knew anything about that." Greg grabbed the handle of his coffee mug and took a sip. "I leave all that up to a local guy to handle for me. I build houses, not websites!" He chuckled.

As if she hadn't been in the back of my mind all night, the thought of the website brought Cora right back front and center. An ache built in my heart. "Yeah, me neither, really. I had someone create it for me, and I can fumble my way through posting new projects for sale on the website. Social media's much easier for me to deal with. Getting lots of likes on the stuff I'm posting, and even have a few interior designers following me and sharing my stuff."

"I bet Cora is thrilled about that." Ryan glanced from Gabby on his lap to his mother. "You know, his girlfriend. She's the one who told him to show off his stuff online and sell it." He grinned at me. "The one who inspired him in the first place."

His singsong taunt cut deep. Of course, he didn't mean it like that. But he had no idea about the conversation I'd had with Mark, or that I'd broken it off with Cora.

"Yeah...well...ahem...actually...it's over. Done."

"What!"

"Oh, dear!"

"Sorry to hear that."

The responses around the table came rapid-fire, and then an awkward silence enveloped the room.

"Mommy, what's 'inspired' mean?" Gabby looked across the table at her mother.

Grace replied, "It means to encourage, honey. Dixon's friend told him he'd be good at his projects, and believed other people would like them, too." She nudged the last piece of pie onto her fork. "And she was right." She swallowed the bite. "So, what happened between you two, anyway? I thought everything was going really good."

"Well, everything was going well. Much better than I could have ever imagined. Cora is the full package...I mean, she's funny, smart, can joke around but not taken any of my sh—" I caught the wide eyes around the table. "I mean, she knows how to keep me in line."

"Like when Mommy gives me her Mommy look?" Gabby asked. "Like when I'm being cranky and dis-disspectful?"

"Disrespectful. Yes. Like that." I smiled at the little girl's words. How Grace ever disciplined such a sweetie—cranky or not—was beyond me. But Ryan's next words swiped the smile off my face.

"Dude, you need to get back together with her. Beg, if you have to. 'Cause I sure ain't going to put up with you mooning over losing her. That one week after you first met her was bad enough. Can't imagine what you'll be like without her around. So fix whatever stupid thing you did and get on your knees, and ask for forgiveness."

Grace nodded, and Gabby clapped.

"Yeah. My teacher always says to say sorry when I step on Marcie's toes, and she always forgives me. Just say you're sorry."

If it were only as simple as saying sorry to Cora. But it wasn't. I was sorry, but mostly because I wasn't the one who could make her dreams come true. Mark was the one with the power to do that. She'd have the life she'd always wanted: the big house, the chance to run the B&B, money, a family. That last one might have been a new dream of mine, but I couldn't see it happening with anyone but Cora.

"Dear, I am sure this is just a bump in the road for you two. Ryan has told us how much happier you are since you met Cora. Even George noticed you've been more helpful on the construction sites, asking more questions. And starting this new business is a step into your future. If you really care about her, you must do what you can to address the situation." Wilma put in her two cents. "Nothing is impossible where love is involved." She smiled over at her husband and held out her hand to him. "You'd be surprised at what can be forgiven. The heart wants what the heart wants, after all."

Greg kissed his wife's hand. "Yes, the heart is a powerhouse when it knows what it wants." He redirected his attention to me. "So, what is this insurmountable problem? Why did she break up with you?"

It was no surprise they'd all think she broke up with me. After all, even Ryan's first words to me about Cora was that she was out of my league, before he'd even known anything about her.

"Well, I was the one to call things off. It's the best for Cora, believe me. There's this guy her father wants her to marry, and he can give her everything I can't. The right life. The right house. The right career. The best of everything." I tapped the fork against the empty plate. "Compared to this guy, I'm the bottom of the barrel." I dropped the fork.

"That's not true, Dixon." This time, Grace laid her fork down before she stared straight at me. "You have plenty to offer. You're honest. A good friend." She looked over at Ryan before looking back to me. "Someone people can depend on. If you really love Cora, and she really loves you, no amount of money—or the lack of money—will change that. Happiness is with the people you love, not the balance in your bank account. I haven't met Cora, but Ryan's told me how nice she is."

I couldn't tell for sure, but there almost seemed to be a twinge of jealousy in her words. But Ryan's next ones had me paying attention.

"Cora wasn't just some notch on your bedpost, buddy. I've never seen you happier, or at ease with yourself. You told me once you could be your best self with Cora, and I've seen it happening. Doesn't matter about this other guy...you are the one for her, and she's the one for you. You need to talk to her and tell her what an idiot you were for pushing her away and into that dude's arms. Tell her you were momentarily out of your mind and you didn't mean it."

Greg put his hand on my arm. "Son, Ryan's right. If Cora is the one to bring out the best in you, even if you pushed her into this other man's direction with the best of intentions, it's likely you'll end up regretting it. Go fight for her. Show her—show yourself—that you've got it in you to be the man she needs. Do whatever it takes."

I began to rethink—not for the first time—my hasty decision and conversation with Cora. *Shit.* I'd truly fucked it up.

TWENTY-THREE

~Cora~

THE DAY OF THE FUNDRAISER, I stopped at my mother's grave. It had been a few months since my last visit, and with no job and no Dixon, time stretched out in a vast expanse...empty and looming.

I parked the car on the gravel driveway and walked through the dew-dropped grass. The towering headstone had an angel's wings outstretched, and the vases in front of the stone were filled with fresh flowers. My father may not have cared about my feelings, but his love for my mother was evident by the attention he paid to her final resting place. There was even a granite bench for visitors.

"Hi, Mom." I sat on the bench and stared at the dates on the gravestone. Only forty-five years old. Taken too soon. "I know it's been awhile since my last visit. Things are...well, complicated to say the least. I met someone." I sniffed. "But it looks like he's not ready to commit." I looked up to the fluffy white clouds. "I was, but he wasn't. At least, he wasn't ready to commit to me." I took a deep breath. "And Dad hasn't let up on his idea that I need to marry Mark. He's got my life planned out for me, and when I stood up for myself, he kicked me out of his life. Out of the business, too."

A cardinal's song stopped my words. I'd always heard that cardinals were your loved ones visiting you, and it was a comforting thought. I listened to the warbling fade as the bird found branches farther away to perch on.

I looked back at the stone. "And he's taken away Grandmother's inheritance. Well, sold the house. I suppose there's not much he can do about the money." I swung my feet, watching the blades of grass get pushed down and bounce back. "Mark bought it. Says I can have it back and have half my dream, if he gets what he wants."

A car drove slowly down one of the other paths, drawing my attention. I watched it stop a few rows over. A middle-aged couple got out of the car, walking directly to a grave with flowers. They stood for a few moments, with the wife placing the flowers down. When she stood, she leaned into her husband, and her husband's hands wrapped around her, holding her close. They were far enough away that I couldn't hear them, but I wasn't sure they were actually speaking, anyway.

I turned my attention back to my mother. "That's what I want, Mom. Someone to hold me in good times and bad. I thought that was Dixon. But, instead, he broke up with me. And with some lame excuse, that I was too good for him. As if he didn't deserve love from anyone." I stood. "But he does, and I do, too. I really wanted it to be from Dixon, Mom."

I FUSSED WITH THE EARRINGS.

Wendy let out a wolf whistle. "Damn, girl. You clean up nice." She hip-bumped me as she tried to get some counter space in the bathroom. "But you're still a bathroom hog. Scooch over."

"And where are you going tonight, huh? I know you passed on my free ticket to the fundraiser, but you never said what those 'other plans'. were. What's his name? And how long has this been going on?" I grinned at her in the mirror as I put on my mother's diamond necklace that matched the earrings and double-checked my lipstick.

"Never you mind. You don't know him. It's just casual right now." She took a dab of hair product and started scrunching, adding volume.

"Casual, huh? Well, you let me know if I need to stay out of your way tonight, in case your 'casual' turns into an overnight party." I hip-bumped her back.

Wendy looked at me, now with that damn no-fun Wendy look on her face. "I know it's going to be a difficult night, but at least you can leave right after the silent auction starts. And remember, even if your father goes through with that sale, you still have options. You can always use your savings to buy a property and start your B&B there instead."

"Yeah, maybe. But I'm not going to think about that tonight. Tonight is about the charity, and the work I can support there." I fidgeted with the ring on my right hand. "If my mother were still alive, things would be different. But she's not, and there's not anything I can do about that. If there's any way I can make things different for some other daughter or son, that's what I'm going to do. Everything else takes a backseat tonight."

Wendy hugged me. "I know she'd be proud of the woman you've become. And she'd want you to plan your own future, not just go with whatever your father or Mark think you should do."

I sniffed. "Thanks." I pulled back from her, a sad smile on my face. "I do wish she was here for me to talk to. I just don't know what to do about Dixon. I can't believe he broke up with me over the phone, without giving us a chance to talk and work things out."

I STOOD AT THE DOORWAY of the ballroom. It was the last place I wanted to be, but I couldn't let my despair over Dixon overshadow how important this night was for the charity. My heart ached, but I put on a brave face. As long as I concentrated on the good I'd be doing here, I could stave off my pain...for a little bit, at least.

"Good evening, Cora." Mark's snobby tone invaded my private bubble. "Care to join me at the table? I believe your father is already there, waiting for us."

I turned around. Mark was about three feet away from me, his handsome, smug face radiating superiority. A custom tux. The stereotypical lawyer attitude. But he was a pathetic man who wanted control, and who had a sad future in front of him...one without me in it. No matter what Dixon said, Mark wasn't the one to make any of my dreams come true. No, that was Dixon.

Even if Dixon pushed me away, it still wouldn't make Mark part of my life. All I had was anger, dismay, the bitterness of betrayal, and an urgent need to get away from him.

"I need to take care of some silent auction details. I'll be at the table later, I'm sure."

I headed over to the tables with the displays and clipboards. There wasn't much for me to do but I double-checked the listings, making sure they were all on the table and nothing was missing. Several of the sheets already had bids past the suggested bid, including one for a package that offered the use of a catamaran for a week in the Bahamas. The starting bid was listed at twenty-five grand.

"I see we've started to get some bids placed." Lila's shrill tone was followed by a sniff. "I certainly hope we do better than last year. I'm not convinced the items offered are quite as...interesting and exciting as we've had in the past."

The past, as when my mother was alive and ran fundraisers like this one.

"Lila," I muttered in acknowledgment. I had turned to face her and her disapproving look. Her face, a layer of plastic covered in impeccable makeup, stayed flat. I'd never seen a smile there, and I guess she couldn't frown either.

Lila looked me up and down, as if a general inspecting the troops...and finding them lacking. "Now, I need you to—"

I had enough of this woman...and her son. I crossed my arms and sighed. "Lila, I am done with my commitments to the event. If you need help with some details or grunt work, I suggest you find the hotel staff and you can lord it over someone else. I am here to enjoy the evening, and that does not include any more time in your company."

After turning away from her and her over-Botoxed face, I went in search of a drink. If I couldn't have Dixon at my side, I'd at least have liquid courage...or drown my sorrows in my wine.

A DRINK IN HAND, I found our dinner table. Technically, my father had purchased the table for him, me, Wendy as my guest, Mark, both his parents, and two business associates and their guests. The ten-person table was large, but not large enough to ignore my father when I sat, or to miss Mark's scowl.

"Hello, Dad." I tried to be pleasant, to not dwell on our last conversation. But the tiny ball of dread had knotted itself into a hard lump. Without Dixon next to me, there was no buffer between me and the two men most responsible for my problems.

My father stood from his chair. "Cora. Good evening. I had expected you and Mark to arrive together. I hope, at least, that you are fulfilling your duties for the silent auction. I need to speak with Lila." After his gruff words, he deliberately...and quite rudely...left the table.

The other people at the table pretended they hadn't seen or heard the awkward scene. I had a vague idea of who they were, but I certainly couldn't expect much sympathy from people who had business relationships with my father.

"Good evening. I don't think we've met before." A stunning woman in a jade-green dress stood and held out her hand. "I'm Emma Sutton. This is my husband, Robert."

I took her hand. "Nice to meet you, Mrs. Sutton. I'm—"

"Oh no, call me Emma. I insist." She smiled at me. "I know that you are Cora Stetson. Robert," she looked at her husband, who had stayed seated but riveted to his wife, "you have met Cora before, haven't you, dear?"

"Emma, I'm sure I've met Cora at some company board event that Warren insisted I be at. But now that I have you in my life, I can't remember any woman but you." His teasing tone and smile captured Emma's attention.

"You big teddy bear." Emma turned back to me. "It is wonderful to meet you. Please, sit with us. I don't know anyone at the table besides Robert, and I think you and I will get along splendidly."

Robert pointed to the empty set of chairs next to him and his wife. "I think the first course is coming soon and then we can get this rubber-chicken dinner done with and get to the fun part of the evening." He gave his wife a look of adoration and a wink.

"Oh, stop, you scoundrel." She playfully hit him with her cloth napkin. "This fundraiser is important. I can't even imagine how I'd be able to go on if someone invaded our home and hurt anyone in our family. Not just physically, but the mental anguish that must cause..." Emma's words faded away as she looked around the table.

My expression must have signaled to her I was one of those kinds of survivors. I took a shaky breath in and focused on breathing out slowly.

"Oh my, I've really stepped in it, haven't I?" Emma looked distressed. "I am so sorry, Cora. I just never...well, again, I apologize." She reached for her wineglass and took a nervous sip. "Sometimes"—her husband snorted—"I get carried away and speak without thinking."

I had dropped into my chair by then. I reached for my wine with my free hand, and it shook as I took a sip.

"It's fine, Emma. I was just momentarily taken back to that time. I miss my mother...I can't believe how long it's been since she was ripped from our lives. That's why participating in events like these, that raise awareness and money for families dealing with this tragedy, is so important. It's the least I can do to keep my mother's memory alive and find some purpose in her death. She would have been the one to start this kind of charity...that's how much she cared for the hurting world we live in. I can only hope my small contribution makes a difference for some other family."

A bit more composed now, I sat back in my chair. The conversation at the table picked up, with our half of the table talking about local events and the other half talking among themselves. Even with the uptick in engaging conversation, only half my brain paid attention. The other half—and all my heart—longed for Dixon's warmth and strength in the empty chair next to me.

I EXCUSED MYSELF TO head to the ladies' room. Emma stood with me, declaring she'd come with me and bring back another round of drinks for us. We headed out of the ballroom and found the powder room.

The room seemed deserted, with no one at the mirrors or the sinks. The guest settee and side chairs were also empty. After we each used a restroom stall, we were at the sinks when a caterwauling sound got louder and louder, until the ladies' room door opened and two women came in. One looked angry, her face in a scowl and her words heated. The other was sobbing, head down; she couldn't have been more than seventeen years old. But most noticeable was her very pregnant belly that kept a distance between the two women.

"I told you that he was no good for you. That all his promises were bullsh—" The older of the two stopped when she caught Emma and me staring at the spectacle they were creating. "What are you—"

Recognition dawned on her face, and probably on mine as well. It was the woman I'd seen at the hotel that night I first brought Dixon to my apartment.

"See! Here she is! This is what that asshole wants...a lady who belongs in his world!"

The words not only made the younger woman cry harder, but they seemed to cut me in half. What had I done to deserve any animosity from either of these two?

"I'm sorry. But do I know you? I mean, I remember meeting you in the hotel lobby when you were talking to Mark, but we never were introduced or anything." I tried to be civil, but my confusion had to be clear to this woman.

"Marcy! Oh my God! When did you talk to Mark? I told you to mind your own business!" The younger woman had stopped crying long enough to berate the other woman. She looked at me and burst into tears again.

"Tina, I told you I wasn't going to let him get away with ignoring you anymore. I went to the hotel and found him. Just to talk to him, I swear. And then"—Marcy pinned me with a glare—"she showed up, and Mark told me to leave. I know he's been seeing her. I heard about their engagement, even."

At those words, Tina let out another gush of tears. "Engaged! He never said he was engaged!" She wiped her nose with a tissue from the counter and looked closer at me.

"I am not engaged to Mark. And I'm not dating him either. We went out a few times about a year ago, but that's it." Horrified that Mark had apparently been involved with someone so young, it was all I could do to make it clear I had nothing to do with him or any of his personal decisions. "And I can only imagine what he said to you, Marcy, but I swear he never said anything to me about you or..."

"My sister, Tina. That's who your boyfriend knocked up and then abandoned."

"Hey! Not my boyfriend." I took a deep breath. "But I agree that he's an asshole. Well, worse than an asshole. But that's just my opinion." I backed down at Tina's indignant look. How she could stick up for Mark after what he'd apparently done, I had no idea. But—not my circus, not my monkey.

"See, Marcy? I told you he loved me. He'll take care of me and the baby." Tina looked back up at her sister, pleading in her tone.

"Then what was that all about in the lobby just now? He told us to leave, in no uncertain terms, and not to call or email him when the baby was born. That hardly seems like someone who's going to take care of you, Tina!" Marcy huffed out an exasperated breath and put her fisted hands on her hips.

Emma, who'd been quiet throughout the entire bizarre exchange, leaned toward me and stage-whispered, "Looks like you dodged a bullet with that prizewinner, Cora. I think it's time we let these two have some privacy and finish their conversation without either of us as spectators." She grabbed my arm and pulled me out of the room.

"Don't talk about Mark like—"

"Go ahead and leave—"

The heated protest and the angry retort were cut off after Emma shut the restroom door.

"Wow. I never expected this kind of entertainment tonight. Almost worth the price of admission." Emma looked at me, trying to hold back a laugh. "I know I shouldn't laugh—that poor girl has quite the reality check coming—but it's not every night out that my bathroom encounters include pregnant teenagers and protective older sisters."

The thought of Mark and that young girl as parents was comical, but more on the side of tragedy. With one overly emotional parent and one parent who couldn't feel a thing, that baby needed a miracle.

WHEN WE GOT BACK TO the table, my father had come back and sat next to Mark. Their heads bent together, and I tried not to be distracted by their whispered conversation.

When I looked across the table, Mark's smirk and my father's disapproval were clear for everyone at the table to see. Even though I'd just sat down, I was ready to get up and leave. I'd done my duty for the silent auction; I didn't have to suffer through any more grief or pointed comments from either Mark or my father.

I turned to Emma and Robert. "It was very nice meeting you. I'm afraid I need to cut my evening short." I stood. As I shook hands with the kind couple, a voice from across the table stopped the action.

"Cora, so sad to see you leave so early. I haven't even had time to catch you up on my latest business deal." Mark raised his glass as if he were toasting me, not trying to pick a fight.

But I could see right through his smarmy attitude. And now that I knew about Tina, I couldn't get away from him quick enough. "Mark, I'd say it's been nice to see you, but it hasn't. And I have no interest in any of your business deals. I don't have to suffer through hearing about your supposed business acumen and star power anymore. We're not together...we're not even friends, because I could never be friends with someone as self-involved as you."

I stepped away from the table, more than ready to get out of there. All I wanted was to go home, get into my jammies, and eat a carton of ice cream to swallow down the misery welling up at Dixon's absence.

"Well, that's too bad, Cora." Mark's voice rose as I distanced myself from the table. "Because I've just bought myself a nice little place in the country...got quite the deal from your father."

The words reached my brain, and despite my best intentions, I stopped while I processed what Mark meant. *A place in the country...a deal from my father?* It could only mean one thing. He'd made good on his earlier threat.

I whirled around. "What? Did you...do you mean..."

The smirk on his face confirmed that this asshole had bought my grandmother's estate from my father.

"That's right, Cora. I hadn't heard from you this week, so I considered your silence as your answer. I now own that precious little mansion that was your grandmother's. Seems your father was motivated to sell...at quite a discount, since we are such good friends. If you have any hope of ever living there again, you'll reconsider my marriage proposal." He walked closer with each word, the smirk firmly on his face. "Otherwise, I might think about some redevelopment of the property. Knock all the buildings down and build some modern house, more suited to my tastes."

He arrived within a foot of where I was rooted to the spot. His eyes gleamed with the meanness, the pettiness, and the joy he got from his cruel words.

"Don't you dare threaten me. You have no power over me and my choices. You are a sad, desperate, controlling asshole. If the only way you can get someone to marry you is blackmail, it doesn't say much for you...or maybe it says everything. That you would hold my dreams hostage to get what you want...I'd say it's unbelievable, but unfortunately, I can believe you'd stoop so low. After all, you're the one who got a teenager pregnant and left her on her own."

Adrenaline pumped through my heart, and I continued to unload on Mark.

"I'm not sure who to pity more, Mark...that young girl or your baby." I glanced behind Mark; my father was watching the spectacle. "You and my father must be cut from the same cloth. Neither of you know how to have a real relationship, how to love another person. I've been nothing but a piece of property to either of you, something to move around your chessboard and sacrifice as a pawn. Well, no more."

Mark stepped closer at my words, surprising me with his guttural tone. "Yes. I will give you more." He bent his head and mashed his lips against mine. He held my arms at my sides, grabbing tight enough that I expected to see a bruise there the next day.

For what seemed like forever, I struggled against his hold until my hand found its way across his face. "What the hell, Mark! Get off me! You have no right to kiss me!"

I stepped back, away from his grasp and in the direction of the ballroom door. I looked to my father again. "First thing in the morning, I will consult with an attorney to handle my upcoming inheritance. An attorney of my choosing. It's less than a year away until Grandmother's will gives me what she intended—even if you have betrayed the spirit of the gift by selling her home, which you know she wanted me to have—but all communication between us will be through attorneys. I have no interest in hearing directly from either of you from this moment on. If you have something to say, you can say it to my lawyer. And Mark, if you ever touch me again, I'll be pressing charges against you!"

I stopped for a moment. The surrounding tables were now watching with interest. "I apologize for interrupting your evening, ladies and gentlemen. But I am leaving now, and I hope you enjoy the rest of the event. There's a great MC tonight for the silent auction prizes, and the dinner has been prepared by a five-Michelin star chef. Please, enjoy and continue your support of SHIELD's programs."

Now that I'd declared my father and Mark to be out of my life officially, the adrenaline was wearing off and my legs shook. All I had to do was turn and walk out of the room with my head held high, before I totally lost it and broke down.

When I did turn, my heart sunk as Dixon's figure retreated from the ballroom.

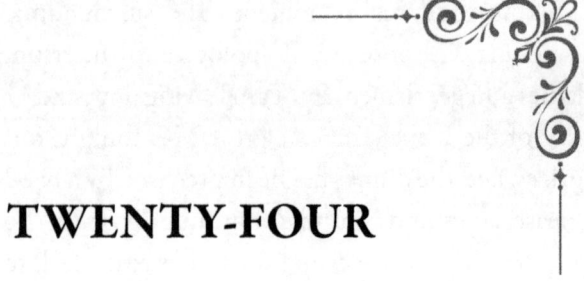

TWENTY-FOUR

~Dixon~

I'D TAKEN WILMA AND Greg's advice to heart. Looking at them and the life they'd built made me want the same kind of thing, with Cora at my side. No matter what life had thrown at them, they'd made it through together. They'd built a family; they'd built a relationship. There was nothing I wanted more than to have Cora in my life, even if she was too good for a sorry son of a bitch like me.

Determined to make things right—and ready to grovel if needed—I had left the Chatfields' house the night of the fundraiser, after raiding Ryan's closet for a suit that would get me through the door at the event. I gripped the steering wheel as I sped through town to get to the downtown hotel. Nerves had my stomach in knots and my mind was a wheel of chaos as I thought about what I could say that would let Cora know what an idiot I'd been by pushing her away. My heart raced when I imagined what she'd say in response.

Pure nervous energy propelled me from the parking garage into the hotel lobby. The ballroom wasn't hard to find...well-dressed couples lingered just outside the doorway, where there was a check-in desk. Shit, I hadn't even thought about how to pay for a ticket, just that I had to be there to find Cora and make things right. Maybe I couldn't even buy a ticket at the door...maybe I was shit out of luck once again.

A hand landed on my shoulder, startling me. I whirled around, hoping to see Cora.

"Hello, stranger. Thinking of crashing the party?" Wendy smiled at me knowingly. "Maybe I can help with that. Follow me." Then she turned on her heels and walked away from the ballroom doors.

I stood there like an idiot until my brain kicked in. If Wendy had a way for me to get in, I'd take it. I gained on her, and soon I was next to her in the hallway. "Thanks, Wendy. Hey, how did you know what I was going to do? And why weren't you in the ballroom yourself?" I took in her outfit and thought she looked as if she fit in with the high-class crowd. She looked great, but my heart and mind was filled with Cora...no one else. "Aren't you supposed to be in there with Cora?" My heart flexed at the idea of Cora in there without me, without her best friend...in the crosshairs of her father and Mark.

Wendy looked back at me. "I had a date tonight, so I skipped the dinner at the fundraiser. But I stopped by to check in on Cora. She's not doing great after you dumped her, you know. I shouldn't even be talking to you for that stupid stunt. You didn't even have the guts to break up with her in person...you did it on the *phone*. She's had to deal with Mark and her father on her own, without your support. I mean, she's strong, but you should have been there, Dixon. She needed you." She stopped abruptly. "But you even being here gives me hope. I do have reason for hope, right, Dixon? You've realized the error of your ways and are coming here to beg forgiveness?"

"Yes. Beg, grovel, plead...whatever it takes for Cora to take me back. I don't care. I made a mistake in letting Mark get into my head—"

"Wait. What? What does Mark have to do with you dumping Cora?" Wendy's eyes flashed.

"Well, he called and basically told me that I wasn't good enough for Cora. Trust me, it wasn't anything I haven't said to myself over and over already. Hearing it from him, though...it just hit me harder. And he talked about what he could give her...the life she could have. I couldn't stand in the way of her having that security, that dream of her bed-and-breakfast. I don't have anything to offer her." Saying the words to Wendy had me second-guessing my plan to get Cora back, the reality of what she'd be giving up for me once again staring me in the face.

"Hey, snap out of it! Cora doesn't care about those things. Well, she wants her bed-and-breakfast, sure, but not with a price tag of marrying that ass. She wants your heart, not your bank account. Hell, she's loaded, remember? She doesn't need you for a business loan. She needs you to light her up from the inside, and trust me, only you can do that. I've never seen her so happy and content as she's been with you." Wendy put a hand on my arm. "So get over any last-minute nerves, and let's get you in that room to make my bestie's dreams come true."

I straightened up. Time to make things right.

WENDY SNUCK ME IN THROUGH the employee access hallway. We stood at the back of the ballroom, next to the swinging doors. The crowd was thick, and it was difficult to see any one person in particular between people mingling on the dancefloor and the tables scattered around the space.

"I'm going to walk along the wall here and see if I can find Cora. Thanks, Wendy, for getting me in here."

Wendy smiled. "Go get her, Dixon. I wish you both nothing but happiness." She gave me a hug. "I'm off to go find my date. I told him I needed a few minutes to freshen up before I could leave. Maybe I'll find my own happy-ever-after, too!" She turned and headed back through the kitchen area.

Now, all I had to do was find Cora in this crowd of thousands. Okay, maybe that was an exaggeration, but it seemed overwhelming. I walked toward the ballroom door, keeping close to the wall to observe everyone within sight. I had no idea what Cora was wearing, but I knew she'd be a knockout in anything.

And then, once I got almost all the way to the ballroom doors, there she was, her back to me. She was at a table, standing in front of Mark.

And then she was kissing him.

I let out a shaky breath. My heart broke into pieces as my brain tried to process what I was seeing. I turned and left; there was nothing here for me now. Somehow, my feet kept my body moving as my mind was stuck in the living hell of seeing that kiss.

A tingle landed on my arm, startling me. It was familiar but impossible. Cora was in Mark's arms, not out here with me.

I looked at the hand resting against the fabric of the borrowed suit. I followed that up, up an arm, to the shoulder, to the face of my dreams. "Cora," I choked out.

"Dixon! Where are you going? What are you doing here? I...I am so glad you are here!" Cora flung herself at me and wrapped her arms around me.

I pulled out of her embrace. "Don't, Cora. I saw you... I saw you and Mark back there. I made a mistake in coming here." I stepped back. "If he's what you want...I want you to be happy, Cora, so be happy."

"What? No, Dixon! I wasn't...well, yes, there was a kiss, but it was Mark kissing me, not me kissing him! I told him that I wanted nothing to do with him or my father. Dixon, it was horrible. My father sold the house to Mark, just to get me to marry him." She gulped. "I can't believe he'd do that. But Dixon, it doesn't matter. None of it matters if I don't have you." Cora reached out to tangle her fingers with mine.

"Cora, are you sure? I mean, there's so much I can't give you. I don't have money. I don't have a good reputation, a name to be proud of. I don't own anything but the beat-up truck I drive." I glanced at the floor before looking back up into those beautiful green eyes. What I saw there kick-started my heart.

"Dixon, you don't have to give me anything but your love. That's all I need. You own my heart. I love you." With that, Cora leaned into me and pressed her lips to mine. "All I've ever wanted was someone who saw me, supported me." She smiled wickedly. "Someone who made me shake in anticipation of our next kiss."

That was all I needed. At that glorious sensation, any doubts were obliterated by my need for Cora, for the love I had for her and—somehow—she had for me. I poured all my love for this amazing woman into my answering kiss, and thanked my lucky stars she was in my life.

"God, Cora. I can't believe you'd choose me, but damn if I'm going to let you back out now. I'm yours, and you are mine. I'm never letting go of you, or letting anyone else try to pull you away. Now and forever, gumdrop...now and forever."

TWENTY-FIVE

~Dixon~

CORA'S HAIR FANNED out on the pillow, and her breath was even as she slept. I couldn't help myself; I couldn't stop watching her in these early morning hours. It was something I couldn't imagine ever getting tired of. So much better than my dreams all those months ago when I envisioned her in the hayloft. Because this was real.

"Ummm. Hey." Cora's eyes fluttered open, avoiding looking at the blowing curtains and the sunlight they no longer hid. She stretched like a cat, twisting toward me. The sheet pulled down, revealing a perfect breast.

I was only a man; there were some things I had no power to resist, and the sight of a naked Cora was one of them. As I bent to take the pebbled nipple in my mouth and give it a little bite, Cora giggled.

"Well, I guess I should say good morning to you, too, handsome." She sighed as my tongue twirled around the left areola and then found its way to the right one, with another light bite on that nipple. Cora reached under the sheet and found my hard cock.

A very good morning, for sure. And it'd been that way for the last few weeks, when we'd moved in together.

The day after the charity dinner, Cora made good on her promise and hired an attorney to handle her inheritance and any interaction between her and her father...and Mark gave up on harassing her into

239

marriage, or any other kind of business arrangement. It hurt her terribly to lose her relationship with her father; without her mother, things between them had broken and the only way she could be her own person was to forcefully cut off contact.

There'd been a few weeks where she'd been quiet about it, but she seemed happier now. More sure. More content. More...everything.

And I couldn't help but revel in being with her all the time. The astonishing thought to move in together was all hers, though. And damn if she didn't surprise me with her entire proposal. One day, we'd been having lunch on one of the main drags in town, and she'd stopped at this rundown storefront.

"You know, this would be a great location for just the right kind of store." She turned and looked at me. "A store where people can find amazing furniture, household items, refurnished and reclaimed from house renovations or flea markets...you know, taking what people think isn't worth anything and making it beautiful and useful and important again." Her wide grin was infectious.

I smiled. "Oh yeah? But you've always been beautiful...and important." I dropped a kiss on her lips. "But there's no way I could afford to rent this place, much less make a living at making reclaimed furniture and house stuff."

"Oh, I don't know about that. I mean, you've had some sales already. And with the website we've been working on and with Jefferson Furniture's ongoing requests, a space for creating the pieces and a space for showcasing them..." She turned and looked at the storefront window, designed to hold large pieces. "It could be exactly what you need to succeed. And, there's even an apartment above the store, where we could live."

In shock, I looked up at the second floor. Sure enough, there were a set of windows up there. It wasn't a closed-off space for storage or something. "You sure that isn't office space?" The idea of owning my own business and moving in with Cora was overwhelming, but one I was cautiously warming up to. If I wasn't careful, my excitement would make me miss some detail that would pull the rug out from under me.

"Well, let's go see." Cora dangled a set of keys in her hand. "I haven't signed anything, so it's fine if you say no. But the real estate agent said we could check it out." She moved toward the storefront door and opened it up.

The storefront windows were dirty but still let in plenty of light. The floorboards were wide...possibly even chestnut. A counter against one wall; shelving behind that. Open floor space. A door at the back led to an office and another empty space.

We walked around, both silent as we assessed the building.

"It'd be a cool store. But I don't know, Cora. I mean, how would I afford this?" I lightly moved my fingers over the countertop, my mind already racing with how to set up the shop windows and how to display the other projects I'd been working on. *And to have my own workspace, with my own tools...*

"You wouldn't. We would. Dixon, I want us to be partners. Equal partners." She stopped, obviously seeing the objection in my eyes. "Yes, equal. I might have the money, but you have the talent. I couldn't do this without you. I wouldn't want to do this without you." Cora grabbed my hand and held it to her chest. "I love you, Dixon, and I want to build a future with you. It's not the future I had planned"—her voice wobbled—"but it's the one I want now. The one with you and me, working and living and being together." She let out a breath.

How the hell could I ever say no to her? Why the hell would I want to? "Well, we better check out that upstairs apartment and make sure there's enough space for the huge bed we're gonna need so I can make love to you properly every night and every morning."

--- ⚬ ---

~Cora~

WAKING UP WITH DIXON every morning was the best feeling
I'd ever had. Every day, my partner, my lover, and my rock was there.
With my hand on his hardening cock, my smile grew wider and my
mind woke up more, eager to start the day with Dixon's love.

I pushed him onto his back and shifted so that I straddled his
body. He skimmed his hands up from my waist and came to a rest
at my breasts, holding them and teasing the nipples. A rush of heat
flushed through me, along with a sense of power. Anything was
possible with Dixon, and there was nothing we couldn't do together.
I leaned forward to kiss him, positioning my body to slide down his
hard length.

"Oh, Cora. Now that's what I call a good morning."

His whispered words in my ear rumbled from deep in his chest
as we moved in a rhythm, at first a slow, languorous motion that
turned into a faster pace as we came closer and closer to climax. My
hair, a curtain around us, created another barrier from the real world.
It was just me and Dixon—cocooned together, joined together...just
together.

Spent from our lovemaking, I snuggled into Dixon's side, my
head on his chest. The thump-thump went from a rapid rate to a
slower one as we both caught our breaths. My mind wandered over
the past months, thinking about all the things that had to happen to
get me—to get us—to this place.

"I can hear you thinking over there, Cora." Dixon moved back
to his side, his hand tracing the outline of my face. "Any more dirty
thoughts going on in that pretty head of yours?" He dropped a kiss
on my nose. "If so, I am totally, one hundred percent behind those
thoughts. Just need some water to re-hydrate and we can go for
round two." His sexy grin grew wider, and he left the bed to grab a
bottled water from the fridge.

Spencer, the tabby from our visit to my grandmother's home, wound around Dixon's legs as he walked across the large space. Tracy, the calico with the broken paw, had fully recovered and joined her buddy, meowing at Dixon for some kibble. Both cats had adapted well to their—our—new living arrangements.

The open floor plan of the second-story space was intended for storage more than a real apartment, but there had been a bathroom and kitchenette space that we'd enlarged. We kept most of the space open, with an open doorway from the bedroom into the living spaces. I had plans to put some gauzy curtains up as some kind of divider, but with just the two of us here, there wasn't a big need for closed-off rooms. And it provided a great view of my naked boyfriend as he walked back to the bed.

"Well, what I was really thinking of"—I slapped his arm slightly before taking the bottle from his hand and having a sip—"was how we ended up here. From that night at Jake's, where you rescued me and Wendy from that jerk at the bar, and then carried me to your place after my ankle twisted."

"I've never been happier to see a broken shoe in all my life." Dixon smiled. "I mean, it was the perfect excuse to get you in my arms. And now, I never want to let go. Cora, I—"

The sound of a dying goat bleating stopped his next words. At least, that was what it sounded like.

I couldn't quite figure out what it was until it sounded again. "I think that might be the backdoor delivery call button. We never tested it out to see if it works, did we? And up here on the second floor, it might not sound as loud as it does downstairs." I had a surprise coming today, and the delivery guy must have gone to the back. Finding the bathrobe up on the wall hook, I shrugged it on while trying to get to the back window before Dixon did.

A delivery truck was parked in the back lot, with one burly guy leaning against the tailgate and another at the door.

"So, Dixon, I have a surprise for you." I turned, practically slamming into that delicious wall of muscle.

"A surprise, huh? At eight in the morning? It's a good thing we got our morning started early, then." He winked and teased me with a light kiss. "So, what is this surprise? And do I have to get dressed for it?"

I pushed him back playfully. "Yes, you need to get dressed for it. We both do." I turned back to the window, pushed it up, and yelled to the delivery guy. "We'll be down in a few minutes."

A returned "Okay" floated up before I shut the window.

I raced around to get dressed, with Dixon shaking his head at me as he pulled on his work clothes of faded jeans, T-shirt, and work boots.

As he finished lacing up his boots, he stood and grabbed me into a hug. "You know, I don't need any surprises. You're the best thing I've ever gotten. You're all I need."

I kissed him, our tongues dancing that now familiar but still passionate dance together. "But you do need this. Trust me." I grabbed his hand and dragged him down the stairs to the back door. "And I can't wait to see it, myself." I smiled back at him as he looked at the lettering on the truck.

"Ma'am. Where'd you want it?" The burly guy had opened up the back of the truck, and pulled the store sign to the opening.

"Well, it's for over the front door. You guys are supposed to do the install, too, right?" At the other man's nod, I continued, "Let's pull it out here and make sure everything is right. Then you can bring it through the store and out the front door. The space should be all set for you to hang it."

I could sense Dixon's curiosity and dawning realization what his surprise was.

"The store sign? That's my surprise?"

He was silent a moment as the guys pulled out the wooden sign. "Reclaimed Life" was in a bold font—rustic but still easy to read—with the logo I'd spent hours on with the designer. The line drawing had intertwining squares and rectangles of varying sizes, representing houses of different sizes and types. Underneath was "EST. 2021" in the same font, but a smaller size.

It was exactly how I'd pictured and approved on the contract. I'd kept the logo and sign a surprise for Dixon, although we'd talked about what to call the store. The name was perfect, as far as I was concerned.

With Dixon, I'd reclaimed my life. No longer did my life include people or things that I didn't love...or who didn't love me for myself. Some of my dreams had changed, but the vision of the future I had far outweighed any feelings of loss.

Dixon was still silent, looking at the sign. He gazed up at me, his expression serious. "I'll be right back." He abruptly turned around and headed back into the storeroom.

Confused, I stood there, looking from the back door to the sign, and then the delivery guys waiting for direction. "Um...I guess he needs a minute. Hey, there's a coffee shop down the street. Why don't you guys grab a coffee—on me—while he's doing...well, whatever he's doing." I fished out a twenty from my pocket and offered it to the guys.

"Sure. We'll be back in ten." The bigger of the two took the money, and they walked in the direction I had pointed to.

"Sorry about that."

Dixon's voice startled me, and I turned back to him. "No problem. I mean, there's no problem, is there? I know I kept this as a surprise, but I thought you'd be excited about it. You like it, right? Did you want to change the name? I mean, we can change anything you want...it's not a big deal to re-do the name or change the font or—"

My rambling was cut short when Dixon reached out and grabbed my hand.

"No, it's perfect. You're perfect. And I had to get my surprise for you."

I was more confused now. He'd come back, but he wasn't carrying anything. He looked exactly the way he did five minutes ago, not even with a phone in his hand now or something.

"Cora, I can't believe how lucky I got when I saw you that night at Jake's. From the moment I saw you, I couldn't stay away. I was drawn to you. You are beautiful, inside and out. You have courage to make new dreams, not be stuck in the past but looking forward to a future. A new life...a reclaimed life. And that's given me the courage and strength to do the same." Dixon dropped to one knee, a hand going into his front pocket.

"Will you marry me? Will you claim a new life with me, with all the joy and happiness that I promise to bring to you?" He pulled out a ring and reached for my left hand.

"I...ohmygod...I...yes! A million times, yes!" I laughed and sobbed my way through my words and reached down to bring him to me. I pressed against his body, tangling my hands in his hair while I kissed him.

Dixon pulled back, his sexy smile firmly in place. "Well, let me put this ring on it, gum drop. 'Cause damn if I don't want everyone to know you're mine and I'm yours." He laughed as he fit the ring onto my finger.

"Oh, Dixon. It's beautiful." I moved my hand to let the jade and diamonds shimmer in the morning sun. "I can't wait to claim our life together."

We held each other, in that back parking lot, with the promise of our new, reclaimed lives right in front of us, ready for the taking.

EPILOGUE

~Cora~

THREE DAYS AFTER DIXON proposed, we invited Ryan and Wendy to the store to toast our new store and our new venture...and to share the news of our engagement. After some good-natured ribbing from Ryan and a squeal from Wendy, Dixon popped the cork on the champagne. I had the glasses ready, but the sparkle of my engagement ring captured all my attention.

I could hardly believe we were engaged. I'd never been happier.

The knock at the door interrupted our celebration.

"I'll get it." Dixon, bottle in hand, went to the front door. When he opened it, I could make out the man in front of him, the fedora on his head the easiest feature to see. "Can I help you?"

"Yes. I am looking for a Cora Stetson. Is this the correct address?" The deep timbre echoed into the mostly empty storefront.

We'd been getting Dixon's pieces ready to move from the warehouse to the workspace here, and had shelving ready for some of his smaller pieces that were completed. Other than that, the space was bare. We didn't have any chairs or a table for our celebration; we were all gathered at the glass display case.

The door creaked as Dixon opened it wider to let the man in. The crisp suit and tie gave away his profession; if nothing else, I knew when a lawyer was in front of me. They seemed to have a know-it-all attitude that others could only envy.

"Yes, I'm Cora Stetson. How can I help you, Mr. ...?" I held my hand out and waited to hear what this lawyer wanted. In my limited experience, a lawyer wasn't a welcome addition to any celebration.

"Mr. Derek. Of Derek, Westing, and Lorde. We represented your grandmother." His hand enveloped mine and gave a firm shake. "I believe we have some business pending to take care of her estate and your inheritance." He looked between me and Dixon, and then glanced at Wendy and Ryan farther back in the room. "Is there somewhere we can speak in private?"

Confused, I shook my head. "I don't think there's anything else to discuss. My father was the trustee, and he sold the property in Atwater Falls."

"Well, that's not entirely accurate. Yes, your father was the trustee, but the trust was an irrevocable trust. He was not authorized to sell any property. According to the terms... I am sorry, but this is a personal matter and we should speak privately."

"No, anything you want to say to me, you can say in front of my fiancé." The giddiness at saying that word for the first time was tempered by my continued confusion. "So let's hear it. My father wasn't supposed to be able to sell that property?"

"Very well. No. He was not to sell any property, of any type, that was held in trust for you from your grandmother. The irrevocable trust was quite clear that you were to take possession of the property in Atwater Falls, as well as your grandmother's shares in the hotel company. You are now majority shareholder in Stetson Suites." Mr. Derek stood still, watching as his words sunk into my head. A small smile and a twinkle in his eyes grew as I started to understand.

"You mean...you mean I own not only the mansion but seventy-five percent of the hotel chain?" I slumped against the counter as that reality slammed into me. "But I never heard about that...it was always about the house, never any of the business." A sudden thought popped into my head. "I thought the company was represented by Franklin, Franklin, and Langdon. My father hired them once he was the CEO..."

The man cleared his throat. "Yes. Your father did retain other counsel once he was CEO. But as this was a personal matter, not a corporate one, our firm represented your grandmother's interests, not the business's. And her will was quite clear and ironclad that the property was to be yours, along with the stocks in the business." He took the hat off, running his hands over the rim. "Ms. Stetson, your grandmother loved her son, but she felt...well, I probably shouldn't say this, but she felt his passion for hospitality was a bit lacking. It was something she remarked upon during our meetings to finalize her estate. She saw within you that spark she felt as she led the company."

Dixon grasped my hand. "She knew your heart...knew how much you truly loved the hospitality business. I know you were willing to give up your dream to be a part of my business, build it up and see it grow, but this is what you were meant to do. It's in your blood...it's in your soul."

I turned to face him. "But we've just started to build this. I don't want to abandon you and your dreams. We are building our life together." I looked at the new ring on my finger. "Our future together...what would that be like if I went back to the hotel? Or started the bed-and-breakfast?"

His strong hands came around my waist. "You can be involved as much or as little as you want, I'd guess. Your father could still run things. Or you could be in full charge and bring the hotel up to the standards you've been pushing for. I'd love for your input on building my business, but you have to follow your heart, too. I'd never make you choose between one job or the other."

I stared at him, still in shock. I could make the cottage a home or turn it into my bed-and-breakfast. I could run Stetson Suites hands-on. I could have a hands-off policy; my father could continue to run it and I could focus on Dixon's—our—business. With all the decisions available, I wasn't sure what I really wanted now. It had been so easy before, when my dream seemed so clear.

My father. That was going to be a difficult conversation. And one I wasn't sure I was ready for. He must have known the full extent of his mother's will, and yet he hadn't shared the details with me. And he'd gone beyond his authority in selling the house. If the sale wasn't legal, how much of a headache would it be to untangle that? As a small bonus, I'd have the pleasure of kicking Mark out. He better not have done anything irreparable to the property.

"Ms. Stetson, I see this news is overwhelming. Please, take a few days to think about your next steps. Here's my card." He pulled a business card from his inner coat pocket and put it on the counter. "I am happy to assist you in any way possible as you take your inheritance and begin exploring your options."

Dixon walked Mr. Derek back to the front door, and Wendy practically jumped up and down like a three-year-old at a carnival as she made her way to me.

"Oh...my...God! Cora, you've got the house! Really and truly, it's all yours. And you can kick that ass-wipe Mark out on his butt!" she crowed.

I could only look at Dixon as he came back to me. Ryan stood by his side now, his hand on Dixon's shoulder.

"Well, gum drop, it looks like you're going to be busy." Dixon grinned at me. "And I can't wait to see you succeed, in whatever you pursue."

I had decisions to make, that was sure, but with Dixon by my side, I'd already gotten what my heart wanted most: his love. Everything else, we'd figure out...together.

Don't miss out!

Visit the website below and you can sign up to receive emails whenever D.W. Alder publishes a new book. There's no charge and no obligation.

https://books2read.com/r/B-A-HZUU-UDECC

BOOKS 2 READ

Connecting independent readers to independent writers.

About the Author

D.W. lives in a small town in Connecticut, with her husband, a dog who is going deaf, and a cat that loves to step on the keyboard. When she's not writing, she's editing, reading, or spending time with family. Read more at www.dwalder.com.